G000153360

heckler

JASON GRAFF

heckler

JASON GRAFF

HECKLER
Copyright © 2020 Jason Graff
All Rights Reserved.
First Edition Paperback.

Published by Unsolicited Press
Portland, Oregon
www.unsolicitedpress.com
info@unsolcitedpress.com
(619)354-8005

Cover Art: Kathryn Gerhardt
Editor: S.R. Stewart

No part of this book may be reproduced or transmitted in
any form or by any means without written permission from the
publisher or author.

Unsolicited Press Books are distributed to the trade by
Ingram.
Printed in the United States of America.
ISBN: 978-I-950730-II-7

All of the poems quoted in this text are appear in The Classics
Club edition of *The Selected Poems* of Walt Whitman published
by Walter J. Black, Inc., 1942

1

Sunlight flashed in The Shelby Hotel's windows as a wave of clouds rolled across the sky. At only four stories, it still managed to tower over every other building for miles from atop its perch on Mt. Kneebow. Since drying out, Angus Sperint had come to accept that much of reality, like the fact that his inheritance wouldn't last forever, was indeed sobering, so it would be dusty hotels like The Shelby, in towns like Pittson from there on out. Not that he was really much for luxury, except when it helped him to recover from other kinds of excess.

Across the street, *Psycho* was playing in an old, rather disused looking movie house. The letters on the marque were of various shades of sun-bleached red -- the 'y' bright, candy-colored, the 's' a dull pink. Angus pushed through the revolving door into The Shelby's lobby, trying not to think of Norman Bates.

A hint of lemon-scented cleaner tucked into the murky air reminded him of the common room back in rehab. He wiped his forehead and sniffed his hand, still unused to smelling of something other than booze. Behind the desk, a young man with the posture of a boy who'd just started to grow into his adult clothes stood before a catacomb of cubbyholes.

"Welcome to the Shelby, sir," he said while attempting to keep his acne-covered cheek averted. 'Bruno' read his nametag.

"Good afternoon," Angus said. "Do you have any vacancies?"

"We could probably squeeze you in, sir." Bruno turned the guest register towards him. "What kind of room are you looking for?"

I'll take the best you have."

"They're all pretty much the same," Bruno said. "I'll put you in 412. It has the best view. On a clear day, you can see all of Pittson."

"I'll take it," Angus said. "I love a good city view."

"Not that there's much to see."

"I'm sure it'll be fine," Angus said.

"How long will you be with us?" Bruno asked, sliding the register towards him and placing a pen in its spine. "If you stay for a week the eighth day is free."

"I... uh..." Angus nervously fingered the strap of his laptop bag. "I'm not sure. I'm in town to work on something, a recording, and I don't know how much time I'll need to see it through."

"Are you a polka musician?" Bruno asked.

"No." Angus chuckled at the vision of himself in lederhosen, sporting a feather in his cap and dancing with his knees high in the air. "Look, I'm unsure how long it's going to take, can I just pay for, say, eight weeks in advance? It'll have to be a check. That's all I have on me right now. My credit cards are..." Angus said, wincing imperceptibly at all the credit cards, he'd left behind in bars.

"Mr. Sperint, is it?" Bruno asked squinting at Angus's signature. "I'm not going to try to talk you out of that. Let me just ask the boss."

Bruno excused himself before disappearing through the apartment door which sat next to the rack of cubbyholes. The living room had the look of a shabby extension of the lobby with its ghostly periwinkle armchairs and tattered blue couch. All had been part of the set that had once sat immediately inside the revolving door. His mother had only moved them in once they were too obviously worn-looking to remain there.

He knew she'd be in the kitchen which was connected to the living room by a creaky swinging door. She sat at the table twirling an ancient phone's cord around her wrist. Bruno grinned nervously and waited for her to finish.

"It's been nearly two years since your office indicated a desire to visit us," she was saying in the robotically bored tone of someone leaving the same message that had been left countless times already. "Any updates you can provide would be appreciated. You have our number here at the hotel."

"Mom, someone's here," he said once she had hung up the phone. "Someone who wants a room."

Threadbare and faded from pink to practically white, her robe flapped loosely around her thin body as she stepped to the sink to pour the dregs from her mug. She rinsed it out beneath the tap until the water started to steam, all the while shaking her head. Bruno never asked about those calls; the fact that she was annoyed by the end of them was all he needed to know.

"That's normally why people come here," she said, just before he repeated himself. "Did you check him in? Why aren't you at the desk?"

"He wants to pay for eight weeks in advance."

"Eight weeks? Well, then. We'll have to think about how much that's going to be."

"He wants to pay by personal check. Will we take one?"

"Bruno, what is your first order as an innkeeper?"

"I wasn't sure if that was possible, so I came to ask. You told me to always get a credit card to cover incidents of damage."

"Incidentals and damages," she said. "At this point, if somebody wanted to pay in magic beans, we'd probably have to accept."

Marianne opened a drawer near the sink, sifting through a mess of expired coupons and a dust-covered phonebook before taking out an old receipt pad and handing it to Bruno. Beneath the receipt pad was a book of poetry left behind by Bruno's last tutor. She'd meant to throw it out but had forgotten. She stepped to the side to make certain Bruno couldn't see it. There was nothing to be gained from having all that dredged up again.

"Charge an even $6,000," she said, after pausing to perform some quick calculations in her head.

He wrote the amount out on the top sheet, which was then transposed by carbon copy onto a pink slip underneath. The bill featured the Shelby's insignia at the top -- a lion's head with the family name crowning its mane like a halo. Returning to his post, Bruno was relieved to find their guest still standing there, one of his bags placed atop the desk.

The young clerk ripped the bill from the pad and handed it over. Angus had his checkbook ready. He simply flipped it open, wrote out the amount, and tore the paper free.

"Don't see too many checks these days," Bruno said, examining it "If you're ready. I can take your bags and show you to your room."

The antique elevator's door gaped open, revealing a spring-loaded metal gate. Bruno pulled it back and motioned for Angus to go ahead. Marked for a maximum capacity of eight people, the car wasn't much bigger than two coat closets. Angus leaned forward to examine the safety certificate framed in glass below the numbered buttons.

"It's never once failed an inspection," Bruno said. "The elevator man says it's the best he's ever seen."

The cable moaned, struggling to lift them. They exchanged wary smiles as it cranked into motion. Then, the floors began sliding by with a soothing hum. At the fourth, it settled to a stop with a shudder.

"Please, follow me," Bruno said.

The floor creaked beneath their steps, sounding unused to any set of feet other than his mother's. Bruno hadn't been up on the fourth floor in nearly two years, not since the last time his father had visited. Standing in the doorway of room 412, he thought he could almost smell the old man's scent: a mixture of salesman's sweat and stale gum. He flipped on the light before placing the laptop bag and suitcase down on a rubber mat at the foot of the bed. As Angus picked up the remote control, Bruno plucked a tissue from atop the television set to wipe the screen, cringing as his blemished cheek grew huge and distorted in the reflection.

Closing his eyes to escape his mirrored image, his memory instead conjured that of his father reclining on the bed behind him, his belly rising and falling as he rapidly pitched his plan. He'd wanted Bruno to join him on a sales trip, travel on the road with him, just the two of them. It was to be Bruno's big chance to get out of the hotel and see some of the world. At the time, he'd been scared of the idea but now, two years on, he would've had more difficulty turning the offer down, especially if anyone other than his typically absentee father made it.

"Is the room alright?" Bruno asked in a voice that suggested the question was more for himself than the lodger.

"Let me see this view," Angus said.

Bruno pulled back the curtains. A cloud drifting in front of the sun turned it a fiery orange as though it were trying to burn through its own shadow. Below, Pittson's modest skyline of factories and church spires appeared dingy in the occluded light. The few smokestacks still in operation billowed out ribbons of purple-tinged smoke but most sat idle and rusting. It was a picture postcard of a town trying to hold on to its past because there was no place for it in the future.

Angus put his hand to the window. The glass was hot enough to sting his soft, pink palm. He quickly withdrew it and sat down on the corner of the bed.

"So that's Pittson," he said.

"A nice view with not much to see. But, as I said, it used to be a big polka spot."

"How long ago was that?"

"Not as long as you might think. We're pretty well behind the times here." Bruno balled up the tissue he'd used to wipe off the television screen and threw it in the small trash can in the corner. "Will there be anything else?"

"I don't think so." Angus gave him a crisp ten-dollar bill. "Thank you."

"Thank you, sir," Bruno said, tucking the money away discreetly in his palm as he'd been trained. "If you need anything just hit 8 on the phone next to the bed. Have a good evening, sir and welcome to The Shelby."

Ray trailed his hand down his necktie, lifting it away from his belly as he reached the end. Perched in the small office chair, he could feel the bulk of his frame listing towards the desk, pulling his shoulders with it, causing his posture to hunch over. His eyes fretted nervously from the travel case he'd placed on the desk to Mark LeSides, who smiled like a man practiced at giving nothing away.

"I just bought three ribbon mics from you not a year ago," Mark said. "What do I want with these?"

"Maybe you need some backups, in case something happens to the ones you already have. Come on, Mr. LeSides, we both know how volatile these musician types can be."

Ray removed a microphone from its foam mold. He showed it to Mark, cradling it in his hands and passing it slowly across the desk. He steadied himself in his chair, sucking in his gut, ready to hold his pose until he made the sale. Mark took the expensive mic, examining it carefully, a faint smile on his face. Ray recognized the smile as one of defeat. Knowing how to move customers beyond temptation by simply putting the object in their hands was one of many tricks he'd mastered over the years.

"When I bought the last ones from you, you said they were the most durable microphones in existence." Mark gently put the mic down on his desk then knitted his fingers together behind his head.

"They are, they are. But they're still delicate in the way any finely crafted piece of audio hardware is, Mr. LeSides," Ray said. "A man with your reputation can ill afford to be caught short in the equipment department."

"My reputation," Mark snorted. "I guess every man can be flattered in just about the same way, huh Mr. Davis?" He took the microphone from Ray's hand. "Fine, I'll take one." Mark opened the top drawer. "You still accept personal checks, I take it."

"Yes, I certainly do. You can make it out to Ray Davis."

"You're a heck of a salesman, Mr. Davis. You just sold me something I don't even need."

"That's not the way I see it, Mr. LeSides. I'm selling you what you will need to ensure the continued growth of your enterprise. Mine is the business of anticipation. I sell people what they need before they even know they need it."

They shook hands at the studio door. Mark hung his head like a man who'd been bested. Rather than get in his car and continue right on to The Shelby, Ray crossed the street towards a squat triangular building with a steeply pitched roof. Not once had he visited Pittson without stopping off at the Northpark Lounge. Situated along the river with Mount Kneebow towering behind it, the lounge resembled a run-down ski chalet. The darkness inside embraced Ray with its fug of old smoke and alcohol. He even relished the sticking sounds his shoes made as he crossed the floor. Pulling out a stool with a cracked leather top, he kept reminding himself of what was still yet to be done.

"Look who it is," Lois said, checking her mountain of high white hair in the mirror. "Ray Davis, Musicman Extraordinaire."

"How is it you always remember me?" he asked.

"I never forget a good tipper, darling. Most salesmen are kind of chintzy that way. You want your usual?"

"You remember that too?"

"Remembering names, faces, and drinks's all I do," she said, putting a pint glass beneath the one working beer tap. "You going up to the hotel to see your family?"

"Family's a big word for what we really are," he said. "I'm in no hurry to get up there."

"Going to be drinking here all night, are you?"

"Not tonight. I do have something I need to do up there before it gets too late," he said. "Something I think I need to do, anyway."

"Man's got to listen to his needs," she said, placing the glass before him.

He spilled some beer as his shaking hand brought it to his lips. The cold foam tickled his teeth, then tongue, before washing across the roof of his mouth. He took a second, much larger sip almost immediately, though he refrained from following it up with a third. This was only a stop-in, he told himself. He'd have the one drink to steady his nerves before making the drive up the hill to see Marianne and his son. It was the same scheme he'd planned many times before but had often failed to execute.

The improved Raymond Davis had come to town to make a point that he was now in control of his appetites. By taking his time and really enjoying the one glass of beer, he kept the urge for another from rising up. Lois even commended him on his self-control when he turned down a second drink. He tipped her generously and relished the feeling of getting in his car without having to worry about the possibility of a DUI.

Taking the back way, he drove up the far side of Mount Kneebow, past the rising line of skeletal towers strung with power lines and the ball field that had been overtaken by weeds. The slightly longer drive allowed the gum in his mouth plenty of time to erase the beer on his breath. Even a hint of alcohol would give Marianne an avenue for attack. The main thrust of his pitch was how responsible he had to be in his line of work and how important it was for Bruce to know that. He just wanted Marianne to see him for the man he knew he really was.

The Thompson Theater's entrance and poster cases were covered up with plywood that the sun had bleached a sickly grey. Letters promising a GRAND REOPENING SOON on the marquee had faded to dull pink, as though distancing themselves from that guarantee. The late evening sun cast the hotel's shadow across the road. 'Shelby,' carved into the marble above the revolving door, had been blackened with soot, making the building seem tomblike.

In the lobby, he noted the periwinkle armchairs, still sitting in either corner across from the door. In such moments, the maniacal consistency about the place, which bothered him even when he was on the best of terms with Marianne, brought comfort. It may not have been his home turf, but at least, it was familiar. She barely moved as he approached the front desk. Her posture was as rigid and guarded as it would've been towards any salesman making an unannounced call. Bruce stood next to her, emulating his mother's stillness. His son's obvious growth in the few months since Ray had last seen him, diminished the reassurance he'd felt in laying his eyes upon the decades-old furniture.

Bruce's lips, nose, and ears were all too big as if grafted from an adult onto his round cherubic face. He squinted at his father - - a sneering look that perhaps said what he could not. Ray couldn't tell if he was just a surprise to the boy or more an unwelcome stranger. He lacquered the gum to the roof of his mouth and quickly checked his breath in his hand.

"I'd like a room," he announced. "A quiet one with a view, if that can be managed."

"Why don't you practice on your father before Julia gets in?" Marianne asked Bruce. She gave Ray a sour frown and disappeared into the apartment.

"Bruce, what's this all about?" he asked, gesturing towards his son's nametag.

"Dad, please don't call me that. I want to be called Bruno."

"What's wrong with Bruce?"

"People still call me Brucey. I'm not a kid anymore," he said in a whine spiked with petulance. "It sounds sissy...like a little boy's name."

"It doesn't sound sissy. Bruno sounds more sissy than Bruce. Don't you think?" Ray raised his palms, as though to plead the obviousness of this point. "Think about it."

"Brucey sounds sissy." His son's posture was now more rigid than his mother's. "I wouldn't be asking to be called Bruno if it didn't."

"Who calls you Brucey?"

"Dad..." Bruno whined again, his voice cracking as it reached for something more like a demand.

"Okay, okay, I'll call you Bruno. But that's not what we named you. Not what I named you. But it's alright. It's just so good to see you, you and your mother." Ray curled his lips into a half-convincing smile. He was well-practiced at letting his frustrations simmer inside until they could be released as a fine steam of insincerity. "Does she call you Bruno? She should be the one to okay things like that."

"Where do you think I got the nametag?"

"When did you make this decision? Has it been done legally or is it more of a nickname?"

"I don't know, a few months ago." Bruno dug his hands into the shallow pockets of his vest. "Since like the last time you were here anyway."

"I've been on the road working," Ray said. "How's your mom doing? Everything okay, family-wise?"

"She's fine." Bruno cleared his throat. "Welcome to the Shelby. How may I help you today?"

Ray raised his eyebrows. His son turned the guest register towards him.

"Mom said I should practice on you. I've started manning the desk on my own."

"That's great. She's really showing you the ropes, huh?"

"Yes, sir. I man the desk." Bruno felt the word 'man' growing inside of him, straightening his shoulders, making him taller. "Now, how may I help you, sir?"

"I'd like a room, young man. I'm in town on some business and will require peace and quiet after my difficult days on the road.

I need a place to lay my head and not be troubled by the outside world."

"Very good, sir. May I recommend Room 412? It's available and boasts a full bath, free HBO, and a fine view of the city."

"Sounds great."

"Very well," Bruno handed his father the pen from his vest pocket, "please, sign right here. Do you have any bags?"

"No, no." Ray signed his name, smirking. "I travel light."

"Excellent. Please, follow me, Mr. Davis."

Bruno led the way to the elevator, maintaining the upright posture his mother had always told him communicated reliability. He held open the gate, looking his father in the eyes. They were grey like his, but also watery, the rims raw with broken capillaries. Red spider webs of busted blood vessels and veins intertwined themselves on the old man's nose, turning the end of it a bruised shade of purple.

"What sort of business brings you to Pittson?" he asked as he pulled the gate shut.

"Sales calls," Ray said.

"Very good, sir," Bruno said as they began their ascent. "Have you been to Pittson before?"

"No. Tell me what I should see."

"At the end of this street is a staircase that descends Mt. Kneebow, allowing you to travel to the heart of Pittson without the need of a vehicle."

"And what should I see in the heart of Pittson?" Ray asked.

"Dad," Bruno said, breaking character to whine again. "Come on."

"What? I'm trying to help you practice. Or did she not prepare you to talk about more than walking to town?"

"I've never been in the elevator before with a guest. I talked too fast I guess. The idea of being able to walk down into town's supposed to speak for itself, at least according to mom."

"Not this town," Ray said in place of a snort.

* * *

Marianne held three tiny bottles upside down over the sink, turning her head from the smell. As she threw the empties into the trash bin at her knees, they made an icy rattle, striking the others that'd met the same fate. Pretending that her dalliance with Ray had been nothing more than a youthful mistake proved more difficult with each of his visits. If he was going to get drunk, it wouldn't be on any of the alcohol she kept on hand for guests.

Coating the sink with Comet, she began scrubbing. White foam washed up through the sponge, stinging her hand. Still, she scrubbed until her wrist grew weak, until the smell of bleach filled her nose, making her slightly dizzy. After she finished, she let the faucet run to scalding hot, until no trace of foam was left.

* * *

Bruno held open the gate once the elevator came to a stop on the top floor. Ray let his son take the lead as they walked down the hall. The boy's posture was so overly erect, so like his mother's that Ray wanted to laugh but only cringed. Once inside the room, Ray sat on the edge of the bed, smoothing out his tie over his belly, as though the thin strip of red and white striped silk could hide his paunch.

"Sold," he said. "Would you please get my bags for me?"

"I thought you said you didn't have any bags," Bruno said.

"That was when I didn't know whether I was really going to stay. I decided just now. It's in my car across the street in front of the theater." He took a pair of dollar bills out of his wallet, pinching them between his fingers.

"You're really staying?" Bruno asked, taking the bills with reluctance.

"If I can." Ray chuckled. "I came to spend time with you."

"For how long?"

"For however long you can stand me, I guess." He flopped down on the bed, giving it his full weight, its springs creaking in protest. "It's good your mother's showing you the ropes."

"I think I should probably put you down in 206."

"The room one door down from the elevator shaft?" Ray propped himself up on his elbows into a half-seated position. "Why?"

"What if someone else comes? You know, like a special guest?"

"It's the busy season, then is it?" Ray asked with a smirk. "Is there anyone else even in this place right now?"

"Well, mom says this room is for special guests. Besides, you never stay for long."

"It's not because I don't want to. Look, Bruce..."

"Bruno. Call me Bruno, Dad."

"Bruno." Ray sat up, fiddling more with his tie. "What would you think of coming away with me for a few days, starting tomorrow? It wouldn't be far."

"I don't know. Where would we be going?" Bruno asked.

"Wheelington, McGill's Landing, Castle Island. Anywhere but this hotel."

"You'll have to ask Mom. She makes the schedule. I might have to work."

"I will. I just wanted to see how much *you* wanted to do it. It'll be fun. It'd help us get a '*yes*' from her if you acted more enthusiastic about the whole enterprise. A young man like you should want to travel. You're not going to learn much about life being cooped up in this stuffy, old hotel."

"Sure, I guess I'd like to go." Bruno offered his hand. Pulling his father up took more effort than he'd expected. "I just don't know what Mom will say."

"I think it'll go over better with her if you asked first instead, then let me jump in and explain a little. You know? Kind of like you talked me into it."

"Do you really think that'll work?" Bruno asked, holding the door open, inviting his father to exit first.

"I'd be right there to back you up," Ray said. "It just needs to seem like your idea and not mine."

"Why? Because she doesn't trust you?"

Ray rolled his head from side to side, neck muscles popping. "Look, this has nothing to do with her trusting me or me trusting her. She just needs to know that *you* trust me and want to be with me. Plus, it'll be a learning experience, about the sales side of things, and all. You're going to be running a business someday and being a good salesman never hurts with that."

"Okay, but you have to tell mom about how the sales side of things comes into it," Bruno said.

Ray reached out for his son, just to lay a hand on his shoulder and remind him that despite the days and distance between them, they were still blood. But he dropped his hand when Bruce turned to the door and walked out into the hall. He followed his son out, keeping behind him as they made their way to the elevator. The boy's overly erect posture seemed now even more pronounced.

At the elevator, he hung back, watching with painted pride as Bruce performed his bellhop routine. Someone that young standing so painfully straight looked faintly ridiculous. Out on the road, Ray would teach him to relax, to disarm possible clients with a well-shaped slouch. He only wanted what was best for him. Marianne seemed determined to turn him into someone like her, someone whose sole role in life was to serve the hotel. In time, Ray's son would become little more than part of the décor, if he didn't do something.

He couldn't look at his son the whole way down in the elevator. He'd thought it was all going to be so much easier. Ray had pictured Bruno leaping at the chance to get out of there. As far as he knew, the boy had never been beyond the crumbling slagheap that was Mt. Kneebow. Maybe his son was wise to fact that all those mill towns looked the same with their deserted main streets being held up by ramshackle bowling alleys and nail salons with paper OPEN signs in the window. It didn't seem possible to Ray but then, there were all sorts of ways to learn about the world.

On his way out of the elevator, he gave his son an impersonal nod of thanks just as he might to any hotel employee.

"You have to come in with me," Bruno said, leading Ray to the apartment door. "You have to be there when I ask."

"Into the apartment?" Ray asked, happy that while there was no excitement in the boy's voice there was a blankness to the way he uttered the words that could've almost passed for determination.

"What's the big deal? You used to go in all the time."

"I haven't been in there in a long time," Ray said. "A real long, long time."

"You have to be right behind me when I ask, like you agreed," Bruno said, something hard and snapping in his voice. "If you don't come in with me..."

"Alright, alright," Ray said.

Ray had planned on facing Marianne down on more neutral ground, like the hotel lobby. There he might be assured that her tone and word choice would be too professional to be truly biting. Every couple of steps inside the apartment, Bruce turned around to make sure he was still there. In the kitchen, they found her washing her hands at the sink. The chemical-clean smell in the air was even less inviting than the look on her face.

"Hey, mom." Bruno said, stumbling forward just far enough to allow Ray in.

"Hello, Bruno," she said, then lowered her voice. "Ray, what in God's name do you think you are doing in here?"

"Nice to see you, too," he said.

"Mom, do you think it would be okay if I went away for a couple of days? With...with Dad?"

"A day and a half really," Ray interjected. "For sales calls. See some of the world."

"And who's idea was this?"

"Bruno's," Ray said and got less of a look of encouragement from his son than he might've hoped. "He wants a taste of the salesman's life."

"Is that what you taste out there on the road?" she asked.

"You want me to spend time with him, right?"

"I'd like to be able to trust you enough to take your son with you. But I can't."

"I'm clean, Marianne. On my eyes, I haven't had a drink in a month. I've got control over it," Ray said, the words rushing out, spilling atop each other, washing away their intent if not their meaning.

There was barely enough room for all of them in the cramped galley-like space. As Marianne took a seat at the table, Ray noted there were only two chairs, there'd only ever been two chairs at that table, even when he was more of a welcome guest there. He leaned against the corner, where the swinging door's frame met the wall. When Bruno stepped back towards him, Ray attempted to pull his son close, thinking, incorrectly, that it was a step towards solidarity. Bruno rolled off of him and through the door. Before Ray fully realized it, he was left embracing the air.

Now alone with Marianne, Ray's perfect pitch, the one he'd spent so much time developing on his way out there, sounded weak. Wearing a meek smile, he approached the same kitchen table where he'd rushed through so many cups of her coffee. Each permitted step was a surprise. Steadying himself on the back of the empty chair across from her, he knew she was one potential customer already well beyond the reach of his usual charms.

"A whole month clean," he said.

"A whole month?" Marianne asked, her eyebrows rising to two ridges of mock appreciation. "Don't you get a pin or a button or something for that?"

"I'm doing it on my own. Meetings..." He winced. "I'm not one of those guys. And I'm up to 30 days, all on my own."

"When it's been a decade, come back and ask me again."

"You can't be serious," he said, pulling out the chair and collapsing into it. "How about this? If I do another thirty days without getting drunk, which I can, standing on my head, what would you think then?"

Marianne pressed her face into her palms, crying out somewhere between a chuckle and a groan. Long ago, she'd promised herself never again to cry in front of Ray, never again to let him see the faintest glimpse of emotion from her. She couldn't stop him from visiting their son, but he was never again to be permitted entrance into the part of the world she held exclusively for herself. Lowering her hands and rubbing them together, she cleared her throat, now certain she could face him down. It was bad enough he was in the apartment, in the kitchen even.

"Okay, Raymond Davis, Salesman of the Year. You want to make a deal? You want to sell me the new and improved model? You can take Bruno when you've been sober for thirty months."

"Thirty months? That's what...two and half years? Marianne," Ray said. "come on. And what's with this Bruno stuff? His name is Bruce, after my dad. You got to give him your last name and I got the first. That was the deal."

"What would you like me to do, Ray? He wants to be called Bruno."

"Jesus," Ray spat the word in a half whisper. He lifted up his hand, fighting the urge to slam it and gently placed it back down. "How about thirty weeks? That's over half a year. I can do thirty days, thirty months, thirty years. That part doesn't matter. But Bruce or Bruno or whatever he wants to be called is growing up so fast. You have him all the time. I just want to spend some time with him."

"Away from me, right?"

"Just away on a trip. I barely know the kid. I want him to learn about my world, so he'll understand why I'm not able to be with him more. I never wanted to be the kind of father who's not around. But this's my life. You knew that when we got together."

"I'll tell you what. Forget thirty months," Marianne said. "If you can do two years, twenty-four months, I'll give you the last six months free. And you don't have to show me any buttons or pins. I'll take you at your word. In the meantime, if you want to see Bruno, it'll have to be here in our home where I can monitor things and where he'll feel safe."

"Two years is still a long time. How about this? What if..."

"It's no longer a sentence than you've earned, Ray."

3

Hilda took more time than usual to tear the ticket from the spool. Her fingers lacked the strength that their thickness suggested. Bruno never understood why she bothered with the ticket as there was no one in the lobby to take it. His pores looked huge in the reflection of the booth's plexiglass, though there wasn't a single blemish on his face. The medicated scrub his mother had been harping about had worked. Bruno hated giving her the satisfaction of knowing she was right, so he hadn't mentioned it on his way out the door.

"Hold it. You're not eighteen," Hilda said after finally managing to peel a ticket free. She pinched it between her press-on nails, waving it in an accusatory manner.

"What?" Bruno asked.

"You're not eighteen. This one ain't for kids."

"My age never mattered before."

"We've never shown a movie like this one before," Hilda said and made a face that approximated a smile.

"My mom says I can see it."

"I don't care what your mom says. You gotta either be eighteen or escorted by a parent or guardian to see *Psycho*. It's got mature themes."

"Says who?"

"Says me." Hilda lowered a black cardboard divider halfway down, leaving only her mouth and chin visible. "It's too violent for a kid your age."

"Let me go get a note from her. We own the hotel across the street. I'm telling you, she said I can see it."

"And I'm telling *you*, you have to be escorted by a parent or guardian. Do you know what escorted means, young man?"

"She can't leave the hotel."

"Not my problem." Hilda said with a snicker, then pulled the divider down the rest of the way.

"It has been recently re-rated an R film, even though it was given an M, the equivalent of a PG, back in the 60's," said a voice from behind Bruno.

"Mr. French," he said with a disbelieving gasp at finding his former tutor behind him on the sidewalk. "What're you doing here?"

"Mr. French? Not anymore. Just call me Rick, please."

In the two years since he'd last seen him, Bruno had been haunted too often by dreams of Rick to compose himself as much as he would've liked. He was aware of his mouth hanging open in a kind of hungry smile. It echoed the feelings he'd experienced when they sat across the kitchen table from each other and he'd been unable to keep his eyes from staring or his body from tensing into a moment of perpetual expectation. When Rick had been dismissed shortly before the end of the school year, it came as something of a relief. Bruno had felt a measure of control over himself again, burying the burning spear of his desire and the febrile discomfort it'd caused him.

Seeing Rick now though, he felt, while not in total control, at least not as uncomfortable, not perched on the tip of something untamable. Part of it had to do with the fact that Bruno had grown enough since that time that he was taller than Rick, no longer were they eye to eye, but this was not the only manner in which his former tutor was diminished. No one could live up to the power that the memories of that time held for Bruno.

"You have to see this one," Rick said. "It's about a lunatic in an abandoned motel."

"I know, I've been waiting to see it," Bruno said. "I've seen lots here since they reopened, but this's the one I've really wanted to see."

"I'll get you a ticket," Rick said. "I'll be your guardian. Pretty sure you can handle this."

Rick brushed close enough by Bruno to disturb some small part of him. A familiar electricity charged the air. Hilda slid the cardboard up, peeking from below it. When she saw it was a different customer, her face, while not exactly brightening, de-scowled at least.

"How many?" she asked.

"One adult and one child," Rick said.

"Found someone to take you, huh?" Hilda asked, pivoting her head to bark at Bruno, who was less than entirely successfully hiding off to the side. "Fine by me, I guess."

The partition slid back down like a guillotine once Rick had scooped up the tickets. He waved off the ten that Bruno tried to hand him and held open the door to the theater.

"Call it a field trip," he said.

The totality of the darkness leant it a thickness Bruno could find nowhere else. It was one of the things he liked most about the theater, especially in the second before his eyes adjusted, when it felt as though he was moving through a plane of nothingness. On their way to their seats, he stayed as close to Rick as he dared, reisiting, somehow, a swelling urge to place his hand on his former tutor's back.

Down in front, shapes moved in the dark. From among them came the sharp whispers of a discussion or even an argument. Strange that the darkness had the effect of making people quiet down, even before the movie began. The show times were mere suggestions, the movie snuck up on you in the dark whether you were ready for it or not. While the rest of the meager crowd still was getting settled, there came a splintering of light to the screen. The whispering stopped. *Psycho* began. Bruno tapped his knee against Rick's as a way of saying thanks and to make sure this all wasn't the beginning of a dream.

* * *

Even more stubborn than usual now that they had a guest, the hospitality cart proved difficult to maneuver from the closet behind the desk. Marianne finally loosened the wheels with a great heave backward. She stacked fresh towels and bed linens on the pull-out shelves inside and placed several more rolls of toilet paper and tissue boxes than necessary in the top bin.

When she reached Angus's room, she found the DO NOT DISTURB sign on the knob. Pushing the cart to the side, she thought she detected the acrid odor of cigarettes. She dropped down to her hands and knees to sniff at the gap between the bottom of the door and the carpet. Before she could drink enough of it in, the sound of his approaching footsteps got her back to her feet and quickly down the hall. The smell followed her as she went, confirming her suspicions. All of the rooms at The Shelby were non-smoking, a policy first put in place by her father long before it was fashionable. The current state of the business didn't really permit her to make much out of this infraction.

The next morning, Marianne held the smile she reserved for guests until Angus vanished from sight down the street on his way into Pittson. She wiped off the RING BELL sign and poked her head inside the apartment. From across the living room, behind the kitchen's swinging door, she heard plates crashing into the sink, the faucet calling out at full blast. She had mere seconds to save the dishes before Bruno put them at risk by attempting to clean them.

"What're you doing?" she asked.

"Rinsing these off." He ran some water over the stack at the bottom of the sink. "This water isn't getting very hot."

"I'll take care of them later," she said. "I have to clean Mr. Sperint's room. I want you to listen for the bell in case someone comes."

"Is it alright if I listen to music in my room?"

"No. Listen for the bell, not your music. I'll be back in a few minutes, then you can listen to music or do whatever it is you do in your room."

Pulling the canvas strap tight, she fastened the vacuum cleaner to the end of the cart. Though the long hose attachment made the cart unwieldy, the sight of the professional-grade Hoover gave rise to a certain giddiness inside of her. For the first time in many months, the vacuum would actually be used to clean a room for a guest, rather than just being run out of habit. Once or twice, she'd used it in the apartment but always thought that ignoble work for something her father had purchased with so much pride.

Outside of Room 412, there was no trace of the tobacco she'd thought she'd detected the day before. Angus's room smelled manly, like cumin and leather rather than the generic shampoo and ear wax his thinning hair and stooped frame suggested. It had been too long since she'd allowed herself to enjoy the smell of a man, like a secret she didn't even know she'd been keeping from herself. She lifted his pillowcase to her face and drank deeply of his scent.

* * *

Perspiration ran down Angus's hand, smudging the ink map Bruno had drawn on a piece of hotel stationery. He'd stopped in the lobby, sheepishly rang the bell, then asked the young man for directions so softly he had to repeat himself, apologizing profusely enough that the boy seemed almost embarrassed by it. Apologizing was one thing he'd not gotten better at since getting sober, though it wasn't for lack of practice.

He wiped his forearm across his brow; the sleeve instantly became thick and heavy, the light blue fabric of his dress shirt clinging to his skin. He started down the metal stairs that led from Mount Kneebow into Pittson, each of his steps echoing in the valley below. He glanced again at the crude map, which was now almost unreadable.

Before he could fully make out a church spire and two tall buildings poking above the haze, he heard the whir of air conditioners and the hum of the traffic below, blending together as if to whisper in protest against the heat. When he reached a landing halfway down, he took a seat. He was too exhausted to care about the hot metal stinging his rear. Even after unbuttoning his collar and rolling up his sleeves, he found no relief.

On the bridge into the city, the Riverway traffic stopped and started, a long metal snake slinking along in both directions. Removing the hanky from his breast pocket, Angus wiped his face. He thought the suffering appropriate and knew that if his brother was looking down, Andy would've smiled at the mess Angus had already made of himself.

* * *

Bruno's finger hovered over the touchpad before he clicked the button promising he was eighteen. When he'd first begun looking at these websites, the lie bothered him. He worried that at any moment a policeman was going to bust down his door, grab the computer from him and charge him with virtual perjury. The fact that no one else could've possibly known he was doing it took time to register. Once it did, he saw the lie as a gift he gave to himself. He was simply doing what any other mature person could.

For a second, the screen went blank. Then came the lemon-yellow frame, then an arrow to be clicked on when Bruno wanted the video to play. A still shot of a blond man shook itself through the pixels. Bruno let his eyes glide over the man's tanned body. He clicked on a flashing sign promising a free preview. Again, the screen went blank and was then quickly filled by that same bronzed blond. When he began to speak, Bruno muted his computer. The man on screen stroked his hand over his subtly barreled chest, down a ridged, muscular abdomen, then plunged into his shorts. He opened his mouth wide as if surprised by the pleasure of his own touch. Then, he closed his eyes and cocked his head back. Just as Bruno tried to make out the outline of the man's knuckles poking at the fabric of his jockey shorts, the screen froze, the image went blurry. A message promised: "More Trent and His Friends For Only $9.99 a month."

Bruno continued stroking himself through his underwear. He liked the silky feel of his boxers -- plus, the extra layer kept him from coming too quickly. With his left hand, he slowly pecked out a new site, typing from memory. The screen filled up with four pictures. The first featured a tiny woman with an unreadable tattoo on her ass straddling a man's hips; the next depicted two women, one a redhead with long hair, the other a black, bald woman, both naked from the waist up locked in an amorous embrace. In the lower half of the screen, two thin young boys sat side by side stroking each other next to a woman with huge breasts pleasuring herself with a dildo. Bruno came before he could decide on a selection.

Exhausted, he pushed the computer to the side and wiped himself off with a washcloth. He was no closer to discovering the source of the riddling lust that felt as though it could consume his entire body. He tried to keep a mental account of his desires, measuring the amount of arousal each scene inspired, hoping that the running tally would tell him more about himself. So far, according to this method, women turned him on more frequently than men but men did so more intensely. It could've been that so far, he'd discovered much more free porn involving women. One thing was clear, more evidence would need to be gathered and weighed before he could fully commit to the idea of who he was. For the moment, due to cramping in each hand, he was forced to suspend his investigations.

After removing the phone cord from the back of the computer, he plugged in his headphones and unmuted the audio. Led Zeppelin's "Stairway to Heaven" came through with its whispering flute and delicate guitar. As Robert Plant began to sing, Bruno's thoughts drifted back to Julia and the kiss he'd tried to force on her two years before, when they were coworkers. Whenever he tried to remember exactly what she looked like, he only got bits and pieces, as though his mind couldn't put all of the pixels together at once. Usually, it was that ponytail of hers, a perfect, honey-colored torch dancing warmly about his memory. Sometimes, he could remember Julia's bright eyes on the morning when he'd made his ill-conceived maneuver to prove something, though he was never quite sure exactly what, to her. He tried to push past that day and recall if she ever turned him on in the same way the images he'd spent the morning viewing did, but uncertainty completely chased away even the most fleeting glimpse of her. In the blank spot, where he'd wanted to find that memory, something else began to stir.

Unbidden thoughts of Rick lurked somewhere just beyond his imagining. He was aware of their shape and movement just as he'd been of the other movie-goers on the previous day's trip to the theater. Bruno struggled against the sensation of blood pumping fervently back into his organ. He blamed Rick for stirring up all of the confusion. Only recently, he'd felt he was managing and understanding his desires better. Now all was again in upheaval, threatening to rage beyond his comprehension.

* * *

Marianne balled up Angus's sheets and towels together and dropped them into the chute next to the elevator. The sound of their descent still managed to inspire the same sense of pride in her as it did when she was a girl. Her father had always encouraged her to be the best bed-maker in the world. Thanks to him, she knew how to slip the fitted sheet on so that each corner was tucked the same amount below the mattress. She knew how to fold the flat sheet under, letting out slack a little at a time until the top six inches were left untucked. A well-made bed was one thing that would keep people coming back, her father had told her. She needn't worry about whether anyone would notice how skillfully it was done. The guests would know at a subconscious level; it would register somehow in their dreams.

4

Julia checked her pockets, digging into each one deliberately almost like a magician letting the suspense build. She brought out a black velvet scrunchie with something of a flourish, winding it around her wrist. She then pulled her hair into a ponytail and rolled the scrunchie up to her skull. Bruno tried not to stare but found the ritual mesmerizing.

"Your hair looks nice today," he said. "I like that thing, that...what do you call it."

"Thanks, Brucey," she said. "I feel like it's so gross today. I didn't even wash it. I'm always running late."

He'd recently stopped asking her to call him Bruno. She obviously didn't care that he'd changed his name. There was no way he was going to tell her he'd done it because she stretched out the syllables in Brucey until they were so long and soft that they seemed t0 measure every second of their small, three-year age gap. He'd thought long and hard of what he might do to impress her, show her that he wasn't the kid she kept taking him for. Nothing had seemed more mature than taking control of his life and changing his name. But she still didn't see him as anything but a boy, and he was running out of time to convince her otherwise.

* * *

Buddy pulled his station wagon behind Ray's rental car, making sure to leave plenty of room. He feared the slightest tap was all it would take for his front bumper to finally surrender to gravity. The faux-wood panels peeling away revealed a flaking exoskeleton of rust. The August heat blanketed him as he stepped onto the road, his cotton shirt and jeans instantly made heavy by the humid air. Looking up at the marquee of the Thompson with its faded letters promising a grand reopening, he remembered going inside on a similarly unbearable day just to beat the heat. He'd snuck in a flask of whiskey which, combined with a Jimmy

Stewart Western, had ushered him into a deep, pleasant slumber. Long after the movie had finished, he was awakened by a woman with breath like a deli counter. She kicked him in the shins, obviously thoroughly enjoying ordering him to leave.

The Shelby was one of the many slightly out of the way refuges he'd come to count on while traveling. It was beautiful to him the way an older woman who'd accepted her age was, imbued with a kind of learned grace that Buddy respected. The faded blue carpet in the lobby made him think of all the great feet that had trod their way to that same mahogany desk, having come to Pittson to further the grand tradition of polka.

"Ready to chase the blues away? How are we today?" he asked in a song. His mellifluous voice briefly turned the lobby into a concert hall.

"Very good, sir." Julia tried to smile. "How can we help you?"

"I'm in town for some work. I could use a room. You got something close to the elevator?"

"Yes, we do sir," Bruno said, turning to the cubbies behind him to find all of the room keys, save the one where his father was staying.

"I'm too old and lazy to walk a long hall," Buddy said.

"Room 404 is available," Julia said, turning around to take the key from Bruno. "It offers a fine view of the city and is right off the elevator. Would you like to see it?"

"That sounds fine."

"I'll take you up and Bruce here will bring up any luggage you might have," Julia said, gesturing towards Bruno.

"It's in my car, the old rust bucket wagon parked across the street. I'll get them later. He doesn't have to worry about that now."

"It's the work of an employee at the Shelby to worry about everything involved with your stay, sir," she said with well-honed, if not entirely convincing cheerfulness.

"They're heavy bags, lots of gear. You sure you can handle them, young man?" Buddy asked.

"I don't think he'll have any problem at all. Will you, Bruce?"

Bruno shook his head. He wanted to tell her she had no right to speak to him that way, no right to treat him like some underling bellhop. He wanted to demand she call him Bruno as the tag on his vest read. But again, he could only watch her and hope that observation would someday reveal the key to changing her mind.

"After you, my dear." Buddy smiled, glancing uncertainly into the elevator. "They don't make them like this anymore."

"It has yet to fail an inspection." Julia said, pressing '4.'

With a shudder, the box began its ascent. The floors whispered by, the cold grey of their concrete briefly coming to light as the elevator passed. Like all tight spaces, the small car momentarily brought out the shyness in everyone, even Buddy. He considered his shoes and listened to the smoker's wheeze coming from his chest.

"You said you have some business in town?" Julia asked as the elevator settled on the fourth floor.

"I'm here to make some music," he said.

"You're a musician?"

"Yes, ma'am. I certainly am."

"Cool." Julia turned around to offer the same kind of curious smile that people always gave when they learned of his chosen profession. Buddy loved getting that smile, especially from a young lady. "What kind of music?" she asked.

"I sing and play accordion, glockenspiel, and piano. I am a practitioner of old-style European Jazz."

"What's that? I don't think I know what that sounds like," Julia said as she held open the gate.

"It's more commonly known as polka."

"Polka?" Julia asked of the air, the word sounding ancient. "I think my grandma liked polka."

* * *

On the street, Bruno found Buddy's car parked in front of his father's latest lease. He'd almost forgotten the old man was still there. The only person willing to treat him as something other than a child was the last person he really wanted to see.

He thought of bringing the luggage up to the room and of Julia bossing him around some more and just broke out running. At first, he just wanted to get away for a few minutes but soon found himself running his usual route, farther away from the hotel than his mother would've allowed. Breaking off the road, through an abandoned lot where weeds and high grass stung his shins, he made for the dirt track that led to the cliffs on the side of Mount Kneebow. Above him, the power lines buzzed between the trees, the sound faint enough to almost not be heard. Once at the cliff side, he paused to rest and found his legs numb, his lungs stinging with each breath. He'd sweated through his shirt and even his vest.

The sun felt merciless beyond the reach of the shade. He sunk down to rest in his secret spot with his back against a cable tower's concrete base, his legs dangling over the side. From there, Pittson stretched below his feet. Smokestacks unfurled their smoggy poetry and cars crawled along the Riverway. Bruno hoped to stand the heat long enough that when he returned to the hotel his father would be gone. Such a wish used to bother him but no longer.

There was a time when Bruno would've rooted himself to the couch in the lobby if there was even a slight chance of seeing his father. He'd passed many a lonely afternoon counting the buttons sewn into its puckered upholstery while waiting in vain. Touching each one, Bruno would count in a whisper, telling himself that his father would appear by the time he reached 20, 25, 40, 50, and so on until he came to the last one. Then, he'd move back to the other end and start all over again. It wasn't long before he'd played the game enough that he could see where his touch had worn away at the fabric, revealing the wood of the buttons. Once they became too well-worn, the couch was reassigned to the apartment. By then, Bruno had grown bitter from too many disappointing afternoons spent counting and having his calculations proven false.

37

He began to sweat profusely from the heat and felt on the brink of a headache. Wearily, Bruno rose, grabbed one ankle and pulled it up to stretch his thigh, then did the same to the other. His body, soaked with sweat, felt heavy. Removing his vest and slinging it over his shoulder, he walked back down, taking his time, stopping to rest whenever he found a cool spot of shade. From time to time, he'd been disappointed in his inability to make it all the way up and down at a jogging pace. But on that day Bruno cherished his limitations. He was in no hurry to get back.

* * *

Before ringing the bell, Ray leaned across the empty desk to peek behind it, thinking Marianne might be hiding from him. He didn't move when the elevator landed, fixing his gaze instead on the apartment door. It was only when a flustered Julia rushed from the elevator back behind the desk did he relax into the idea of saving his best face for his ex.

"How may I help you, sir?" Julia asked, moving the bell just out of his reach.

"I'm staying in 206 and I....look...is Marianne in the apartment? I know she lives here, we're...old friends. Do you remember me? You're the new girl, right?"

"I'm not sure," Julia said.

"Where else would she be? She never leaves this place."

"I'm not sure what to tell you."

"Would you just mind checking? Just poking your head in the apartment? I know she's there," he said. "I just want to talk to her before I leave for the day."

"She really doesn't like to be disturbed in the morning, sir. Would you care to leave a message?"

"Morning's not her time? Come on, she rises with the sun," he said. "Tell her it's Ray and that she needs to see me. I know she's in there. And if she's mad about being bothered, I'll take the heat. Just tell her I put you up to it."

Julia's nervous smile dipped into something less certain. She turned and knocked on the apartment door, her hand tapping it so timidly there was no chance of it being heard. When she looked back apologetically, Ray motioned for her to knock a little harder. She used a fraction more force, leaning closer to the door listening for any movement inside. When the deadbolt clicked open, Julia leaped back. On opening, the door echoed ominously with something between a yowl and a moan throughout the lobby. Marianne was still in her robe, her hair wet, a toothbrush in hand.

"Yes, Julia," she said.

"There's a Ray here to see you. He says he's an old friend." Julia stepped to the side. Marianne looked at Julia and Ray with the same frown.

"Where's Bruno?" Marianne asked her.

"Good morning," Ray said in mock cheer.

"Getting someone's bags, I think," Julia said. "We have a new guest."

"Did he tip you?" Marianne asked.

"A little," Julia said, raising her hand to show Marianne the crumbled bills stashed there.

"I need a minute is all," Ray said, drumming out a beat on the front desk.

"Make sure you and Bruno get together and split the tip. I don't want you getting less just because you didn't carry any bags," Marianne said.

"So, you don't want to..." Julia nodded in Ray's direction.

"Mr. Davis and I have nothing to discuss," Marianne said. "If he has a question or needs something to make his stay more comfortable, you're more than capable of assisting him."

Julia wanted to tell her how Bruno had actually not yet appeared with the guest's bags, but Marianne shut the door in her face before she could even think of how to phrase it. Unsure of what more to say to Ray, she turned to him with a shrug. They stood for a time facing one another, exchanging the uncertain looks of business concluded but still left unfinished.

"We used to be...together; is what I should have said." Ray tapped the desk with the flat of his hand. "Marianne and me, believe it or not, were..."

"I'm sure she's just busy," Julia said in the flustered manner of someone who wished to know no more.

5

After tossing and turning well into the morning, Angus gave up on sleep. Since drying out, he'd found getting a decent night's rest more difficult than staying sober. Of all the changes to his life this was the most severe. Even as a boy, he'd always been a heavy sleeper; his head to the pillow never more than a few minutes before drifting off. His mother had to wake him for school every day. Then after Father had sent her away and packed the boys off to prep school, the job fell to Andy. In time, Angus's drinking made the task much more difficult for his brother.

At the clinic, they'd informed him that passing out after drinking didn't really count as sleep. Just another in the long list of things he didn't even know he'd been doing wrong. His therapist had predicted the insomnia could take years into his recovery to get over. When he did manage to sleep of late, he'd wake with a start, expecting to find Andy over him. Slowly wakefulness would overtake him, and Angus would realize that was never going to happen again.

He cupped his hand beneath the bathroom faucet and alternated splashing cold water on his face and drinking some. It would be all that he'd have in him until lunch. Regularly taking breakfast, like sleep, was a habit he hoped to get back into some day. But for now, he'd have to settle for trying to talk himself into being hungry later.

He dressed, leaving the top three buttons of his shirt undone, daring to expose more of his chest than he was typically comfortable showing. As further concessions to how the heat had treated him the day before, he also left his sports coat and laptop behind as he set out for the studio. He carried only the disc which he still wasn't certain he was ready to hear.

The air proved cooler that morning. A threatening crop of clouds slowly overtook the sky, turning it a foreboding green.

Thunder growled, first faraway then suddenly closer, like the storm was clearing its throat. A cool wind pushed at his back. It felt as though autumn had come to wring the last of summer from the clouds.

Angus wrapped the disc in his handkerchief and held it close to his chest, when the skies finally opened. Balancing on the steep, rain-slick stairs was difficult, he had to hold tight to the rail. As the rain came down harder, he stooped forward, offering his entire body as cover. Nothing could happen to the disc, the one thing that had given his life purpose or at least, gave him a reason to walk out of rehab.

* * *

Marianne cracked open the apartment door just enough to see Bruno without calling attention to herself. He slouched against the front desk; facing away from the door, biting his nails. She regretted the fight they'd had earlier that morning, but he'd started it, coming to breakfast full of his usual complaints. She wanted to give him a normal life, let him get his driver's license, visit colleges, but theirs wasn't a normal life. He was too young to understand that what made the hotel important was that it was something bigger than himself.

He complained about being trapped there without ever once considering her position. She would like to leave, go to the movies, go for runs, do whatever else it was that he did, but she couldn't. Change crept silently from the walls, change happened when you weren't vigilant. Bruno didn't understand how important it was to her to keep change at bay, to keep The Shelby to the same standard her father had set. She'd bought him that computer and still, he wasn't satisfied. But one day he could be, if he ever learned to appreciate the notions of duty and constancy.

"Bruno, would you please go and clean Mr. Sperint's room?"

"Who'll watch the desk, then?"

"You beg me for independence. I give you some, and then it seems you don't want it."

"Great. Independently cleaning a stranger's room. Just what I asked for."

"If you had an ounce of the maturity I'm supposedly keeping you from realizing, you'd understand how having a different life than other children is actually an advantage. My dad, your grandfather used to always say..."

"Fine, I'll do it," he said. "I'll do it right now. I don't need to hear any more about your dad and his wisdom."

Bruno threw open the door to the utility closet. Using one hand, he jerked the cart so hard that the vacuum cleaner's hose fell off and the cans of Pledge on the top rack banged nervously together. He picked up the hose and put it back on the vacuum upside down while propelling the cart towards the elevator.

"No, no. It's fine. You can't do it? You can't take pride in your work? Fine." His mother chased after him, pulling at the slide buckle on the back of his vest. "You know what? Just stay and watch the desk. That seems to be as much as you are capable of right now."

"No, no. I should want to take on the duties of a mature employee, right? That's what you keep telling me."

"I keep wishing you will. Yes, I want you to."

"If I do it, can I then please go down into town or something that normal people my age do?"

Bruno stepped in her direction, turning his cheek towards her -- acne plagued, a bubbling rash. He hadn't used the medicated scrub for several nights, too preoccupied about meeting Rick in a dream that never happened anyway. His mother had once told him that acne was simply part of becoming a man, that there was nothing to be embarrassed about. Lately, it seemed to Bruno that the horrors wrought upon his skin and the opportunity to change a stranger's bed was all he had to show for this supposed maturation that was taking place.

"Nothing in your duties is to be treated as a bargaining chip, Bruno. Leave the cart there," she said. "I'll do it. You can just watch the desk."

"We've had our guest for this year," Bruno said, shoving the cart away.

Marianne pulled it back towards her with a gentleness meant to counterbalance her son's violent haste. She rearranged the cans of Pledge, pushing them back together and righting the vacuum's hose. She wanted so badly to tell him that the sooner he accepted the life she was making for him there, the sooner he'd be content. Instead, she pushed the cart towards the elevator and tried to pretend nothing had happened.

All of this was hard for him to understand, she realized. Though, she did wonder if she'd kept the reality of what life running a hotel truly was like from him for too long. She'd been in and out of the rooms, cleaning and making the beds and doing whatever was needed since she was a little girl -- far too young to work anywhere else. It was all she'd ever wanted and was sure someday Bruno would see things the same way. It might've been a small world, but it was theirs completely.

* * *

Angus stepped cautiously onto the last of the metal stairs. The closer he came to the bottom, the deeper his fear of slipping and falling grew. He imagined the disc tumbling away from where he lay in a bloody heap, rolling down the side of the road, then carried away by the muddy runoff into a storm drain. Andy had always joked that he wished his filthy act came directly from the gutter so that at least he could brag it was going somewhere, someday.

Cars lined up in both directions waiting to cross the bridge, their windshield wipers squeaking away in a cock-eyed rhythm. Angus squeezed his way between two vehicles. Behind the windshields, blurred motorists tapped on steering wheels and eyed him with impatience. The walkway of the bridge was almost as slick as the stairs. Under the last and thickest of the bridge's struts,

Angus stood in a patch of dryness to check on his parcel. The disc was still dry.

* * *

Rain struck the windows like nails. Alone on the fourth floor, Marianne stood over Angus's bed, drank in his scent, and let his smell caress her like a pair of rough calloused hands. It made her shiver inside.

Marianne couldn't help but still think of Room 412 as Ray's. She'd put him in it on his very first visit. He'd an air busyness, of always needing to be elsewhere, of not having laid down any roots that made her want to give him a home. The musicians who frequented the hotel were on the road a lot too and had things to do but seemed more like leaves being buffeted by the wind. Ray, on the other hand, came in more like the wind itself, rushing through the revolving door like it couldn't spin fast enough for him. She wasn't even sure she knew how to flirt with him, until he asked her if she would go to the movies. She agreed without a second thought. It was only when he came down to get her later that evening that she worried about leaving her post. There would be no one there to take care of the other guests or sign in new ones.

Marianne just wanted to be with him, felt she needed to be with him. She'd only been on her own running the hotel for a few months at that point and thought she could find the source of the confidence Ray carried with him, as though it was some spring from which they both could drink.

Later, when they came back from the movies, the guilt she'd pushed to the side seemed suddenly poised to overtake her. Then Ray said, "Feels like coming back home to me," and, as they crossed the lobby hand in hand, the feeling again subsided. They kissed good night, and she took up her post again behind the desk.

When, up in his room on a subsequent visit a few weeks later, they kissed again, she found herself short of breath, blood beating desperately against her temples. The years of isolation had been cracked and sent something both uncontrollable and perfect rushing forth. It was *their* room and in it, everything was perfect. Now, she chased away the memory as she gathered Angus's towels from the bathroom floor and stuffed them into the hamper.

As the storm moved on, thunder rumbled in the distance. She pressed the pillowcase to her lips, taking in another dose of Angus Sperint, before dropping it into the hamper. Then, she dusted off the nightstand, where she'd put her hairpins that night years ago before sitting on the edge of the bed, waiting for Ray to peel the spaghetti straps from her shoulders.

Marianne finished cleaning the room. In the hallway, she took a rag and wiped the 412 over the peephole. She wanted that one place to be perfect. She cursed her memory for allowing Ray to intrude again and for granting him some part of her hotel.

* * *

Mark unwrapped the slightly soggy handkerchief from around the CD. Placing his index finger through the center and resting his thumb against the edge, he held it up to the light and checked for scratches. Then, he inserted it into the studio console.

"So this is what you want remastered? The one you forgot to bring yesterday?" he asked, watching track after track appear on the monitor before him. "What's the nature of the content we're looking at here?"

"It's my brother. Live performances of his standup comedy," Angus said.

"Lot of tracks. How long do you want the finished product to be?"

"I want as many good bits as can be found. You may need to accentuate the laughs," Angus said. "Many of the jokes are repeated on different tracks with slight variations. I just want it to all sound...more cohesive, more vibrant. I want it to sound like someone good enough to have their own comedy album."

"Remaster, remix. Sure. We can do that."

"Maybe get rid of some of the heckles, too."

"Heckles?" Mark asked. "Why's there a heckler on here?"

"I guess I didn't think my brother was very funny."

"*You* guess you didn't?" Mark asked, laughing. "Don't you know?"

"No," Angus said. "I don't remember doing it. But all the evidence's on there."

"Okay. Are there any tracks you'd like me to start with?" Mark asked.

"That'll be for you to decide, Mr. LeSides. Word is that you are the best record producer around."

"Can't argue with that," Mark laughed. "I'm more music than comedy. But I think I can work this for you."

* * *

On the curb outside the hotel, Bruno jumped over a puddle to keep from soaking his shoes. The previous day's storm had washed the sky to a cloudless blue. He peeked inside the theater door. The lobby was empty. He worried he'd missed Rick or worse that he wasn't coming. Just as he was about to return to the hotel, in case Rick came for him there, his former tutor rounded the corner at the far end of the street. He pulled right up to the front of the theater.

"You'll like James Cagney," Rick said, through the open passenger window. "You could probably get in without me, though there's no telling how old Hilda thinks you have to be to see *White Heat.*"

"I was just about to find out," Bruno said.

"This is one to see." Rick squinted at the marquee after getting out of his car. "*Yankee Doodle Dandy*'s pretty good too. Cagney can dance as well as he acts. A true Renaissance man from a time when that phrase meant something."

"What did it used to mean?" Bruno asked.

"I can see there're some important things your mother's not teaching you," Rick said, laughing.

* * *

47

"Good afternoon, Mr. Sperint." Mark stroked his goatee, black hairs sprouting through his fingers. "Let's take a listen to what I've got so far. Make sure we're cool before we get too far into this thing. Follow me." Mark led him past a couple of unoccupied recording booths down a hall lined with gold records. "I've got a room back here where we can listen."

Beneath a lit plastic sign that read PLAYBACK was a door leading to a room of almost blinding white. In the center were two metal desk chairs at either end of a long steel table atop which sat an old Sony reel to reel player. Its empty rollers looked like two eyes above the crooked open mouth of the PLAY button. Mark loaded each of the reels. One held an empty disk, the other was several inches thick with tape.

"Let's see what we got," he said over the sound of static. "I think my embellishments and subtractions sound best on analog. When we transfer them back to digital, we can layer them more. But analog's how life actually sounds, to me anyway."

The tape crackled on the ancient machine. "Last call's in fifteen, folks," a club owner's voice called out. "Now, let's welcome to the stage Andy Spearmint. Uh, Sperint. Andy Sperint"

This was followed by more applause than Andy had ever received.

"Hi folks," his voice came through clear if shaky. "If I seem a little nervous, it's because I just escaped from a cult."

Here, Mark had inserted a couple of mild guffaws.

"Too much?" he asked.

Angus shook his head, not so much to answer the question but to fight off a shiver of anxiety at hearing his brother again. Closing his eyes, Angus prepared to hear his own voice croaking with drink. At that moment, he so desperately wanted a shot of whiskey that he could almost taste it.

Andy's voice came on again.

"It was kinda tough on me. Kirk, the Neogod, saved everyone by having sex with their wives, daughters, and girlfriends. He took one look at my Shawna and said we were good. He didn't need to save us." Mark filled what had been an awkward pause with some chuckles. "He said I'd be saving a lotta men by keeping her all to myself."

The end of the joke was punctuated by a roar of manufactured laughter. Angus tightened, waiting to hear his own voice but he'd been subsumed by the crowd Mark had conjured. He relaxed in his seat, gave Mark a nod of approval. His thirst had, for the moment, been curbed.

* * *

"I wish the world were black and white," Bruno said to Rick during the credits as they made their way out of the aisle. "I wish that's how everyone looked."

"That's all you have to say about the end of Cody Jarrett?" Rick asked. "You don't have any thoughts on the relationship between him and his mother?"

"I don't know. I just think it'd be cool if everything had that shadowy glow to it. It seems like there would be a lot more places to hide." Bruno shrugged.

"What're you hiding from?" Rick asked.

"I was just telling you what I thought," Bruno said, summoning the petulant tone he usually reserved for his mother. "I didn't know there was going to be a quiz after the movie."

"There isn't." Rick laughed and opened the door to the lobby. "I just wondered what you thought about the story. What it meant to you."

Bruno smiled. "Tell me, Mr. French, what did my comment mean to you?"

"A question for the teacher? I like that," Rick said. "Well, Bruno, the very fact that the world is in color is, I feel, the reason we respond as we do to black and white. I don't think it would seem nearly as mysterious or beautiful or...dark, if the whole world looked like that. Do you?"

"If that's all we could see? Black and white? I think I'd look better," Bruno said.

They paused before the theater door, facing one another. Bruno kept his head slightly tilted, dipping his cheek into a shadow just in case some pimples had bubbled up. He wanted to say something, even just to hint that Rick, on the other hand, most definitely looked amazing in color.

"I think *Hello Dolly's* next," Bruno said quietly.

"I don't know that I'll be in the mood for a musical," Rick said.

"I've never seen a musical. I'm not sure what kind of mood I need to be in."

"Never?" Rick asked. "Maybe I'll stop by the hotel sometime soon to see what kind of mood you're in," Rick said. "Hope you'll be able to join me."

"I hope so, too." Bruno put his head down as they came out of the theater. He didn't even watch Rick walk away.

After noting how well it'd worked on the film's hardened henchmen, Bruno mustered his best Cody Jarrett face. He hoped it would keep his mother from interrogating him. As he approached the desk, it occurred to him that nothing Jarrett did seemed to shut his own mother up and that he'd gone insane when she died.

"How was the movie?" Marianne asked.

"Fine. Do you need me for anything?" he asked.

"How did you like James Cagney?"

"He was fine."

"I guess we know that *fine* is the baseline of your ranking system," she said. "Is there anything else you would like to share, Mr. Bruce Shelby?"

"What do you want me to say, mom?"

"I want you to talk to me, Bruno," Marianne said, raising her voice. "To actually talk to me."

"I'm not in the mood, Mom," Bruno said, slipping by her and through the apartment door.

* * *

"Then, there was the time I accidentally switched on the closed-circuit television I had accidentally wired to a camera hidden in my parent's bedroom. I accidentally watched them have sex for more than an hour." Andy rushed through the joke, practically breathless by the end of it. "It might've been less disturbing if the picture weren't so clear. Goddamned Sony."

Though Mark had added a vigorous round of cheers, Angus was too difficult to cover up this time. He could even hear himself slurping down the last of his drink before he yelled out: "And you still didn't know what to get your mom for Christmas, faggot."

On the ugliest of those nights, Angus didn't just heckle; he took over the room. His cruel barking bounced off the walls. The silence that followed would be punctuated by the shocked gasps of the audience. Some even turned to find him at the back of the room. More often than not, Angus was too drunk to notice, let alone feel embarrassed. How the shame burned him now, crumpling and blackening his soul as though it were made of paper.

"I think I can get rid of that." Mark stopped the playback, removing the tape from the reel and marking that spot with a white pencil. "I understand about you wanting to honor your brother, had a younger one myself who passed not long ago."

"I never realized how much pain my brother was in until he..." Angus turned his head to break from his words, his thoughts. "What was your brother like, Mark?"

"Mike was a real biker. Designed, built and rode them. One day last summer, he took one out..." Mark paused and pinched his goatee between his forefinger and thumb, straightening out the hairs. "It was a fine, sunny day. I remember he came riding over here, revving his engine in the back parking lot, loud enough for me to hear. So I come out, all pissed, tell him to knock it off." He let out a tired laugh. "Truth was, I think I envied him `cause I had to be inside all day recording some old polka band. It was some real unknowns. Not like Buddy Cyzek or anyone like that. This was real boring work. Anyway, there he was soaking up the sun, shades on, riding around the city, speeding up and down Mount Kneebow. I guess he must've hit like a pebble or rock or something over there near the bridge. They said he died on impact. He didn't suffer."

"My brother's death was an accident too." Angus enjoyed the sound of the lie enough that he hoped one day to actually convince himself of it.

Mark laid his huge hand on Angus's shoulder. They sat, sharing a moment of peace with their departed siblings. There in the silence of that room, Angus was aware of the heft of his past deeds. The weightless feeling was the thing he missed most about drinking -- the brief period when it seemed absurd to worry about anything because he'd floated above and beyond all the pain he felt or caused. Not until he got sober and had been made to feel it, did he realize how accurate it was to describe that state of mind as "high." Finally, when the air around him began to feel like it was swelling and Angus felt close to tears, he told Mark he wasn't ready to hear any more of his brother's recordings.

"We did something today," Mark said, lifting his hand from Angus's shoulder. "It's a good start."

Across the street at the Northpark Lounge, Angus grabbed the last stool at the end of the bar. A half-smoked cigarette, long and white with a gold band where the filter met the tobacco, lay at the end of a snake of ash. He leaned forward and smiled at Lois.

"How about a menu?" Lois asked, showing him a stack of them fanned out in her hand.

"Please," he said unwrapping the cellophane band from the top of a pack of cigarettes.

She handed him a laminated piece of cardboard the size of a legal pad. All four corners were curled. A stain had somehow penetrated the plastic, darkening the white to beige in a large amoeba-shaped spot. He traced the edges of that spot with his finger, staring at it, trying not to think about the drink he really wanted. His hands began to shake badly enough that he couldn't strike a match. Lois saved him with a lighter.

"When you work at one of the only places where folks can still smoke indoors, you learn to get pretty handy with one of these," she said. "What can I get you?"

"I need a drink," Angus said, "but I'll settle for a Coke for now."

6

The tailgate of Buddy's station wagon fell open like it was getting too tired to hang on much longer. Atop a faded leather suitcase with worn, rounded corners, his accordion sat clasped shut and compact. He wiped the dust from the closed bellows and strapped it on. Unlocking the instrument, he played a chorus of flat notes to the rhythm of Pittson buzzing off in the distance. He fought the urge to continue improvising on his way across the street. Locking it closed again, he took the accordion off and tucked it under his arm, holding it tight to his side. He slung his suitcase out with a great deal more abandon, letting it scrape the ground as he half-dragged it across the street.

Marianne smiled from behind the front desk. Her hair, fading from chestnut to light brown with a smattering of grey along the temples, marked her as maybe one generation removed from what Buddy thought of as the zenith of polka's popularity there in what had become known as the "Rust Belt." The smile lines encroaching around her lips, the wrinkles just finding their way across her forehead, told of possible childhood memories dancing atop a great uncle's shoes to an old accordion band. Buddy unlocked his instrument and played around, just hinting at a song as he approached the desk.

"Fine acoustics in this lobby," he said as his fingers tickled over a three-note jig.

"How can I help you today, sir?" Marianne asked. "If you're looking for a room, we do have a few vacancies."

"I checked in yesterday. Thought someone was going to bring my bags up but they never showed," he said, placing his suitcase atop the front desk. "Can't believe I left my squeezebox out in the car."

"Sorry about that, sir," she said. "I'll have a word with the staff."

"Nothing to worry about. Probably couldn't get in the thing. The tailgate on my old rattletrap's just about rusted shut," he said, squeezing out a few more notes. "I've always liked this hotel."

"It's wonderful to have you back. As always, if there is anything we can do to make your stay more comfortable, please don't hesitate to ask," Marianne said. "Let me help you with your bags."

"Won't hear of it," Buddy said, turning away from her. "Forgive me but I'm old fashioned enough to think a lady shouldn't be doing that."

"Let me get the gate for you, at least." Marianne walked ahead of him to the elevator. "It's an old-fashioned kind and can be temperamental."

"Like me," Buddy said.

He slid his suitcase into the elevator. It toppled over with a thud. Then, he carefully leaned in, accordion first, practically on one-foot dancing through the gate as Marianne held it open. Buddy made sure to keep the instrument from banging against the door's steel frame. Never light on his feet otherwise, he moved with grace whenever he had his favorite instrument strapped on, as though it were a dance partner leading him in a waltz.

"Are you sure there isn't anything more I can do for you?" Marianne asked.

"Not right now. But I'm sure I'll be bothering you about something or other later."

"It won't be a bother, sir."

"Please," he said as he closed the gate. "Call me, Buddy."

* * *

Knowing he'd be working with Julia later had Bruno pacing his room, talking to himself in a deeper voice and casting his eyes about in a desperate search for something that might help him become what he thought she wanted. The bottle of English Leather had been sitting atop his bureau for so long, Bruno wondered when the last time he'd even noticed it.

A gift from his father many years before, the cologne was inextricably tied to suspect claims just like anything else the old man had given him. Bruno unscrewed the bottle's fake wooden cap, then sniffed at it hesitantly. Smelling of leather and melted plastic, it was strong enough to make his eyes burn.

There would come a day, his father had predicted, when Bruno would become interested in getting girls' attention and in the bottle lay a secret way of doing that. He went on to explain his theory of chemical attraction to Bruno, who'd been too young to even think about such matters. It wasn't about the smell, his father had assured him but something ancient and mysterious.

Looking at the bottle, Bruno realized one of his father's predictions had come true. He'd changed his name but that hadn't impressed Julia. Feeling out of ideas, it didn't seem like testing his father's theory, if only just to disprove it, was much of a risk.

He splashed some in his hands, sniffing at it and again doubting his father. He slapped at his neck with it, rubbed it under his arms, then at a loss as to where else he should apply it, he ran his hands through his hair. As he was doing all of this, it became apparent that he was making a mistake. He no sooner should've followed his father's advice than his own.

With time yet before Julia's shift, he paced the few steps from his door to the wall and back, half-listening to the innocuous pop song spilling lightly from his bedside clock-radio and trying to walk the overwhelming smell off of him. He searched for wisdom in its lyrics, but the idea that no time was a good time for good-byes was as much as the singer was able to offer. The astringent odor of his mistake soon filled the room.

In the bathroom, he turned on the faucet, letting the water warm, before rinsing the cologne off his neck, from his armpits and out of his hair as best he could. While his armpits and neck no longer smelled so strongly of it, the cologne still wafted heavily from his hair. The scent only seemed to get more powerful the more he ran his wet hands through it. Lathering up with soap now, he ran them through it again and again, bubbles covering his scalp like a hairnet. His head wouldn't fit in the sink enough to rinse all of the soap out, so he stuck it under the faucet in the tub. The water pounded his face. As he dried his head, he noticed how brittle and sticky his hair had become. He tried slicking it back, which only made it worse.

* * *

The same male receptionist who had blocked Ray at Mym's Sound and Motion on each of his previous visits sat bored before a computer, a ketchup stain on his collar. Chase Taylor, as his nameplate identified him, had long thinning hair and a puffy face. Ray was pleased to see him as Chase, like the best of the worst musicians, turned out to be a shameless self-promoter, the sort easily undone by the merest flattery. The last time Ray was there, Chase had left his band's flyer under Ray's windshield.

"How can I help you?" Chase asked without looking up.

"Hey, aren't you in Crane?" Ray asked. "Oh, no, that's right. You're in Vultan."

"Yeah, I was in Crane." Chase looked at Ray without any of his usual venom. "Vultan is the future."

"You guys sure play fast," Ray said.

"Loud and fast and not for very long," Chase said. "It's not some bullshit all-night commitment to come to one of our shows. Get you in, get you rocked, get you out, that's our motto."

"I like that about your guys almost as much as the music." Ray leaned over the desk and offered Chase one of his readymade smiles -- broad, self-assured, friendly and just short of sincere. "You playing around here soon?"

"No offense but you don't look like one of our typical fans."

"Hey, don't judge an album by its cover, right? I may be old but I still rock."

"Really? Where do you still do your rocking?"

"Saw you guys at The Red Loom a few months back."

"Wait, were you there the night we got arrested?"

"Barely got out of there myself," Ray said. "Everyone thought I was a cop."

"Yeah, you may be old but you sure ain't no cop."

They shared a laugh, but the sound had hard edges. The fact that their sudden camaraderie felt forced meant Ray had broken through. Forcing things came easy to him, getting others to force them was the real trick.

"I'm here to see Mylissa," Ray said.

"Take a seat." Chase pressed a button on his phone and called into his intercom. "Someone's here for you."

"What's its name?" Mylissa's voice cracked through the speaker.

Chase looked at the salesman to introduce himself.

"My name is Ray Davis," he said. "I have some microphones she'll want to see."

"Microphone salesman," Chase said into the intercom.

"Wouldn't you just know it," Mylissa said. "Send him right damn in."

"Down this way," Chase said as he rose from his desk.

The white linoleum floors reflected the records hung on the red-carpeted walls. All were of bands Ray had heard of, but only in passing, mentioned in terms of faded glory. Not finding any by Vultan, Ray smirked behind their bassist's back. When they reached the end of the hall, Chase knocked on the door.

"You got the mics on you?" Mylissa asked from behind door.

"Yes, I do," Ray said, stepping past Chase.

The door whooshed open with a gust of air. Mylissa remained in the threshold for a moment, inspecting Ray. He needlessly straightened his tie and looked down at her, trying not to stare. With a grunt, she maneuvered her wheelchair back behind the desk, nodding for Ray to come inside.

"Close the door." She growled. "It's your lucky day. I just had my best one get thrown up on by some sloppy-ass punk. I got another act coming in less than an hour. Show me what you damn got."

Ray propped his sales case on his lap and flipped its locks open. He lifted the lid slowly in order to give the impression that great and wondrous treasures were waiting inside to be discovered at bargain prices. He said nothing for a moment, preferring to watch Mylissa's reaction.

"Shiny," she said with a snort. "Tell me about them."

"This one was made to handle vomit." He carefully removed a microphone from its spot nestled into the case's molded foam.

"Really?" she asked. She took the expensive microphone from him, holding it to her mouth. After inspecting it from all angles, she hit the button on her phone for the intercom. "Chase?"

"Yeah," he said.

"Is Dewey still in the damn bathroom?"

"Think so."

"Well, Mr. Davis, let's find out if you're bullshitting me." She motioned to Ray as she propelled herself towards the door.

Ray followed, feeling as though he was being borne along in her wheelchair's wake. Long comfortable in the habit of making questionable claims, he found the ground much less steady when someone wanted to test one in his presence. They rounded the corner where Chase sat. Instead of his ironic smile, the receptionist appeared sad and defeated, as though plagued by the still unfulfilled dreams that Ray had evoked to get past him.

He knew they were near the bathroom before he saw the sign. The familiar acid punch of liquor and regurgitated food slapped Ray in the face. He pulled the collar of his shirt over his nose and tried not to breathe. A skinny kid lay prone on the floor resting his head against the toilet, his tongue, too small for the large silver stud that pierced it, lolled from his mouth like a dog's.

"About done Dewey?" Mylissa wheeled herself into the bathroom.

Dewey nodded.

59

"For sure? Nothing left? Not even a little bit?" she asked.

"No. Nothing." The kid struggled to his feet using both the toilet and the handicap rails.

"Anything left in the damn bowl?"

Dewey sighed and reached for the flusher.

"No, don't," she said.

Mylissa wheeled close, practically pinning Dewey against the toilet. She leaned over the edge with a grunt and dipped the mic into the bowl. Ray balled up his fists, trying to calm himself as she shook it off. Dewey crawled to his knees to avoid the spray from the regurgitant covering the microphone which she'd turned into a sort of aspergillum, the kind that might be used in some punk rock baptism.

"Want to lay down some tracks, Dew?" she asked, holding the dripping mic away from her body.

"I guess," he said. "I, uh, sound better with my throat all tore up."

"Splash some water on your face and meet me in Booth Four." She backed out of the bathroom with one hand. "Come on." She nearly wheeled over Ray's feet. "We're going to find out about your damn wares here, pal."

"I assure you that mic will work like new," Ray said, swallowing to keep his voice from quavering.

"We'll see," Mylissa said, spitting the words behind her.

* * *

Buddy pantomimed playing his accordion with his eyes closed -- the silent notes, a vivid sonic texture rendered as waves of shapes and colors across the canvas of his mind. Though he'd played "The Beer Wagoneer's Lament" dozens of times, the notes still felt like they might bring revelation if first fully reconstructed within his imagination. It was like being a child again, picking up the squeezebox for the first time. The real stuff always hit him like new, like neither it nor he had aged a day.

"Alright Budman, about ready to roll in here," Mark said into the intercom.

Buddy adjusted the strap and hugged the accordion to his chest.

"Give me a high one," Mark said.

Buddy squeezed out a soaring C.

"Sounds good." Mark made another adjustment to fine tune the timbre. "We're ready."

"This one is called *The Beer Wagoneer's Lament.*" Buddy arched his back a bit and aimed his mouth at the microphone. His voice deepened as he began to sing: "I got two fat barrels in back/And no sign of you on the road/I got two fat barrels in back/Won't you help me with my load."

Until recently, he'd always considered himself young for his age. It was the music that he felt kept him that way. Now he found himself having push through, struggling to find the energy the music usually gave him. His fingers felt heavy, his voice strained and tired. The process was taking more out of him each time. Erin had predicted that their having kids later in life, or in Buddy's case very late in life, would help keep them young. Time, he was finding, would not be cheated.

* * *

Bruno itched at his scalp. Little white flakes swirled beneath the single naked bulb dangling above the basement's laundry area. Looking like gossamer scabs, they came to rest on his shoulder as well as on the linens and towels he and Julia were folding. Each time she brushed some away from the newly folded laundry, he tried to stop scratching, but his head felt so tight that it was the only relief he could find. As he picked up the pile of towels she had made and stacked them on the linen cart, he tried not to act like some creature in the midst of shedding its skin.

"Are we having a problem today?" she asked, touching the side of her head.

"What? No, I just.....no I'm fine," he said. "You mean this?" He brushed some from his shoulder as though it were the most normal thing on earth to have a pile of crusty skull flakes sitting there.

"It might be your shampoo." She sniffed at him. "Smells kind of odd. And strong. What kind is it?"

"A new kind. My mom got it. I don't remember what it's called."

"You should talk to her about it. It doesn't seem to be addressing your needs. In fact, it seems to be making things worse."

"Yeah, she'll probably make me use it up before getting me any more," he said, an undeniably true statement that helped better bind together his lies.

"Dandruff's so treatable, you know?" she asked, compounding his embarrassment.

After brushing off more of his debris, Julia handed him another stack of towels. He held them to his chest before putting them on the rack. It seemed there was nothing he could say now to save the moment. Though he'd tried shifting the blame onto his mother, it was he who was standing there molting before her eyes.

"It's okay Brucey." She reached into the dryer for another clutch of towels. "You don't have to be embarrassed. I get it sometimes, too."

"*You* have dandruff?" Bruno asked.

"It just means you have a dry scalp. It's nothing to be ashamed of," she said.

"It's not...I mean I don't...You? You have it?"

"I'll bring in a little bottle of the shampoo I use. Should clear it right up."

"Your shampoo?"

A pulse of excitement flipped inside his chest at the notion that they'd have something in common, something to share. He took another stack of towels from her, trying not to smile too broadly, trying to keep hold of himself. Not knowing what to say, he bit his lip and let the feeling melt through him.

* * *

When Ray awoke the next morning, the smile he'd won at Mym's remained on his face, until he remembered his failure at selling Marianne on the idea of Bruce going away with him. Here he was, waking up in her hotel like a prisoner, forced to obey her rules if he wanted to see his own son. No matter what he did, the mother of his child wanted to keep their son locked in her little world, in what Ray saw as her failing family hotel. At least, he had some money to leave her. He guessed she probably liked him better when he took the form of a personal check.

He ripped the sheets from his body, jumped out of the bed, and threw open the curtains. The late summer sun cast an orange veil across the morning sky. Taking the hotel notepad and pen from the bedside table, he turned over on his side and began to write.

Marianne-
Have to go. Got to make some money. As always, if you want me to send more, you just need to say so. Hope this sees you through the next couple of months. I'm always happy to help with Bruce. I just wish you'd let me do more.
-R
PS – Next time I come. I will be sober again and I hope you will reconsider my offer. A father <u>should not have to wait</u> two years(!!) to spend some man-to-man time with his son. Think about it.

He tore it out and reread it, cringing at his handwriting. Marianne was always quick to complain about his sloppy cursive. He folded up the paper around the check and placed it on the table.

Bruce-

Bruno-

Sorry for leaving like this. It must seem like I'm always slipping out before saying goodbye. I am sorry things didn't work out for our trip. Next time, I'll do the asking. I promise.

-Your Dad

After he got dressed, Ray took the folded notes, writing *Marianne* and *Bruce* on each respectively and tucked them in the inside pocket of his blazer along with the check. In the lobby, he was relieved to find only Julia at the desk. Dropping off the notes and just leaving seemed the perfect goodbye for the way he'd been treated.

"How can I help you, Mr. Davis?" Julia asked.

"I'd like to settle my bill," he said.

"Are we checking out today?"

"Afraid I am."

"Will we be using the credit card on file?"

"That's the one," he said, handing her the key.

She put it in the cubbyhole, then ran his credit card. The machine beneath the desk made several electronic noises before spitting out the receipt. It was an ancient device and took a long time. Julia didn't understand why Marianne didn't get a new one.

"Here you go." She handed the slip of paper and a pen. "Is there anything else I can help you with?"

Ray took out the notes and tapped them against the edge of the desk. He began to extend them to her but stopped halfway. Looking at them there in the lobby, he found what he'd written insufficient. That hotel seemed like the one place where he always struggled to put forth the proper point of view of himself. He placed the note for Bruce back in his pocket.

"Please make sure Ms. Shelby gets this," he said and handed the other note over..

Buddy propped himself against the bed's headboard and rested the accordion in his lap. Fingering the keys, he listened for the notes in his head. With alternating taps of his feet, he beat a rhythm against the mattress. It was a song he no longer remembered the name of, one of the first his father had taught him. He could still hear his pop's voice, so deep had it sunk itself into his bones. With some effort, he rolled his large body to the other side of the bed and picked up the phone. He took a couple of deep breaths, then dialed. It only rang twice before his soon to be ex-wife picked up.

"Hello," Erin said, the children could be heard shrieking for attention in the background. Their shrill cries, as always, made Buddy glad to be on the road.

"Good Morning, Erin," he said.

"Morning, Buddy. How's the road?" she asked.

"Glamorous as I remember."

"Oh yeah?" Erin laughed. "Having fun out there? Running around making music, seeing exciting places, staying in luxurious hotels?"

"I'm in an exquisite fleabag called the Shelby Hotel at the moment," he said. "It looks like it used to be something grand but was probably never quite as grand as it wanted to be."

"Well, I'd imagine you're quite the expert on hotels and motels by now."

"Can't say you're wrong." He pulled the receiver away from his mouth and cleared his throat. "How're the kids?"

"Essie's curious about when she might catch a glimpse of you again," Erin said.

"What did you tell her?"

"I told her you'd be back when you got around to it."

"Erin." He sat up and allowed the accordion to tumble off him onto the mattress. "Why did you say that?"

"What am I supposed to tell her?" she asked.

"Something like *when he can*, I don't know…anything else. I'm trying to do something here."

"That's tough for kids to wrap their minds around, you know? I mean, you're there and they're here and that's all they can understand. They're too young to realize you're just selfish by nature and they shouldn't take it personally."

"Jesus, how long before you start telling them shit like that?"

"They'll learn. I won't have to."

"Did you get the check?" Buddy asked, his lips curling from the taste of spite.

"Yes, I did. Thank you. You're only six months behind now."

"Four."

"See you when we see you, Bud." Erin hung up.

He used to be better at telling himself he wasn't running from the family he'd started. A musician's place was on the road, or so he'd always claimed. Since polka's popularity had gone from declining to almost nonexistent, he'd started searching more and more for reasons to get out on the road. And though he would never admit it to himself, the idea of his polka almanac project -- conceived as an aural way to document different styles of the genre from different areas across the country -- had more to do with him being able to stay on the road than it did with the actual music. Having so recently traded the house and life he'd shared with Erin and the kids in for a trailer, the road appealed more and more to him all the time.

* * *

"Vomit?" Burt Newhouse asked, looking at the microphone Ray had practically forced into his hand.

"I've seen them do it. Sold one at Mym's Sound and Motion for that very reason just yesterday," Ray said, watching Burt's blue eyes trace the body of the microphone.

"No shit?" Burt looked up at him. "Mylissa's a no bullshit type of gal."

"She's tough."

"Vomit." Newhouse chuckled, handing the microphone back to Ray. "I only record artists who are right with Jesus. I don't have drinkers or partiers here."

"You only record Christian acts now?"

"Fucking right."

"Since when?" Ray asked.

"A few months ago." Newhouse shrugged. "I had to find my niche or some shit like that."

"Well, I think I've got just the thing Christian acts will go crazy for."

"What, is it sprinkled with holy water?"

"Close," Ray said, not sure quite yet of what was about to come out of his mouth next, but totally confident that whatever it was would work.

* * *

Marianne carefully lowered herself into the bathtub, the heat and steam taking her in a profound embrace. With her foot, she turned the hot knob, warming the water even more, enough that she began sweating. After submerging her head, she listened to the muted flow of water as it encircled her body. The sound could carry her far away; it could've been the river or even the sea.

She wanted to find a quiet place inside herself, a place where her mind could grow blank. She'd follow the sound to where it floated off into nothingness. She wanted to search behind that nothing, find its source. As always, no sooner would she begin to approach that place, than her mind interfered.

The state Board of Education's deadline for finding a tutor for Bruno was approaching. Demonstrating he was receiving an adequate education at the hotel had never been a problem up until now, but there had been some changes in the home schooling procedures. There were new standards in place, a new regime running things that seemed to her to be anti-business, especially small business. It was none of their concern how her son was educated. His place in the future was secure, he'd be running a hotel. The form they expected her to fill out was so long it was a joke. Meanwhile, the information she'd requested from the town of Pittson about possibly applying for landmark status had still not arrived. That was government business for you, she thought, always wanting you to do things quickly while they took their time.

She ushered these thoughts from her mind. If she let reality intrude on her bathtime, she'd risk inviting doubts regarding the value of the type of study she felt Bruno really needed. She'd stretched Daddy's money as far as it would go to keep the hotel running. Now, she was starting to feel up against it. And there was this tutor she had to hire. Again, she wished she could let her son have a normal childhood, but the school down in the valley wasn't going to teach him the things he really needed to know. At least with a tutor, she'd have some control.

She turned the knob again to refresh the quickly cooling water. The steam rolled up and tickled her bare skin. Closing her eyes, she went searching for quietude again.

When she'd told Bruno about Ray leaving, he'd just about managed a shrug. That shrug used to pain her, as though it were evidence she'd failed at making a real family for him. Now, she saw it as proof that it wasn't she who'd failed him but Ray. The slight peel of Bruno's shoulder and the dip of his head betrayed little emotion. If anything, this time he'd looked so apathetic, so lethargic that it confirmed that she was right in denying Ray's request to take the boy away.

* * *

Ray threw his sports coat over the back of the barstool. Its leather upholstery had worn away in places allowing the foam beenath to bubble up, evidence that Gregg's Lounge's best days were long behind it. Hooking his tie with his index finger and thumb, he loosened it. The smile on his face relaxed into something almost like joy. Dark and expansive, Gregg's was the kind of place one could pass a whole day without noticing it had turned to night.

Three sales in three days had earned him a drink. Ray thought of ordering a Coke, but that felt too much like admitting he had a problem. He was in control, in total control. He could have a real drink if he so chose.

He took the note for Bruce out of his pocket, wondering what he could've said to convince his son to be more excited about going out on the road. It seemed impossible to Ray that his son didn't feel trapped there. Using this angle on Marianne had proven useless several times before. Bruce wasn't trapped there according to her, but rather, learning the importance of family through duty. He should've written a new one to the both of them that addressed her concerns about Bruce's future. Ray might've even slipped in something about his certainty that Marianne's father must've been a great salesman to have built that place up to what it had become. But then, he had to admit he didn't know either of them well enough to be assured of success. He knew some studio owners better than his own son.

"Good afternoon. How are you?" the bartender asked, nattily attired with a vest and bow tie.

"Good. And you?"

"Fine, sir. Would you like something to drink?"

"A beer," Ray said.

"What kind?"

"What's local that you have on tap? The Horace?"

"Horace Ale, yes sir." The bartender pulled the tap. The amber nectar flooded the glass in a foamy explosion. "Here you go. Would you like something to eat?" He waited a moment for the foam to settle and slid a menu in front of Ray.

After ordering some food, he tried to nurse his beer, by taking tiny sips, barely enough to wet his lips. After ten minutes, only a quarter of the glass was gone. Soon, however, his sips grew to large gulps. In another ten minutes, with a long final swallow, he'd finished it.

"I'm sorry sir." The bartender reappeared after a lengthy absence. "There's been a mix-up in the kitchen. It might be awhile until your food's ready."

"That's okay. I'm not in a rush." Ray admired the rings of foam on the glass.

"Let me get you another," the bartender said.

"I wasn't going to..."

"Please. It's on the house, an apology for our mistake."

"Sure, what the hell," Ray said. "I should celebrate anyway."

"Everyone should," the bartender said.

When dinner finally came, Ray was four beers in. He tore into his sandwich and found he grew thirstier with each bite. He had two more during the course of his meal.

By the time a group of tired businessmen shuffled through the door, Ray was drunk enough to enjoy himself without any guilt. The men in suits slogged from their tables to the bar and back, looking so beaten down at chasing the same dollar that Ray had just made so easily. He toasted the air as one of them approached the bar, receiving a glare in return. Ray swallowed the last of his pint. It tasted warm. One more would be just enough.

"One more?" the bartender asked.

"I made three big sales on consecutive days."

"Congratulations."

"And I'm not done celebrating yet."

"That's the spirit," the bartender said.

"I don't overdo things too much," Ray said. "I'm too old."

* * *

Finally, the application she'd requested weeks before arrived. Marianne sliced through the Pittson town seal on the back of the envelope, after a moment's hesitation. She looked down at the trash as she did so, still unsure if she'd be able to go through with it. She slid the forms out over the desk, reading the first paragraph of each page -- full of technical jargon, broken up by lines for answers to questions she wasn't ready to ask herself. All she really wanted to find out was if she registered The Shelby as a historic building, would they be able to afford to continue living in the apartment, even if business never picked back up. She knew it might mean giving up on the idea that it would still be a real hotel; it'd become like a museum that people sometimes slept in.

There will still be much for Bruno to learn about, she thought to herself, as she began to fill out the forms. In fact, it was going to be even more important for him to be involved as the business shifted to this next phase. He sure wasn't going to learn how to turn his childhood home into a landmark in the Pittson Public School System. When the time came, he could take business classes at the community college down in the valley, if it was deemed necessary. The screeching of the elevator broke her off just as she neared convincing herself of all of this. She slipped the forms back in the envelope, then locked it inside the desk. No one should see her even deliberating over such a thing.

"Mr. Cyzek, how are you today?" she asked.

"Fine. And you?" he asked. "Must take a lot of work to keep this big old place up and running."

"We aim to make it look easy, Mr. Cyzek."

"It takes a lot of work for something to look effortless. I know that for sure." Buddy looked down at his accordion. "I wonder if you would do me a favor?"

"Anything for such a valued guest, Mr. Cyzek," Marianne said.

"If anyone calls for me, would you mind telling them that I'm out working? If it's no imposition, that is."

"Not at all, sir."

"I appreciate that. Would you like to hear a song?" he asked, unlocking the accordion. "What's your favorite song? I can play just about anything."

"I couldn't trouble you Mr. Cyzek..."

"Give me a try," he said. "Pick a song, any song."

"Do you know *Night and Day?*" Marianne asked.

"By Cole Porter? Of course."

He launched into a forlorn version, full of notes that wheezed and cried. Marianne swayed in an off-kilter rhythm, unable to keep from getting caught up in the melody. Her chest tightened as though Buddy's fingers felt out the source of the song's longing.

When he finished, Buddy took the instrument off and locked the sides together. With their clicking, Marianne opened her eyes, freed from the spell. Blushing slightly, she felt embarrassed to be caught acting in such a way in front of a guest. In returning to herself, she considered that she might be betraying her father's memory in turning the hotel over to the town as it were. She bid Buddy farewell and slid open the drawer but could only look at the forms.

* * *

Morning sunlight blasted through the curtain. Ray rolled away from it to face the dark. The traffic moving by on the road outside sounded so close, it made his head throb. It took a moment before he remembered he was in a hotel room on Castle Island. A memory of staggering up to the front desk earlier that morning came to him. He could almost make out the face of the woman behind the desk. She'd been wearing glasses, he was fairly sure. She'd handed him the key that now sat atop the digital clock on the nightstand. It was 7:17. Ray pulled back the sheets to find he was still wearing the same slacks he'd worn the day before, their dryness came as a relief.

He took a lukewarm swig of water from a small plastic cup at the bedside. When the air conditioner rattled to life, Ray hugged the sheets around him and hauled his body from the bed. The hotel's carpet felt thin and cold beneath his bare feet. After shutting the air off, he risked peeking outside. His car was parked squarely in its spot with no obvious signs of damage, a further cause for relief.

Hoping for recovery in the shower, he got as close as he could to the showerhead and faced its flow. The water pounded his face, massaging the tightness beneath his skin. He tiptoed higher into the force of spray. The sting of heat against his eyelids even began to chase his headache away. Opening his mouth, he felt the stream hot against his teeth and gums. In another moment of relief, he realized the unmistakable tang of vomit was absent from his tongue.

* * *

"Buddy, it's after dawn. The sun's up." Mark slouched away from the soundboard, his arms limp at his sides.

"Let me go one more time. I'll pay you for two extra hours." Buddy dabbed his face with a red handkerchief. Where the accordion's bellows rested against his chest, lines of sweat soaked through his checked flannel shirt.

Mark swirled the coffee in his mug and leaned towards the board begrudgingly. Were it anyone else, he would've packed it in long ago. With Buddy, he wouldn't even think of accepting more money. The big man had already poured so much into the microphone that night and morning, that it didn't feel right not to let him get it all out. After slurping down the last of his coffee, Mark pushed record.

"Ready when you are, man," he said.

Buddy stretched out the instrument, flexing its bellows with a soft honk that sounded almost like a sigh. He cleared his throat. Tapping out a rhythm with his foot, he leaned into the microphone.

"Last one," he said. "Last take of *Milwaukee Digger.*"

When he brought the bellows together and tapped at the keys, it sounded like an enormous harmonica played by a giant, huffing and puffing his way over the notes. His fingers sped up and down in alternating synchronization on either end. For more than three minutes, the big man struggled to keep up with the swinging *Milwaukee Digger,* speaking the words more than singing them.

When he was finished, Buddy removed the accordion from his shoulders and rose unsteadily. His face was flushed. A thin wheeze rode the air coming from his chest.

"Ready to hear it?" Mark asked.

"Later," Buddy huffed. "Cigarette?"

"You sure you need one?" Mark asked.

"No, but that's the best time to have one in my experience."

Down the hall that led to the back door, Buddy grinned when he spotted one of the records he'd done years ago hanging on the wall -- "Road to Buckland," a single, one of his own compositions. Above the record was a picture of him with his band, many of whom had passed on. He looked so young and thin then, even though it was only a handful of years before. The accordion propped on his thigh was the same one he'd just played. The youth on that record sleeve had no problems finding the necessary energy. He could play for practically days at a time with only a case of beer and pack of cigarettes for fuel, maybe with a cup of coffee thrown in.

Mark put his key in the lock next to the alarm switch. With half a turn, it blurted out part of its call and went dead. Outside, the brittle orange of morning struggled to break through a light blanket of smog. The air had a bit of an autumn chill to it, as though summer was slowly taking off its coat. Buddy squeezed a cigarette from his pack.

"So, what do you think?" he asked.

"Sounds good. No problems getting it down."

"Did you have any fun in there?"

"No doubt, you really know how to make that thing sing," Mark said.

Buddy wanted to ask if he sounded old, worn out. But he knew enough to just take his producer's compliment. He coughed on his first inhale -- the smoke thick in his lungs. Mark looked a little worried. Buddy wanted to reassure him that his work on this earth was far from finished but just smiled and had another toke.

* * *

It didn't smell like booze in the room, not the way Ray used to sweat it out -- a thick oily cloud of sourness. Though Marianne had put off cleaning his room for a day, so the smell might not have been so telling. It'd been years but she could still recognize the imprint his head left on the pillow, the shape of his body impressed on the mattress. After putting her hand to his pillow, she ripped off the sheets.

In the trash, there were none of the tiny bottles that were customarily strewn about any room in which he stayed. There were none under the bed or in the drawers of the dresser or behind the dresser; towards the end of their romance, Ray had taken to trying to hide them from her. It forced her to consider that he might've gotten sober for just as long as it took her to plug in the vacuum cleaner. She worked quickly, wanting to get away from him as fast as she could.

Back at the desk in the lobby, she might not have noticed that the doors of the theater across the street were no longer covered in plywood, if it hadn't been for the man in the grey jumpsuit coming out of them. He cradled a ladder under one arm and squeezed a cardboard box against his hip with the other. After putting the ladder up under the marquee, he climbed it and began dropping letters until it no longer read *Grand Reopening* but *ran on in*. He then went down to his box and took out some letters, affixing them so that it now read *Strangers on a Train*.

Marianne might've taken some encouragement for the sign that hers would no longer be the only business trying to survive there on the top of Mt. Kneebow had her eyes not dropped down from the marquee to what was undoubtedly Buddy's station wagon. It reminded her of the talk she'd yet to have with her son about tending to guests properly. She'd tried starting her lecture on this topic in the apartment once or twice but could never be as certain that she'd have his full attention in there the way she could in the lobby. It would be a good test for Bruno as well to see if he could take professional criticism maturely and not turn petulant.

* * *

Foam washed down Bruno's face, stinging his eyes, tingling his scalp. He deciphered enough of the tiny print on the bottle to read that he had to wait ninety seconds before rinsing. He obeyed that directive and found his reward as the water caressed his head like a cool hand. The sensation counted as proof or so the bottle implied that his nonexistent dandruff was being cured.

He wanted Julia to notice and comment on it. Back in his room, as he finished dressing, he saw the bottle of cologne still on his dresser. He took it to the bathroom and dumped it out, stashing the bottle at the bottom of the trash under a pile of tissues and other detritus he was satisfied not knowing more about.

Normally, there were few conversations he dreaded more than those in which his mother tried to tell him what a handsome young man he was. It produced the same petted puppy feeling that he so hated from Julia. But now as he tugged at his vest and opened the apartment door, Bruno was struck by the need for his mother to recognize his efforts.

"What's this?" she asked when he appeared practically strutting out of the apartment.

Blushing mildly, Bruno stood straight, eager for her examination.

"Your hair looks so...healthy and...full. Very handsome, Bruno."

"Mom," he whined in false protest.

"Sorry. Can't I compliment you when you look nice?"

"Thanks, Mom," he said, settling next to her.

"Look across the street," she said. "Is there anything out there we should be talking about? Can you see anything that you might've missed."

Bruno squinted through the revolving door at the theater as though he'd forgotten it was even there. It'd been years since he'd daydreamed about going inside. When he saw that the sun-bleached letters on the marquee had been replaced by new ones and that a movie would soon, apparently, be playing, all he could think of were all the broken promises his father had made about taking him, when he was a boy.

"*Strangers on a Train*?" he asked.

"No, not the theater possibly reopening."

"I don't know what? Dad's gone? I know. You told me."

"Is one of our guests parked out there?"

"Yeah, the station wagon. I see it. It's falling apart. So what?"

"Were you supposed to retrieve some luggage from it for that guest and bring it to his room?"

"I guess," he said, huffing as though exhausted.

"Did you?"

"No."

"Why not?"

"I don't know."

"You don't?" Marianne said, steadying herself and remaining calm. "When I let you work with Julia, I expect you to work as a team not to neglect a guest."

"I don't like the way she talks to me," he said. "She acts like she's my boss. I've been here longer. This is my home. It should be the other way around."

"Calm down, calm down," Marianne said, pleased it had taken at least that long for things to turn spiky. "She's just older than you so probably finds that role more natural."

"She's not that much older than me."

"Bruno, the fact is, I was really embarrassed when Mr. Cyzek came through the lobby carrying his own luggage," she said. "If you want people to treat you differently, treat you like you're not a kid, then you have to act more responsibly."

Bruno tried listening to his mother, but looking at the theater, he found his mind wandering. A movie might offer him the chance to get Julia to see him as something more than just the boss's son. He imagined her following him into the dark interior of the Thompson, so close he could feel her just behind him. Like a gentleman, he'd find their row and allow her to go first, her ponytail like a golden torch lighting the way. They wouldn't sit too close at first, but when the scary parts came, she'd squeeze his arm. There in the dark, she'd finally see he was not a boy but a man who could protect her. By the time his mom had finished with her lecture, he wasn't even sure what she was talking about, just more family and duty and her usual lines. He said whatever he thought she wanted to hear just to make her go away.

Of course, Julia was ten excruciating minutes late. When she saw it was Bruno behind the desk, she panted a laugh dripping with relief. Slightly pinker than flushed, her face glowed even more radiantly than it had in his imagination. He knew there wouldn't be many more chances to show her that he was not just a little boy. In a few days, she'd start school down in Pittson; the summer would be over and so would his shifts with her.

"Hi Brucey," she said, "Where's the boss?"

"I'm manning the desk on my own today in case our guest needs anything," Bruno said, trying to deepen his voice.

"That other guy checked out. He said he was a friend of your mother's, I guess." She looked down at the register. "Ray Davis, I think was his name. He left her a note. Do you know who that is?"

"No," Bruno said, glancing down at the name and running his finger over it. "He's no one I know."

"I think your mother knows him," Julia said. "They had kind of a thing in the lobby right there in front of me."

"Did they?"

"I don't know what you'd call it, almost a fight but not quite, but like it would've been a fight, if they were alone together. It was weird like they used to see each other or something."

"Probably just some loser who's stayed here before. We used to get lots of losers like that, bothering my mother. Don't worry about him."

"Brucey, are you like doing something to your hair? It's kind of..." she began, sounding so close to giggling that it made Bruno nervous.

"Did you, um...notice the sign above the theater?" he asked. Julia turned and looked across the street.

"I've never heard of *Strangers on a Train*. What is it?".

"A movie, I guess. Maybe we can go together," Bruno said barely containing his excitement.

He laid his hand atop hers. She tried to squirm it from beneath his grasp, but he didn't let go. She tried lifting it away and he only pressed down with greater force.

"Bruce, stop," she said in a whisper that rose to something sharp. "This is making me uncomfortable."

"I hear *Strangers on a Train* is good," he said, withdrawing his hand finally.

"Just keep your hands to yourself, freak," she said. "Just cause you never get out of this place doesn't mean you can act like it."

"Julia, I like you," he said and though it was true, it was also a cover for the discomfort he was beginning to feel -- an altogether less enticing one than Julia normally aroused.

"Do you even know what that means?" she asked.

"I've been meaning to tell you all summer. I think we..."

"I'm going down to the basement to grab some towels for the cart or something," she said, walking away from the desk. "You need to get a grip, Bruno."

Utter disdain rather than love or even kindness, rode on that word when she finally said it to him. The moment was so far from what he dreamed it would be that it made him want to change back to Brucey. He went after her, but she slammed the door to the basement hard enough to communicate her feelings even more clearly.

7

Bruno awoke unable to think of anything but Rick. He was sure he'd dreamt about him but couldn't latch on to any details. The need to hold something concrete that would remind him of his former tutor was suddenly very strong. He thought he'd stashed a book of poems from their too brief time together in the top drawer of his bureau. Beneath the underwear he never wore and the monogrammed handkerchiefs his father had given him, he didn't find the book but unearthed an even older relic, a brochure for The Fireman's Arcade.

Its corners were curled, the photos and print both fading, but despite being unable to remember the last time he'd looked at it, he saw in a flash all of the things he used to imagine doing there and the glance it offered of the world that lay at the foot of Mt. Kneebow, of which he knew even now only as flat images on his computer screen. He flipped it open to what it'd once meant to him, hoping it would staunch the need for his former tutor.

When he was a boy and the hotel and Pittson still something of a destination, his mother would display information about local attractions discreetly on the side of the front desk that faced the elevator. Bruno couldn't remember any more of them but there had certainly been others. He'd only ever really been interested in the arcade. He thought the prizes to be redeemed from tickets earned playing games like skee-ball looked wondrous. The thing he wanted the most was pictured on the back of the brochure, a stamp made from the letters in his name. It had been years since he even remembered what he thought he'd do with such a thing.

His father had promised to take him there, but it never happened. Bruno had come to see the notion that his father broke his promises wasn't really accurate because his father didn't really care enough. His promises didn't break so much as disappear the moment they were uttered. Flipping backwards through the brochure's pages, he wondered if the arcade was still in business or if the former warehouse with tall windows where it was housed, was even still standing. On the cover, though freshly painted, the building was unmistakably old, here and there bricks were missing -- black rectangular voids in the red.

It was absurd that he'd yet to run down the stairs into the valley, into the town that lay at their feet. He had a purpose for going now though, he thought, looking again at the brochure. There would be no more waiting for his father to take him. There would be no more waiting until he was sure his mother would allow it. He took one last look at the brochure before putting it in the drawer and pushing it closed.

In the living room, his mother was pushing a vacuum beneath a tattered blue armchair that had been in Bruno's life in one spot or another for as long as he could remember, and yet he could never recall anyone ever sitting in it. Surrounded by objects that never seemed to change, he now was sure he wanted to run down to the arcade. He wasn't even that interested in the games. He just wanted to make it there, to run until the Shelby and Mt. Kneebow and everything of the life that he knew was but a speck in the distance.

"Mom," Bruno yelled over the vacuum. When she didn't answer immediately, he shouted -- his voice cracked and shrill.

She pressed her foot on the button in the back, and it wheezed to a stop. "What is it, Bruno? What is it? Why are you lurking behind me like that? Come where I can see you if you want to ask me something, don't just stand there hollering yourself hoarse for me."

"Can I have some money?"

"I just gave you money yesterday to go to the movies," she said winding the cord around her wrist.

"I need some more."

"More?"

"Come on, Mr. Sperint paid all that money in advance. I just want like a hundred."

"A hundred?" she asked, her eyebrows riding a wrinkle on her forehead. "No way. We need that money to last, Bruno. What do you need it for anyway?"

"Okay ten, then," he said. "I won't have to bother you next time."

"Already down to ten? You're a shrewd negotiator Bruno. Take ten from my purse."

"Can I take 20?"

"Ten," she said and stomped the vacuum back to life.

Her purse sat in its usual spot against the armrest of the couch. Another former lobby item that had been decommissioned and placed in the living room. It had been there for years, and he hadn't so much as slung his vest over it. If it wasn't for the fact that his mother's purse often sat on it, he would've never gone near it. The worn buttons on the back of it, once symbols of the fatherless afternoons of his youth, now struck him more as a series of counted and wasted seconds.

He undid the silver clasp of her wallet. Coupons and tattered receipts fell out around his hand as he tried to gather them. The ten-dollar note sat alone in the billfold. After taking it, Bruno sat the purse on the end table next to the couch.

"I'm going for a run," he said.

"A run? Where?" she said, turning the vacuum off again.

"Just outside. Just up the hill and back."

"Wear a watch. Don't be long. I don't want you straying too far. I might need you, later."

"Like for what?"

"Does a run cost ten dollars?" she asked as he opened the door. "Someone charging for that now?"

Bruno tucked the money in the waistband of his shorts and jogged out of the lobby before she changed her mind. Increasing his pace to almost a sprint, he soon put the hotel and theater behind him. Determined to go too far, he jogged past the abandoned shops boarded up with plywood bleached almost white by the sun. Ghost neighbors whose businesses he failed to recall even from the deepest recesses of his childhood.

With perspiration stinging his eyes, he felt he could finally outrun the border his mother had drawn around his life. Pulling his shirt up, he wiped his face and thought about how all the things his mother claimed caused his acne to breakout were also linked to things she didn't want him doing, like eating sweets or sweating. Bruno couldn't help wondering whether being bisexual or gay might also be part of the problem, and how many more barriers she'd place around him if she found out what he was.

He ran the very path she'd trained him to draw out for guests down to the stairs that led into Pittson. For a time, his schooling under her watch seemed to consist of little more than memorizing the streets down in the valley well enough so that he could reproduce them in ink, drawing for guests what would one day be his own forbidden zone. The notion of finally going into the town he knew only a series of intersecting lines was always brighter just before he got to them. One moment, his determination felt at its peak, then that first step sat just below his feet. The two last working smokestacks coughed purple ribbons up into the air before him. He stood at the edge, waiting as always for the will to carry on.

* * *

After brushing his teeth, the coat of nicotine remained in Angus's mouth, a taste becoming a texture. He rinsed over and over, spitting out yellow globs of saliva. His stomach felt swollen and uneasy. He filled a glass in the bathroom and sat on the edge of the bed before dialing the front desk.

"Mr. Sperint, how may I help you?" Marianne asked.

"Would you have any mouthwash available for purchase?" he asked in a voice thick with phlegm.

"For you, Mr. Sperint, it's complimentary," she said. "I'll bring it right up."

Angus breathed into his hands. The residue of cigarette smoke struck him even more without the sour stench of booze to hide it. He gargled hot water, spitting it out when he heard the elevator. When Marianne knocked, he tiptoed from the bathroom and unlocked the door.

"Come in," he said, stepping aside.

As she handed him the bottle of Scope, he noticed how long and slender her fingers were. They wrapped their cargo elegantly. He wasn't sure he'd noticed things like that until he'd gotten sober. Rarer still was the experience of being alone with a woman without the emboldening effect of alcohol warming his blood. He felt flushed in just thinking about telling her what beautiful hands she had.

"Thank you very much," Angus said, instead. He avoided looking at her face.

"Just one thing, Mr. Sperint."

"Yes?"

"All the rooms at the Shelby are non-smoking."

"I wasn't smoking in the room. I'm afraid that's me...I mean my clothes. I had dinner in a bar." He sniffed at himself.

"If you'd like Mr. Sperint, I can cook for you," she said. "That is if you'd rather not eat in some dingy bar."

"Thank you. I'll think about that. I didn't realize..."

"We pride ourselves on being a full-service hotel. You'll just let me know." She left, closing the door so softly that it barely made a sound.

Putting his ear to the door, he listened to her feet tracking softly down the hall. The small bottle felt warm in his hand. This new way of seeing and being in the world was still so new to him that he felt lost in the clarity -- being drunk had always obscured things, shrunk the perceivable world down. In such moments, he found he missed it so much, he almost felt ill.

After unscrewing the cap, he took almost half of the bottle's liquid into his mouth. He was on his way to the bathroom to spit it out when, without thinking, he swallowed it instead. The first notes of warmth began to creep through him with such terrifying familiarity that he poured the rest down the drain.

* * *

Bruno rubbed a dime-sized dot of cleanser it into the areas most affected on his face with the tip of his finger. The foaming wash tingled as he gently worked it into his skin. He counted to sixty. Then, after rinsing, he turned down the heat of the shower.

As he crossed the hall back to his room, he took the ten-dollar bill from his jogging shorts. It was soggy with sweat. He'd have to wait to spend it, having failed once again to make it down the stairs. Two years since his father had offered him the chance to leave town and still, he couldn't bring himself to even go down the hill.

Back when his mother first allowed him the freedom to go for his runs, he had to promise her never to go into town. From that point forward, he knew exactly what she thought was too far. As he'd stood at the top of the stairs, on the precipice of crossing the boundary earlier that morning, his body had seized up. It seemed that the very molecules that made him resisted trespassing from the world she had designed for him.

When she knocked on his door, he thought about not answering or pretending like he was down in Pittson at the arcade blowing the ten she'd given him. She pounded harder. He remained still, trying not to breathe, trying not to be there. The doorknob began to twist.

"Wait, mom," he called.

He threw a dress shirt over his shoulders and pulled on a pair of jeans. Her knocks were announcements, not questions, and lately, he'd been in the habit of answering merely to preserve his privacy. Bruno cracked open the door just enough to show her he was fully, if defeatedly, there.

8

Marianne dusted and polished the reception desk as her father had taught her, not stopping until she could make out her reflection in its mahogany surface. It had been weeks since she'd dusted it like that. Her father would've been shamefaced by her procrastination; he'd dusted that desk to a dark mirror every morning of his life. When she was a girl, Marianne used to crouch behind him and watch. As he worked, he'd tell her of the importance of making sure the little things were taken care of. For him, there was no such thing as a petty task when it came to his hotel. Everything about The Shelby deserved his constant attention. Things out here, he'd say referring to the hotel, couldn't be put off, while things in there, pointing behind him to the apartment, could always wait.

She came to think of the hotel as solely her father's domain. In the apartment, her mother ruled but Marianne wasn't there much, if she could help it. When forced to, she'd assist with the chores - - the dishes, the dusting, the making of beds -- none of which had the same prestige for her as what needed to be done out in the hotel. As she worked, her mother would complain about how much time the hotel took up. Your father has no concept of delegating, her mother would say, a turn of phrase that baffled Marianne even in memory. He cares too much about the petty things, she'd continue from the kitchen, holding the swinging door open with her back as Marianne scrubbed the pots and pans.

Even as a very young girl, she bristled at any notion that her father cared too much about the hotel. From an early age, she'd understood as her father did that the Shelbys and their business were inseparable. The hotel held them together. It made them who they were. It was a concept her mother never seemed to grasp.

Bruno reminded her of her mother that way. She couldn't help but blame him a little for her letting things slide. Now 14, he was becoming more difficult to manage. Lately, he'd begun pestering her constantly to let him go for runs. It annoyed her but at least he'd given up on the idea of going to school down in the valley. She'd only relented and let him run to prove he wasn't trapped. He'd be happier, she thought, if he took more pride in the hotel. It was his life, his future. Only in accepting the necessity of his duties would he understand freedom

Opening the drawer, she took out the letter specifying the type of tutoring required if she wished to continue having Bruno's education done where he belonged. It was as if the government had allied with her son in an effort to make her life more difficult. From the wording of the letter, it was clear they discounted the need for him to get two educations, one from books and one from the hotel. She hoped to find an individual who would see things the way she did and would meet the guidelines without getting in the way of his real education.

* * *

Ray stopped in at a small diner off the highway for lunch, the kind with chipped glasses and greasy food served on paper in plastic baskets. His chicken fingers and fries were dry and overcooked. To compensate for their dryness, he ordered a bottle of beer. Trying to savor it, he drank slowly, but never put the bottle down. The stool felt comfortable, and the idea of running up a little tab seemed like a relaxing way to spend the afternoon. He'd made his month already. He'd earned a right to cut loose.

"You must be thirsty." The bartender glanced up from filling a plastic cup with straws. She wore a faded blouse with a tattered blue ribbon in the middle of the collar.

"I'm celebrating. Sold some expensive equipment this week. Microphones," he said. "Makes my whole month easy."

"You sell microphones?" she asked.

"Sometimes I tell people I work in the music industry."

"You kind of do. Right?"

"Thank you for seeing it my way." Ray saluted her, then downed the rest of his bottle in one large swallow. He placed it on a coaster, tingling with happiness from his toes to his teeth.

* * *

"I was just coming to make up the room, Mr. Cyzek. Sorry to have bothered you. I can wait until you've left," Marianne said, moving the cart to the side.

"I'd like a wakeup call for seven tomorrow morning. If it's not too much trouble," Buddy said, removing the tag from the door that requested house cleaning. He'd meant to display the DO NOT DISTURB side but had been too tired to notice the difference.

"Seven tomorrow, that we can do," she said. "I hope you've enjoyed your stay. Please, just drop your key at the front desk before noon."

"Much obliged."

Buddy wasn't ready to leave but had to move on. He could've happily stayed there in Pittson and done a whole suite of records with Mark. But if he was going to finish his project, if that really was what was keeping him from seeing his kids, he needed to be out on the road. There were other notches in the rust belt that he needed to hit, if his polka almanac was going to be what he wanted it to be.

He could only hope to have the same experience he'd had there in Pittson. During their final morning cigarette break, Buddy had known for certain that he and Mark had shared something real. Something about the music had gotten to them both. For true music lovers, who understood how one squeezed their soul from the notes they played, it was impossible to describe or deny the feeling. Producers like Mark could only capture the passion of the music when they allowed it to take them on a journey to a place they didn't even know they wanted to go.

* * *

Unsteadiness buckled Ray's legs. Woozy enough for the room to start spinning, he held on to his stool for a moment then slid back up on his seat. Things had gotten away from him, but they were still close enough that he could breathe through it until he regained control. He closed his eyes as he gave each cheek a slap.

"Thirsty boy's back," the bartender said as he reclaimed his seat. "Find the men's room okay?"

"I should eat something else." Ray spoke carefully, making sure to form the words one by one in his mouth. Experience had taught him to hide his inebriation by delivering each syllable as deliberately as possible.

"More food's probably a good idea," she said. "You left one chicken tender and barely touched the fries."

"Anything you'd recommend?"

"How about something hearty, like a fish sandwich? It comes with coleslaw rather than french fries."

"Sounds good," Ray said.

"You need something with a little green in it."

"Why green?" he asked.

"It'll help settle your stomach. Give your system something to work on."

"Do I seem that drunk?"

"I've seen worse. But I can tell you're drunk. Looks like you got a little water on yourself," she said, smiling.

He looked down to find a large wet spot just to the side of his crotch. If he stayed seated long enough, no one else would see. It didn't matter so much that the bartender had noticed. She wouldn't tell anyone. Bartenders were like priests.

"You're not driving nowhere I hope," she said.

"No. I'm staying down the street at the motor lodge. Got here on my own two feet."

"Let's try to make sure you can get home that way then," she said. "You look like you're about ready to fall off your stool."

"I thought you said I didn't look that drunk."

"No," she said, chuckling, "I said I've seen worse. It's not the same thing."

"Quit pacing, man. You're making me tense." Mark said, hunched over the soundboard.

"I don't want to hear my own voice," Angus said. "Please make it go away."

"Breathing down my neck won't make anything good happen."

"I want to be erased."

"I understand what you want, Mr. Sperint...Angus," Mark said after a weary chuckle. "But I can only do so much. Tell you what, why don't we go take a breather? Come with me."

Down a hall lined with records in glass cases, Mark led the way to the back door of the studio. Most were little-known rhythm and blues records, with some polka acts sprinkled in. Never a fan of music, Angus gave them no more than a passing glance.

Mark put his key in the fire alarm and disarmed it before opening the back door. The bright afternoon sun exploded across the parking lot, the heat rushing at them. Angus took the cigarette offered to him from between Mark's thick fingers, then leaned into his flame.

"God, I have to quit," Mark said, exhaling through his nostrils.

"A nasty habit," Angus said before taking a long drag then spitting.

"How long you been a smoker?" Mark asked.

"I'm not really," Angus said. "I mean I do when I'm nervous or have been drinking."

"I've been at it for about twenty-five years," Mark said through a cough. "Still remember my first one. Lucky Strike. Better because it's toasted, the pack said...old school. I was just a kid, fifteen, sixteen something like that."

"I'm pretty nervous it seems all the time nowadays," Angus said, quietly almost to himself. "My brother got me started. He smoked Pall Malls because Johnny Carson smoked them. He thought they were necessary for a comedian, I guess."

"That's old school too. Can't remember the last time I saw someone smoking a Pall Mall. Sounds like your brother was kind of a bad influence."

"Sometimes he was," Angus said. He considered the burning end of his Marlboro Light, glowing orange. He'd forgotten what Pall Malls tasted like.

* * *

Bits of chicken skin stuck to Marianne's fingers as she peeled the flesh, trying not to burn her hands. It was still very hot in some places. After she'd finished skinning it, she cubed the cooked meat, waiting for the water to boil. Once it was hot enough, she added stock cubes, then the chicken, before adding the carrots, radishes, onions, and celery she had diced earlier. She hadn't made anything that substantial in some time. Bruno had lately taken to making his own meals -- sandwiches and ready-to-heat things as far as she could tell. The work of the hotel rarely allowed them to eat together.

From his appearance, she'd judged Angus to be a modest type, the kind of man who didn't overindulge or expect more from life than he could handle. Her experience hosting so many musicians had taught her how to spot the hedonists. They were always more demanding, always asking for things with confidence, as if they expected to be given more of everything. They never were happy with the simple things.

She felt that Ray's problems arose from this inability to enjoy and relish simplicity, to ask for no more than that which was placed before him. He always wanted more, wanted something different, begged to be indulged. Marianne stirred the pot, refocusing herself on her guest. She still had Mr. Sperint's room to clean and didn't want any thoughts of Ray to follow her into 412 again.

* * *

"What can I get you, hun?" Lois asked

Her hands gripped two of the draft beer levers. She only had to lean back a little, accidentally let some come out and Angus would've taken it as a sign to start drinking again. It was a mistake to keep going there. He couldn't trust his sobriety enough to continue putting it through these tests. Looking at his own hands on the rail of the bar, he was struck by something of a novelty -- a clear memory. Though he didn't remember the name of the bar and it looked nothing like The Northpark Lounge, the emptiness, the atmosphere of soon to be thwarted expectations that permeated the air felt the same.

He was to meet Andy to help him go over some new material, and Angus prided himself on being early, especially when the rendezvous point boasted generous happy hour specials. Andy had tried to wring a promise from him that he'd hold off drinking until they were together, but Angus could no more make that promise than Andy could vow to be punctual. Fifteen minutes past the appointed time Angus ordered his first beer, then fifteen minutes became a half an hour, then forty-five minutes and one beer became two, then three, then a couple of shots.

As the day rolled into evening, a road crew shuffled in, still wearing their hard hats and reflective vests. Angus bought them a round and then each one of the three of them reciprocated. They made an odd-looking party, those dusty blue-collar types with Angus, the perpetual prep school kid, in his blue blazer and khakis. He listened to them grumble about their day, about their wives, lives, and paychecks.

By the time his reliable and yet too often unfortunate urge to speak came around, Angus found himself complaining about having Father's money doled out in monthly stipends. Even though it would've been much less, he surmised he should've just taken the lump sum. From there on the rounds were on him and his new drinking companions began to regard him with barely disguised contempt.

Andy never showed. Angus would not find out what had happened to him until getting that terrible phone call the next morning. He was so hungover sick that the news his brother had hung himself only made him numb. It'd happened in the next room probably while Angus had been passed out in his clothes atop his bed -- a familiar oblivion. He pushed himself off his stool at The Northpark Lounge, having again *just* passed another of his tests.

On the sidewalk, the heat of the day coiled up from the concrete. Crossing the bridge, Angus began to swim in the sweat clinging to his shirt. His thighs burned as he hiked the metal stairs to the top of Mount Kneebow. It felt as though he'd been drinking but had somehow skidded past the high right into the dehydration of a hangover. By the time he reached The Shelby, the sky had turned dark. The thickness of the air seemed more determined.

* * *

Plant wailed over Page's stabbing guitar line while the backbeat collapsed and reformed. "Immigrant Song" from *Led Zeppelin III* had lately become one of the things in the world Bruno loved best. Its speed and weight so bracing, he felt compelled to listen over and over in hopes of discovering the source of its power. As Plant sang of hammers and gods and driven ships and new lands all while cymbals crashed behind him like a storm at sea, Bruno imagined himself singing on stage, playing guitar, or sitting behind the drums. Looking out at the crowd, he tried to find a familiar face to fixate on, but the images scattered before he could completely fill them in. He began to wonder what the minds behind those fleeting faces might've thought of him, what anyone saw when they looked at him. He wondered what more he could be for people than the kid showing them to their room, giving them directions into town. The fantasy evaporated at this intrusion. He turned off the music. Lying on his back, he looked up at the ceiling and found it impossible to imagine any other world where he might exist.

* * *

On the fourth floor the next morning, Marianne hesitated before opening the gate. She ran her hand over her hair, not to straighten it but to simply feel that all was in place. The coarseness of the grayed hairs tickled her palm. It'd been years since she last prepared food for a guest. She wanted to hear that Angus had enjoyed it. She needed assurance that she could still run a full-service hotel. There was no card hanging on the door of 412, so she knocked.

He opened the door, half-dressed. His tight white undershirt stretched over the sharp outline of his ribcage like a layer of cotton skin. The hearty ambrosia of chicken soup still hung in the air.

"You must be here for the bowl and silverware," he said, smiling.

"Only if you're finished with them." Marianne nodded. As Angus handed her the bowl, their eyes met, lingering for a long moment.

"The soup spoon," he said with a failed snap of his fingers, as though trying to answer the uncomfortable silence.

Marianne thought it odd that he went into the bathroom to find it. She stood by the doorway, smoothing out her skirt, wondering why he'd turned on the faucet. Finally, after far longer than necessary, he emerged, wiping off the spoon with a washcloth.

"Have you eaten breakfast?" she asked.

"No, no," Angus said shaking free of himself. "I'd like some, though, if it's not too much trouble. Dinner was delicious. Dinner was perfect."

"Was it? We are certainly glad to hear that," she said, fighting the joy she felt from blooming on her face. Her smile would've been too wide, too brimming with unprofessional self-satisfaction. Things needed to look effortless for guests to feel at ease, or so her father had always said.

* * *

By the time he'd run to the end of the block, past the disused baseball field overrun by dandelions and other assorted thick-growing weeds, Bruno was sweating enough to make his hair and clothes feel heavy. Behind where home plate had once been, he slipped through a chain link fence that was rusted and fell away like a curtain. He followed the uphill path into the small forest of oaks and poplars bordering either side of a set of power lines.

As he picked up the pace, the gathering swelter made heavy work of moving his entire body. He tried keeping under the trees, but their shade offered no relief. Soon, his lungs began to tingle as though he was inhaling pure heat. When he reached the top of the hill, he sat down, leaning his back against the warm concrete of one of the transmission tower's bases. Letting his legs dangle over the sheer cliff that sat high above Pittson, he looked straight down until he felt dizzy.

He'd lately taken to spying from that vantage point on all of the lives being lived at a distance. He tried putting himself in one of the cars moving along the Riverway, picking out one to watch until it rounded the bend and went behind Mt. Kneebow. He wondered where they were going. He watched a barge drifting atop the brown water and thought about what it would be like to be sitting atop all its coal with a view downstream. As the concrete he sat against cooled his back, he thought about staying there all day, until the sun began to set. He wanted to be gone too long. There, overlooking the city, he felt less alone even if the signs of other life were fleeting and indistinct.

Words came to him as if borne aloft by the breeze: *This moment, yearning and thoughtful sitting alone / It seems to me there are other men in other lands yearning and thoughtful.* Since they were most definitely not Zeppelin lyrics, he couldn't, at first, be sure from where they came. Then he remembered that they were part of a poem he'd been made to memorize by Rick, a poem from the very book he'd been looking for. He searched his mind for other bits of it but couldn't recall any. He repeated the words he did remember aloud over again, hearing them echo back. He thought of Rick at home somewhere down there, hearing him.

Bruno had his number but the thought of calling Rick was even more daunting than taking the stairs down into town. Whatever it was that kept him from doing these things, whatever had bred this fear into him, he was unable to face it long enough to understand. Leaning his head back against the concrete, he kept saying the poem's lines over and over again as though they were an incantation, which might summon Rick.

* * *

The eggs sizzled as Marianne swirled a fork from the outside edge of the pan inward. She added dashes of oregano and basil with ecstatic pinches from her fingers. She felt like a girl again, making it up as she went, showing her father what she could do. Considering a tomato for a moment, Marianne shook the inclination away, deciding Angus was a basic egg, toast, and black coffee man. Her father had always stressed keeping the cooking simple. That way, you can never fail your guest.

When she reached 412, she rested the back of her hand against the mug to make sure the coffee was still warm. She knocked and leaned towards the door, straightening her vest as she waited. Inside, Angus coughed. Marianne took it as her cue to lift the tray from the cart, holding it aloft. He opened the door and invited her in with a wave of his hand.

"I hope you like scrambled eggs and toast," she said, placing the tray on the dresser.

"Yes, yes I do."

"I also brought you some coffee." She presented him with the saucer and cup.

"Thank you. Smells perfect. I haven't been eating breakfast often enough." He took it from her with a hand that shook slightly. "I got out of the habit somewhere along the way, but I do like my eggs cooked like this." He looked at her with a shy smile, then turned away.

"The service here's excellent," he said. "I feel very well cared for."

"I'm glad." Marianne took a courteous step back into the hall. "If there's nothing else Mr. Sperint, I'll be on my way."

"Nothing at the moment. Thank you, again."

She felt she'd float down the hall if she let go of the cart. Marianne sensed in Angus something she hadn't experienced in a long time. Not in years had she reduced a man to a disquieted bundle of nerves. She cast her mind back, knowing that she'd find Ray and his salesman's bravado lurking in some private place. Looking down the hall from the elevator towards Room 412, she remembered the day after the night that she'd allowed Ray to seduce her.

The following morning, Ray had rung the bell at the front desk so lightly that, had Marianne not been in the apartment's living room, she wouldn't have heard it. He was fit back then, barrel-chested and, while not exactly skinny, trim at least in proportion to his build -- an athlete's body. She found something pleasing in the way he nervously balled up his fists then stretched out his fingers. It seemed such a dainty a gesture, so disconsonant in the context of his frame that she couldn't help but be charmed by it. Without thinking of it as the start of something, she invited him into the intimate space of the apartment where no other guests had ever been permitted. He hesitated at first, unsure it seemed of taking this next step. She closed the door behind him once he did and worried that he'd find her apartment tiny and dark. Marianne so wanted Ray to like it there, like it as much as he claimed he liked the hotel.

10

Something under the hood of the station wagon rattled then hissed. The steering wheel jerked in Buddy's hand. Smoke curled up from the radiator. Easing the vehicle off the road, he turned off the engine and lit a cigarette. A geyser of white ashes exploded from the ashtray when he clicked it open. The engine would be ready to start once he'd smoked two all the way down to the filter, or so he hoped. It'd been the case before and, over the years, the station wagon, much like its owner, had become a slave to the methods of time. He still hoped to make his sister's before it got dark. Olivia was waiting on him to eat.

On his last trip out to McGill's Landing to visit her, they, along with their brother Merrill, had all played together on a raft floating out in the middle of a crater-formed lake. The way the sunset painted the placid water a blazing orange made it seem like they were gigging on the surface of the sun. It was the last time they'd made music together, the last time Buddy had seen them both. He wondered if they'd be able to recapture the brilliance of those moments out on the water, where it seemed they finally understood each other, at least everything that mattered about each other.

Olivia, four years Buddy's elder, talked fast and loud. She loved music, loved to dance. She threw herself into everything with the passion of his father, mother, brother, and Buddy combined. She played every instrument, every style. She played all night, talked all night and drank all night, any night she chose.

Her band, The Cleveland Steamers, had played fast and sharp, a kind of bebop polka. She left them behind a couple of years before, complaining her bandmates were getting too old, though she was the group's eldest member by at least a decade. Buddy knew she'd be itching to play with him. He was the only one who knew the old songs that she loved as well as she did.

Merrill, a good five years younger than Buddy, was more like the regular session musician of the family, a player close at hand but never at the forefront. He taught music at McGill High School and dabbled in every fashionable health fad that came along. Something about him had always seemed frivolous to Buddy.

Once the second cigarette had been smoked down, he said a prayer and turned the key. After a couple of rattles, the vehicle roared back to life. Buddy jerked it back onto the road and pointed his dying machine out of the shadows.

* * *

Candlelight flickered on the tiles, orange and distorted across the shimmering surface. Marianne settled deeper into the warmth of the bath, stirring the lights' reflections. She turned on the radio perched atop the toilet's cistern. Mozart's *Moonlight Sonata* floated through the air with a gentle insistence. She sank even deeper, letting the water cocoon her. Before she could focus fully on the lapping sound, Bruno pounded on the door.

"What?" she yelled.

"Mom?"

"Yes, Bruno? Aren't you supposed to be at the desk?"

"Is Julia scheduled to come in and work with me or is she done for the season?"

"She'll be here. I thought you were ready for more time at the desk by yourself?"

Bruno grumbled something to himself without answering. After he stomped away, Marianne tried to return to her relaxation, but the bath had gone lukewarm. Using her toes, she tugged on the drain plug's chain. Its ugly, gurgling sound mocked her attempts at meditation. She ran a towel delicately over goose-bumped skin, trying to prolong her solitude.

Though the bustle and noise that had once filled The Shelby had long since receded, true, prolonged peace and quiet remained elusive. When she was a girl, there were nights when the hotel, full of sleeping guests, seemed stilled, awash in their collective dream.

Back then, the lack of noise was slightly frightening. A hush fell over the floors and down the elevator shaft with a weight she could feel pressing down on top of her as she tried to sleep, making her afraid to close her eyes.

After tugging on her robe, she stood in front of the mirror. The bags beneath her eyes seemed better defined, set in more indelibly. Marianne flipped off the light and stood there looking at her silhouette, a form darker than the darkness surrounding it. She closed her eyes and tried to measure out her breaths, concentrating on just the air flowing through her. Then, the pipes screeched from behind the walls. Marianne thought about how she would soon need to worry about them freezing. The disruptive sound also reminded her of the two educations she still wanted for her son and that the ad she'd placed for a tutor had yet to be answered.

* * *

With his eyes fixed on the revolving door, Bruno now almost dreaded Julia's arrival. The slow trickle of moviegoers coming out of the theater that afternoon served as a painful reminder of the fantasy he had of taking her there one day. He planned to apologize the minute he saw her.

An immovable look sculpted the features of her face as she crossed the lobby, fifteen minutes after her shift had started. Bruno cleared his throat, hoping to cough up the right words. It was as if the air inside of his chest was strangling the ones he'd wanted to use. When she got closer to the desk, he found he could barely speak at all.

"Hi Julia," he said, meekly, almost under his breath.

"Hello Bruno," she replied in a distant voice.

She took her position next to him behind the desk, her eyes fixed on the revolving door as if expecting a prospective lodger to arrive at any minute. Bruno smiled and leaned into her sight line. Her concentration didn't waiver. He leaned back into position and took on a posture as straight as hers.

"When did you decide to start calling me Bruno?" he asked. "You always called me Brucey. Not that I mind. It's just, you know, I got kinda used to you calling me Brucey."

"I'm just trying to be professional, Bruno."

"Julia, if this has something to do with the other day...I didn't mean anything by it. I just thought that we could be friends outside the hotel. We may not see each other much anymore and I want you to know that I have feelings for you...mature feelings and I..."

"Mature feelings? Do you know what those are?" she asked. "You're barely fourteen. I'm seventeen going on eighteen. Don't you see the difference?"

"At least I show up for work on time."

"Congratulations on that," she said, "you live here."

"Our job requires punctuality. My mother might get upset if I told her you were late...again."

"Are you threatening to tell on me?" she asked with mocking chuckle.

"You mean like how you told her about me not getting that polka guy's bags?"

"What? I didn't..." she said. "Is that what this is really about? You're being a brat because you think I got you in trouble?"

"No, no. Look, Julia, I like you..."

"You told me that already."

"I used your shampoo so I could smell like you. I don't even have dandruff."

"You need to get out more if that's your way of expressing your so-called mature feelings. It's not mature, what you just told me. It's...creepy."

"I'm sorry," he said. "I'm not trying to be creepy. I just don't know how to..."

"It's okay," she said. "You're just a kid. You don't know what you want. You don't know how to act. You're like an animal, almost, caged up here day after day."

Bruno scowled at her, he wanted to yell, not just at her but to fill the lobby with his rage. He didn't open his mouth for fear that what came out would sound more like a great, seeping sob. It seemed he couldn't, in any way, trust his body to express his feelings to her. He kept quiet, back straight and silently vowed not to speak to her, unless absolutely necessary, for the rest of the day.

* * *

Buddy belched with enough force that he banged against the wall. Gripping the handrail, he pulled himself up the stairs. Inside the guest room at the end of the hall, he steadied himself with the help of a bedpost. Once he felt sure on his feet, he lifted his accordion from the bed. After hooking the strap, he gingerly made his way back downstairs. As soon as he took the final step, Olivia started an old Moravian work song, one of the first their father had ever taught them. Buddy no longer remembered the title. He fell in quickly though, his fingers fast to the notes before he knew what they were doing.

He could always hear his father's deep baritone crying inside the music, a voice filled with a yearning for something lost, for the land of his forefathers. Felled by a dizzy spell, he sat down, just making it onto the armchair without pausing his playing. To an outsider, the music would've sounded sloppy, as though the musicians were just learning to play. Buddy and his siblings heard only beauty, though, the beauty of their shared memories, memories of their father and mother and childhood home. Music was the only reminder left of what they'd once all shared.

* * *

Ray got undressed in the bathroom while the shower heated up. Once behind the moldy curtain, the steamy water melted away the edges of his latest and most surprising hangover. He hadn't even drunk that much the night before. Cutting back even more would be necessary, if he wanted to be sure of always being at his best. Looking for signs of last night's debauchery, he inspected his face in the mirror and practiced a smile until it looked sincere.

"Ben Marcus, good to see you again," he said to his reflection. "Good to see you still have...what's that nasty cat's name...eh, it won't matter. Mr. Marcus, you were the first man I thought of when I got these new Voxhowl microphones. I said to myself, Ray, there's only one man I can think of who would appreciate technology like this. I rushed all the way down here to see you from the home office. These babies can make just about anyone sound like a choir of angels."

Marcus had been one of his earliest clients. When Ray checked up on who he'd been working with, he'd been surprised to find the former heavy metal producer was also now working with Christian acts. Somewhere along the line, foul-mouthed Marcus had signed up to do the Lord's work. Having had some recent experience with just such a studio and situation, Ray felt confident of closing another sale before lunch.

* * *

Olivia handed Buddy a large green mug, chipped and faded from years of use. It was the biggest mug she owned, so big she only used it for soup and Buddy. Sipping coffee from her more modestly-sized cup, she took the seat across from him at the kitchen table. They both wore their headaches with smiles, neither wanting to let on how much it hurt. After going so long without seeing one another, it was a foregone conclusion that they were going to get after it a bit.

"Cigarette?" he asked, removing the crumpled pack from the breast pocket of his flannel shirt.

"You know I don't smoke," Olivia said.

"Hoped you might've changed your mind by now."

"Don't think so. Would you mind going outside?"

"You let Pop smoke indoors."

"No, I didn't."

"He smoked sitting right here in this chair, all the time."

"If he did, it wasn't with my knowledge. I can tell you that," Olivia said and took another sip from her cup.

"Coffee," Merrill cried, wearily shuffling across the linoleum. He rubbed his palms over his temples, making no effort to hide the pain creasing his brow. His wispy grey hair stood on end from the top of his head and his eyes were red and watery.

"Jesus, Mer. You look like hell had its way with you, then spit you back up," Buddy said, snickering.

"Then I look how I feel," Merrill said, taking the seat between them.

"Didn't Pop use to smoke in this kitchen?" Buddy asked Merrill. "Right here, right where I'm sitting?"

"Not true." Olivia handed Merrill a black mug with an emerald 'M' on either side.

"Yes, it is," Buddy said. "You were always trying to curry favor with him."

"Not true," she said. "I never let anyone smoke in this house."

"If you think Pop's looking down now, you should let Buddy smoke inside," Merrill said. He held his mug with both hands. "He was always the favorite, always the most like Pop."

"No, I wasn't," Buddy said. "The old man had no favorites."

"Yes, you were." Olivia said. "He probably still is, isn't he?"

"No, no, no." Buddy finished the last of his coffee.

"He's looking down smiling on you, Bud." Merrill laughed. "Shoot, you look just like him with a cigarette in your mouth. Let him smoke one, Liv. You'll see what I mean."

"No need to see him do it in my kitchen, I've seen him smoke thousands of times," she said. "You're right, though. He looks exactly like Dad."

"Come on," Buddy protested. "I do not."

"You look even more like him when you play, Bud," Olivia said. "You dance around the room like him, the accordion strapped to you like it's your sweetheart. Your foot stomps even sound like his."

"You stagger around when you're drunk in the same way he used to," Merrill said.

"Ha! That too!" Olivia concurred, lifting her mug in tribute.

"You two see what you want." Buddy put a cigarette between his lips. "You hear what you want. What you forget is how he and I used to fight like hellions."

"Of course. You both always thought you were right," Olivia said.

"Pour me another cup to take outside with me," Buddy said forcing his mug into her hand.

"Black." Olivia filled the mug and handed it back to him. "Just like Pop." Merrill joined her in a laugh.

"Fine." Buddy took the cup. "Now, unlike Pop, I am going to have to step outside to enjoy my damn cigarette."

* * *

Included in the usual pile of past dues and second notices was a response to the tutoring ad Marianne had placed several days before. Beyond being the only one she'd received, Rick French's résumé did little to distinguish itself. His experiences ranged from work as a dog groomer to an artist's assistant and most recently, a clerk at an antique shop on Castle Island. Despite possessing the proper state license, he had no tutoring experience. Since the time mandated for Bruno to start his year of homeschooling was fast approaching, Marianne didn't have the luxury to wait much longer.

When she called, Rick answered so quickly it felt as though he'd been expecting it. Discarding her own instincts to play coy about the number of applicants competing for the job, Marianne asked if he could come over that same day. He arrived barely half an hour later, working his hand nervously through his short blond hair. Dressed in a dark blazer and pressed slate-grey slacks that were several sizes too large, he looked younger than twenty-six.

"Hello," he said. "I'm looking for Ms. Shelby."

"You've found her." Marianne extended her hand. He shook it with an assured grip.

"I'm Rick French. Pleasure to meet you, Ms. Shelby"

Marianne put the bell out along with the sign requesting guests ring it for service.

"Let's go in here," she said, opening the door to the apartment. "We can talk in peace."

She watched as he looked around the living room and then the kitchen, wondering what he thought. It was rare for anyone other than her or Bruno to set foot in the apartment. Then she recalled Ray forcing his way in there on his last visit, using Bruno as a kind of battering ram no less. Fortunately, his stay had been mercifully if typically short.

"I've been reading about you," she said, indicating he sit in the chair across from her at the kitchen table. "Your experiences are interesting. You've done so many different things."

"I've had a lot of nice opportunities," he said, smiling. "I've been blessed."

"I guess the first thing I'd like to know is what brings you to Pittson."

"Well, my mother lives on her own down in the valley and was having a hard time with things." Rick began then paused, prepared for the question but not for the answer that came spilling forth. He ran his hand through his hair and regained his composure. "She needed me to come home and help to deal with the things going on in her life. I'll be staying with her for a while. Probably for the foreseeable future."

"There's nothing wrong with that," Marianne said, approvingly. "I lived here my whole life, since I was born."

"You mean here? In this hotel?"

"This apartment, this hotel. I wouldn't know how to live anywhere else," she said.

"That must have made for an interesting upbringing," Rick said. "All sorts of people coming and going. It's a beautiful place."

"Thank you. We try to keep up appearances," she said. She rearranged the papers before her. "What I really wanted to ask.

Well, not ask. I guess I don't know how to put it, but you don't seem to have any tutoring experience at all."

"That's...I suppose that's true," Rick said. "But I have a degree in education and passed the state licensing exam. I have a copy if you'd like to see it."

His hand shook as he took the certificate from his bag and handed it across the table. Marianne smiled, grateful to not be the only nervous one in the room. She looked it over, while intermittently catching his eye. She thought she could tell how much he wanted and needed the job.

* * *

The cat rubbed the crown of its head against Ray's ankles. He didn't let it bother him. His attention remained firmly fixed on Ben Marcus, who was studying the slender Voxhowl mic. The cat purred and lay down at his feet.

"Iggy warmed up to you awful fast. You spray tuna juice on those pants or something?" Marcus asked.

"Animals like me," Ray said looking down, fighting the urge to kick the cat and make it go away.

"He's usually more standoffish when I have someone in here. He thinks my office is his room."

"Maybe I should throw something for him into our negotiations, like a pound of catnip or a year's supply of mice. What do you say down there?" Ray asked. The cat was too busy cleaning itself to notice. "What do I need to do to make this work?"

"I'd love to tell you that since 'ol Iggy approves of you, we got a deal. But I'm afraid I'm going to have to say no, Mr. Davis."

"Shouldn't you confer more with Iggy first?"

"Afraid not. The room's his. The studio's mine." Ben sat the microphone back down.

"I understand, Mr. Marcus. But, if you'll permit me." Ray picked up the microphone and pointed it in Marcus's direction as if preparing to interview him. "This is the future in voice recording. If word gets out that you got top-of-the-line Voxhowl microphones, you'd have more business than you'd know what to do with. You'd be the first studio on Castle Island to have one. You know what they say: the equipment makes the studio almost as much as the man. You've always been cutting edge out here on the island."

"Sorry, Mr. Davis. Not this time. I ain't some cat just rolling over waiting to have his underside scratched," Marcus said, standing up and offering his hand. "I don't need anything I can't afford right now."

"Mr. Marcus, if you'll permit me..." But it was too late. Marcus was already shaking his head with the look of a man unwilling to succumb to any tactic, no matter how well-planned its charm. Ray hadn't tasted failure in some time. As he left the studio, he could only think of cleansing his palate.

* * *

Marianne felt she had run out of questions too quickly. She and Rick attempted to fill the silence by testing slightly different facial expressions on each other, each hoping the other would speak first. Rick kept thinking of ways of reassuring her that his lack of experience wouldn't be an issue but found no way of phrasing that sounded simply true rather than honestly desperate. While Marianne didn't realize what a paucity of suitable positions for a man of Rick's modest accomplishments there were in Pittson. Unless he experienced a sudden yen for pressing out nails in the last still operating building of the Nazareth Steel Works or wished to run the machine testing asthma inhalers at Gregson's Plastics, this really was the only job in town.

"I have one last question," she finally said. "I think teaching my son about the family business is frankly more important than going to school."

"I'm sorry but was that a question?" Rick asked.

"What do you think of that?"

"I think he needs both. One day he'll be running this place. Is that right?" Rick asked.

Marianne nodded.

"So he'll need to use his education in order to relate to guests and better understand them, understand their needs and how he can best serve them. After all, I don't know much about this business admittedly, but I'd guess the personal touch is what keeps people coming back."

"Okay," Marianne said, wondering if something like relief had registered on her face enough for him to tell. "I think I'll see you out, Mr. French." She stood up and motioned towards the kitchen door. "I'll be making my decision tonight."

Only after he left, did it occur to her that she should've just offered him the job right there in the kitchen. It wasn't so much that she was uncertain about Rick, though due to his lack of experience, there certainly was some of that. She resented having to hire him, having to spend money she barely had so that the state would be satisfied with her son's education. She knew what Bruno needed to learn, what would really make a difference in his life. But like any wise small business owner, Marianne also knew she had little choice but to follow the rules.

Bruno didn't even need to see the name of the movie. JAMES CAGNEY on the marquee was enough to send him racing back through the revolving door and across the lobby. Believing that the few extra steps it would've taken to get inside the apartment would've cost him his nerve, he took the phone from the front desk. He squatted behind it and dialed Rick's number. He'd memorized it much more easily than any poem, if only to dial it in his sleep.

When no one answered, he felt relieved. Bruno cleared his throat to leave a message. After fumbling around a bit, he mentioned it was a Cagney movie, cursing himself for not finding out which one and listed the show times. Not until after hanging up, did it occur to him that the voice he'd just heard had been a man's but certainly not Rick's. Bruno reasoned it could be a brother or father, but Rick had never mentioned anyone but his mother. Since the message only reiterated the number he'd reached, it could have been some neighbor that had recorded the message for Rick's mother, maybe she'd been too weak, her voice too soft.

Whatever scenario Bruno came up with, the thought that Rick had someone else troubled him. He'd always seen Rick as a kind of twin soul, alone in the world with only a demanding mother for company. If he let it, the thought that he really didn't know Rick very well at all might've shattered Bruno's dreams, but he had the strength just then to keep such thoughts at bay. The fact that he'd made the call and had a way of luring Rick back up there was enough for now. It was as close to joy, albeit a fragile one, that Bruno dared dream.

* * *

For years, Marianne had been in the habit of rotating and washing all of the sheets and towels from each room no matter the number of guests. If she started early enough in the morning, it might take a day, never more than two. She'd tried getting Bruno to do it, but he was never good for more than a couple of loads before getting careless or whiny or both. Now with Mr. Sperints's fitted sheet tangled around the washer's agitator, she remembered how important the laundry used to be to her. As a teenager, it was the first major project that she'd been entrusted with, though she'd hardly felt the same pride in journeying down into the dank basement as she felt in changing and cleaning a room.

It took some work to unspool the sheet from the bottom of the washer. Once she did, it lay wet and heavy in her arms as she struggled with the dryer door. She put it in the dryer, along with his other sheets and towels and turned it on. It rattled to life in the cool darkness of the basement. As a girl, she was often afraid to be alone down there and would run back upstairs as soon as she could. Now though, she could look without seeing and know what was around her -- the bits of the hotel that no longer had a place or function but she couldn't bring herself to throw away. Memories lingered like the shadows Of ghosts, and more and more lately, she wanted to be touched by them.

* * *

"So what did you think?" Rick asked, exiting the aisle ahead of Bruno.

"I don't know." Bruno thought they were going to watch Rick's favorite actor James Cagney in *The Public Enemy*. But there had been a problem with the print so they'd shown *Oklahoma!* instead.

"They were wearing those ridiculous costumes. And the music, God, it actually did damage to my ears, I think," Bruno said.

"Guess you weren't in the mood for a musical."

"How do you get in the mood for something like that?"

"I guess I don't really know how, but I can," Rick said. "There were a lot of beautiful, heart-rending things going on. Don't tell me you didn't notice or didn't care."

"I noticed it was like an hour too long."

"Okay, okay, I get it. You didn't like it. It's from another age."

"The stone age," Bruno said with a self-satisfied chuckle.

"Easy now, easy now, I have a friend who loves musicals and that one in particular."

"Don't know how anyone could get into stuff like that," Bruno said, pausing to linger in the lobby. He didn't want to go back to the hotel just yet and now wished he hadn't been so hard on the movie or that he could recall the lines of that poem that had come to him, seemingly from nowhere -- anything to keep Rick near him.

"Tristian's an old soul," Rick said with a note in his voice like he was going to cry.

"Is that whose voice I..." Bruno began, stopping when he realized what he was asking.

"Yeah, I don't have a phone of my own. No landline. No cellphone."

"So you live with? Is your mom sick or is..."

"I live with Tristian. My mother's fine. She lives in Tallahassee, Florida, of all places," Rick said, leaning into the door of the lobby but not opening it. "I first came here to live with Tristian two years ago and when the tutoring, like every other thing I've ever tried, didn't work out I had to move on."

"Why did you tell my mother..."

"I can't be certain how people, especially people around here, will react to the truth, the whole truth about me. So, I try not to give them even the smallest piece."

"The truth about yourself?" Bruno asked. "What do you mean?"

"Tristian's sick," Rick said. "He's very frail. There are a lot of things he needs help doing right now."

"I'm sorry. I didn't mean to..."

"He always asks about you," Rick said. "You and your mother are pretty well-known down in the valley."

"As weirdos?"

"I prefer the term eccentrics. Suits the both of you better."

Bruno wanted to ask what was wrong with Tristian but saying anything more seemed vulgar, out of place. From the way Rick's eyes softened when he talked about him, from the way his lips trembled, as if in anticipation of being wounded by more words, Bruno felt he didn't really want to know what it was. When they parted, he told Rick he hoped Tristian would get better, rather than ask him more questions; so many, he felt, had just been answered.

* * *

Angus turned the stool so that his laptop faced him. He was about to insert his pebble-sized headphones, when he motioned to get Lois's attention. Stealing a glance at the bottles of brown liquid on the shelves behind her, he licked his lips. He knew how badly he'd want a drink when he was finished.

"Are you sure it's okay?" he asked.

"Go ahead, hun. You're the only here right now."

He thanked her with a nod and started the disc. Mark had somehow produced a smattering of polite applause out of nothing. Angus braced himself once it stopped. He heard his brother clear his throat. The once loud hack had been softened. Angus said a prayer for his own voice to sound even softer.

"Thanks for coming, everyone," Andy said, an anxious edge to his voice. "Glad to be here. Listen, I want to tell you about my girlfriend. She just loves getting fisted." The silence that followed did not seem as biting and shocked as Angus remembered. "Especially after I take off my boxing glove." Mark inserted a strong but not overpowering bit of laughter. "She keeps asking me if I'm more of a tits or ass man. So I told her whichever she can afford to improve I'll be happy with." Though Mark had amplified the laughter, he hadn't been able to cover Angus yelling in a gruff, intoxicated voice that Andy was breastfed from his mother's ass. Listening to the replay, he didn't even remember

114

what he'd meant. It was just another thought borne of some drunken logic.

He plucked out the earphones and closed his laptop. Hearing his voice soaked with whiskey made Angus sick with shame. He hated the sound more than the words. His thirst came back, stronger then than any time since he'd stopped.

"You okay, hun?" Lois asked. "Your computer broken?"

"Could I have my tab?"

"Your tab? You've only had a couple of sodas. It's on me, hun."

"No, no. I've got it," Angus said. He threw down a crumpled ten-dollar bill and walked out of the bar before his thirst could overwhelm him. He'd not ask to hear any work in progress again.

* * *

Bothered by the persistent stirring inside of him from his meeting with Rick, Bruno put the phone cord into the back of his laptop and hopped online. He went to some of his favorite sites but found the feelings he now had made them all seem tawdry and depressing. When he thought of Rick's face, the slight glaze of sadness that held and shaped his features dominated his thoughts. There was no pushing past it into the realm of fantasy.

He couldn't help wondering what Tristian looked like and how he and Rick looked together. Bruno wanted to know everything about Tristian but couldn't think of a way to ask. Even more, he wanted to tell Rick that he knew something of what his life was like. It just wasn't a thought that came to him in words exactly.

The ones that did come just then were those he'd been searching his mind for less than an hour before: "This moment, yearning and thoughtful sitting alone/It seems to me there are other men in other lands yearning and thoughtful." The rest of the poem still eluded him, not that it would've done any good now.

He closed his laptop, unplugged the line. After trying to listen to some music, he put his head down on his pillow. In that instant of realization outside of the theater, Rick had become attainable in a way he'd always fantasized about and unattainable in a way he didn't even know enough to fear. It was like finding out a dream he'd been wanting to have was real but already happening to someone sleeping in another bed, far away.

12

Marianne called Rick French before going to bed to offer him the job, hoping that by putting that issue to rest she'd sleep more soundly than she had of late. The day-to-day issues like cleaning and dealing with the bills bothered her but only so long as she kept her eyes open. They were easy to push into the darkness.

Turning on her side, she could feel her heartbeat in her ears. Rick had agreed so quickly, it made her think her offer had been overly generous. It was barely above minimum wage, little more than she'd been paying Julia. Still, it was almost more than she could afford.

She opened her eyes to the familiar dark of her room, the outline of her dresser, its mirror faintly shimmering like a black sea. Applying for the landmark status bothered her more than she'd admitted to herself. It felt like failure, a crutch. What was worse was the realization that she needed one, desperately almost. There was no other way she could think of to make things work. She could never, would never sell the hotel, even if forced to.

* * *

Buddy rolled his jeans to his knees and braved the cold water of the lake at dawn, slowly submerging his legs, sending out long ripples across the icy water. To his back, Olivia sat in a rickety lounge chair made of thin plastic. She hugged her guitar close to her body and cracked open a can of beer. She took a sip, then spat some back out.

"Yours warm?" she asked.

"Yep." Buddy swilled from his can.

"He likes it warm in the morning," Merrill said from the middle of the large wooden raft, lying on his back with a can perched atop his belly. "Just like Pop."

"Will you two please quit?" Buddy turned to his siblings.

"Don't be so sensitive. We're just kidding," Olivia said.

"You two are ganging up on me like you always do." Buddy finished his beer. He squinted in the direction of the sun as it began to assert itself on the horizon. "So what if I do things like Pop? What's wrong with that?"

"I don't think there's anything wrong with it," Olivia said. "It seems to bother you though, Bud."

"You just love to pick on me don't you, Liv?"

"Buddy, come on." Merrill propped himself up on his elbows. "We're just having a little fun. You don't have to get so surly."

Buddy belched. He pitched the empty can out into the lake and kicked the water, triggering larger and larger ripples towards the shore. Merrill stood up, grunting. He walked to the side of the pontoon and took two more beers from the cooler in Olivia's rowboat.

"I didn't want to drink again," Merrill said as he dropped a can into Buddy's lap. "Not after yesterday. I don't want to go into the studio either. I promise I am not about to let you talk me into that. Two bad ideas in the same week is my limit."

Buddy couldn't care less, really, if Merrill came, but Olivia wouldn't go without him. He kicked in the water again and watched the ripples curl off towards the shore. Buddy wouldn't be able to consider his project complete without getting a recording with her. His little brother threatened to ruin things for him just by being around.

* * *

Ray put his tray down at an empty table and surveyed the motel's little breakfast nook. A couple of old-timers in worn pinstriped blazers were sitting near the small television mounted above the coffee machine. They sipped from styrofoam cups and pushed their paper plates to the side with the remains of their toast. Their eyes glued to the news; they said not a word to one another. A woman in an orange pantsuit that was tight in all the wrong places examined the cereals atop a nearby table. She picked up each mini-box before settling on the Cocoa Puffs.

With a jittery hand, Ray brought a spoonful of cornflakes to his mouth. Looking around the room once again, he wondered if waking up sober was really worth it. Last night, he had kept himself from tying one on because of his early morning appointment in McGill's Landing. He knew he had to be sharp. George Lyfus, one of his oldest clients, could be a tough sell. What little luck Ray had with him had always taken place before 9 AM.

On the outskirts of McGill's Landing, he took an off-ramp into an industrial park beside the river to avoid traffic. Between him and the river sat an abandoned scrapyard, then a chemical plant with towers releasing clouds of greenish-grey. Parking in the shade of a bridge's undercarriage, he couldn't help but think of how aptly Troll Recording Studios had been named.

"Good morning," he said as he stepped into the lobby. "I'm Mr. Davis, here to see Mr. Lyfus."

"You're early," said the receptionist, her glasses resting low on her nose. "Have a seat in the waiting area. Mr. Lyfus is running late."

The modest waiting area featured three metal folding chairs next to a red water cooler with a large plastic jug. A young man was resting his head against it, his arms and legs sprawled out, his complexion like ash disintegrating into dust. After he'd given Ray the once over, the young man scratched at his scabrous arms.

"I'm next, pal," he said.

"That's alright with me," Ray said.

"Lyfus has been ducking me. I've got to see him."

"No worries."

"It's not..." the young man shook his head. "It's not what you think."

"I don't make any assumptions. My name is Ray, by the way. Ray Davis."

"I'm Mike Crier. I'm in a band that's recorded here called Grand Plasma."

"I thought I recognized you," Ray said.

"Shut up. You didn't recognize me."

"I saw you at the Bass Theater about a year ago."

"We played there. We played lots of places," Mike said. "What you doing here?"

"These are microphones." Ray patted his case.

"You sing?"

"No. No. I'm just a mic salesman."

"I bet you know more about mics than that asshole Lyfus. I sound like I'm singing from off the floor half the time."

* * *

The crushed aluminum can made a splash then disappeared for a moment before bobbing back to the surface. Buddy lit a cigarette. Already tipsy, he kicked up more waves, admiring the ripples.

"Quit throwing cans in the lake," Olivia said, plucking at her guitar without purpose. "I thought we came out here to play. That was all you talked about last night, Bud."

"He didn't bring his squeeze box," Merrill said.

"Hey, I want to play." Buddy turned to face them. "But I want to do it in a studio, so we can get a decent recording."

"There're untold taped hours of us playin'. Playin' with Pop, with Ma, playin' ourselves." Merrill spoke in a jovial slur. "We got plenty of tapes already."

"Not as adults. The only tapes of us playing together are the ones they made of us as kids," Buddy said, then shook a flake of ash from his thumb.

"I love our jam sessions on the lake. Remember last time out here?" Olivia asked. "You played like your hands were on fire, Bud. I never saw anyone play the accordion like that."

"I only ever play like that with you two," he said.

"Then, why didn't you bring the accordion?" Merrill closed his eyes and turned his face into the sun.

"I've already explained myself. Come on! Let's book a studio session. There's that nice modern place under the bridge up the road."

"That studio's terrible," Merrill said. "The only people who record there are wasted, druggie kids who can't even play."

"What difference does it make?" Buddy asked, pulling his legs out of the water. After shaking them dry, he rolled his jeans back down. "Those kids ain't going to be playing with us."

"They'll be there's the whole problem. They give me the creeps some of these young guys," Merrill said.

"None of us are getting any younger," Buddy replied.

"Jesus, Buddy." Merrill chuckled. "Is there something you want to clue us in on? You're not dying, are you?"

"Not that I know of," Buddy said. "All I know is that we've all got less time than we did back in the day. Who knows how much time any of us have?"

"That's a grim way of thinking," Merrill said.

"Buddy, don't be so morbid," Olivia said sternly. "I don't want to talk about those sorts of things."

"You both know I'm right." Buddy squinted at the sunlight glinting off the lake. "We're old enough to face the facts, aren't we?"

He sucked the last drops from his can and crushed it. Rather than toss it in the lake, he turned and threw it in the direction of his sister. Olivia fended it off with the neck of her guitar. The can crashed against the strings and bounced across the raft. Buddy pinched his cigarette butt between his thumb and forefinger and flicked it out into the lake, earning another aggrieved "Buddy" from Olivia. Leaning towards the rowboat unsteadily, he reached for the cooler and found it empty.

"We got at least one more problem," he said.

* * *

After finally getting the call from the city office for historic preservation, Marianne found herself even more beset by doubts about going through with it. The idea of turning some of the hotel over to government inspectors and being partially reliant on the state to keep the business going was less palatable as she looked upon her lobby in the morning light. She also could not shake the feeling that her father wouldn't have approved. A date had yet to be fixed, so she could still back out, if business suddenly picked up.

When her father had gotten off the phone with her mother after she'd left for the last time, he'd wailed. It was a terrible sound Marianne had never heard before. She'd crept from her post at the desk into the apartment to find him clawing at the living room wall; the phone beeping dead at his feet. There were guests in the lobby at the time, so she shut the door quickly. As a girl, his voice crying "no" over and over lingered in her head for a long time afterwards, now she wished she could hear it again, so she could have a reason not to continue to seek outside assistance.

She went to work cleaning the lobby, hoping her labors would push those thoughts further away. Cleaning the glass of the revolving doors managed to steal her attention. Every smudge, streak and dried rain drop had to be wiped away. She got the vacuum out and using the hose cleaned the upholstery of the couch and chairs. By the time Julia arrived, they looked almost new and the money issues again reasserted themselves in Marianne's thoughts.

"Has anyone checked in today?" Julia asked, finding her crouched behind a chair.

"It's been slow today. Slow all season. But things might be changing here."

"Changing?"

"I haven't even told Bruno yet," Marianne said, "but the city is interested in making us a historic landmark."

"Really? That's so cool."

"I wasn't sure about it doing it at first, but now I guess that I'm glad I did. I want people to know it's a special place. That's all I've ever wanted."

"Will it still be a hotel?" Julia asked.

"Yes," Marianne said, her voice dipping at having to face the question she'd avoided asking herself, "We'll still host guests. I'm not sure how that part works but..."

"So will it be like part-museum, part-hotel or what?"

"A bit of both," Marianne said, fully conscious of having all of the excitement drained from her voice. "We'll have a plaque out in front."

* * *

The salesman's grin turned into a smirk as Ray left Lyfus' office. The junkie in the waiting room had been right -- he knew much more about the new technology than Lyfus did. It had taken him a while to break the old man down, but i'd been inevitable. Lyfus would've rewarded almost anyone who listened to him talk about all of the sweat and blood it took to build his studio up. It'd been so easy, it hardly felt like a success.

The secretary ignored Ray with almost righteous glee as he passed her desk. He shot her a smile anyway. Grand Plasma's Mike was leaning against the water cooler sleeping. Looking at his frail body, Ray thought about the triviality of his own drunkenness. He never showed up for a meeting so obviously intoxicated.

He resolved not to drink beer at dinner. One celebratory glass of wine would be it. The new Ray was in control, total control. He planned to leave town the next morning and head up north. As long as his case had some microphones in it, he'd stay on the road.

* * *

Buddy sat the plastic sheath of bread next to piles of ham and turkey, looking practically luminous atop their wax paper sleeves. After drinking all morning into the afternoon, he knew the three of them needed something in their stomachs if they were going to be in any shape to record the next day. He hoped Merrill would remember agreeing to go. He'd been pretty far gone by the time Buddy had worn him down.

Twilight filled the back porch's windows in a sleepy orange. A soft breeze banged the blinds against the window frames. Merrill lay on his side on the dilapidated couch that Buddy had given Olivia as a house-warming gift, one of the only things he'd ever given her. Seeing Merrill passed out like that did make Buddy feel a little guilty. He should've watched out more for his little brother.

"Hey…" Buddy nudged him with his elbow as he tried to balance three paper plates in his hands. "Hey, Merrill."

Merrill turned to the side, eyes springing open with momentary surprise. He pressed his face into his palms. For a second, he looked lost and afraid, a stranger awakening in a strange place. After a yawn, he gathered himself enough to sit up.

"Here," Buddy said, pushing the plate under his brother's nose.

"What is it?" Merrill asked.

"A sandwich."

"What's on it?"

"Turkey and ham."

"Buddy, I'm a vegetarian."

"Still?" Buddy asked.

"Leave it." Merrill took the plate and put it down on the floor. "I'll pick at the chips."

Buddy snickered as he left the porch. In his estimation, Merrill was too old to be a vegetarian. It was the kind of thing younger, flakier people took up, like a fashion trend. No matter how many grey hairs dotted his chin or how many wrinkles crowded around his eyes and mouth, Merrill would always be the baby of the family, someone whom Buddy would struggle to take seriously.

Cobwebs sewed every corner of Room 304 together. Marianne couldn't remember the last time she'd cleaned it thoroughly or indeed when a guest had last been there. She'd run the vacuum in it, even glided a dust rag indifferently over the furniture from time to time but the neglect was obvious, when she examined it closely enough. She had no idea when it was going to be yet but felt more vigilance was necessary in the light of their upcoming inspection.

Right next to the elevator shaft, 304 was a noisy and undesirable -- possibly the worst room in the hotel. It was where she would've put Ray when he'd last visited had she been on the desk. She began to sweat and so turned down the thermostat. When the air conditioner kicked on, it made a strange rattling sound that grew louder.

She'd thought about sending Bruno to clean it but then he'd ask why, not to mention do a less than thorough job. She hadn't yet told him anything about the hotel's impending landmark status. She'd yet to even tell him about his new tutor. She would wait until things were closer to happening. Her son had become enough of a teenager that anything that didn't go according to plan was seen as a broken promise, to be weaponized, no doubt, at some later date.

She had no idea how he'd react to news that he'd be learning from a tutor. Past discussions about his education had, no matter her approach, always devolved into weepy shouting matches about him wanting to go to school down in the valley. He never missed the chance to hold the fact that he didn't have a normal childhood against her.

When the AC unit's rattling grew thunderous, she took out a screwdriver rom the small tool kit she kept on the bottom shelf of her cart. After shutting it down, she removed the front panel and out spilled three tiny bottles. They were covered in a moss-like layer of dust. Wiping them clean, she knew the label before the name had been completely revealed. They were bottles of Rymner's Gin, her father's preferred brand.

Marianne went from room to room and found the same brand of tiny bottles inside every older AC unit she came across. She dumped them in the bathroom sink of each room and if she'd already cleaned the sink, she'd clean it again. A day that had started wholly of her own momentum, her own sense of purpose was slowly being darkened by something about Daddy that she'd forgotten or at least tried to forget. She wanted not to think about him or the bottles, but every one of those units old enough to have been touched by his hands held the same evidence.

Once she was finished with the third floor, she'd collected enough plastic bottles to make the bag on the end of her cart bulge. When she took out the trash, the bottles jingled like loose change when the bag hit the bottom of the dumpster. She had no time to dwell on such things, though, there was still more to do.

* * *

Ray woke before the alarm, alert and ready. He'd kept it to two glasses of wine the night before. Further proof, he didn't need to get in a program or go to meetings. Beyond not needing to go to meetings, the notion of doing so was a little ridiculous for someone out on the road as much as he was. Was he supposed to find a different meeting in each town he visited? Sit with a bunch of different strangers every time and tell them of all the woe booze had visited on his life? It just wasn't practical. Over the past months, he could count the number of times he'd really gotten drunk on one hand.

He made himself a coffee in his room. The machine next to the TV produced an impressive amount of steam for its size. As he sipped it, he realized he was learning to enjoy mornings now rather than trying to wrestle a few more hours of sleep from them. Sober days were about thriving rather than just hanging on until he could crawl into the next motel bed. He only wished he'd gotten things under control sooner.

He took his time getting ready, showering solely to clean and ready himself rather than trying to revive his body. He ironed his shirt and slacks and took an ancient lint roller from his bag to clean off his blazer. Taking out his phone, he called the other recording studio in McGill's Landing. He didn't have an appointment but feeling bright decided to squeeze yet another sale in on his way out of town.

"Phillips Sound and Motion," a bored voice answered.

"Rich Phillip, please," Ray said.

"This is Rich."

"Good Morning, Mr. Phillips. This is Ray Davis. We've done some business before. I have some gear I'd think you'd like to at least check out."

"Ray Davis?"

"I had the good fortune to visit your studio about a year ago," Ray said, clearing his voice. "I happen to be in McGill's Landing again and thought you might like to see some of the latest models, absolute state of the art."

"So this's a sales call?" Phillips asked.

"Absolutely, sir. No point denying it."

"You sell microphones, right?"

"I like to think the microphones sell themselves. I just transport them," Ray said.

"Yeah, I remember you," Phillips said, sounding almost amused. "You might as well come by. I know you will anyway. But I'll tell you Davis, you're wasting your time. There ain't nothing I need."

"Well lucky for you, Mr. Phillips, I'm not interested in selling what you know you don't need," Ray said. "My specialty is selling products that keep businesses like yours ahead of the curve. Just wait until you see these mics."

"Sure, sure, better pick up, purer sound all that," Phillips said. "Just ask for me when you get here."

"See you soon, Mr. Philips."

Ray couldn't tell where he stood. Phillips had been a bit of a pushover the last time he'd been through town. Ray tried to remember if he'd needed something specific that time. He'd been drinking pretty heavily then, so there were a lot of blank spaces where that part of his past should've been. When he was younger, he prided himself on remembering every detail of every sale, no matter how hammered he'd been the night before or got the night after but those days were long gone.

Before leaving, he called The Shelby. He hadn't spoken with his son since leaving the hotel. He was determined to call more often than he had in the past. A lot of times, he'd been too hungover to do it, too busy trying to collect himself for the day ahead. Part of it though, he could also see in the light of a sober dawn, was that he didn't think he was worthy of being the boy's father, when he'd been drinking. Marianne answered, so he hung up, and thought that the drink wasn't the only thing that had convinced him of his lack of worth.

* * *

"Easy around the bend, Liv," Merrill moaned from the back seat, his hands partially covering his mouth.

Olivia sighed from the driver's seat. Buddy gave his brother a quick glare of pity in the rearview mirror. He was about to lecture him about what he saw as the connection between his crippling hangover and his vegetarianism but decided not to risk upsetting Merrill before they got to the studio. He'd save it for the ride home. Yawning, he closed his eyes and leaned against his window.

"Hey, you don't get to doze off," Merrill said. "It was your idea to drag us out here. I could be in bed right now."

"How can a sleeping man drag anyone anywhere?" Buddy asked.

"Only you could pull off something like that," Olivia said.

Merrill rolled down his window and leaned his head out. He opened his mouth into the oncoming wind, taking gulps of it. To passing motorists, it might've looked like he was a dog trapped in a man's body.

"I wouldn't do that, Mer." Olivia peeked in the rearview mirror. "A mailbox's going to decapitate you."

"Just trying to stay alert," Merrill said. He brought his head back inside and gave each cheek a slap.

"How about you, Olivia?" Buddy asked. "You ready to record?"

"I guess," she said. "It's not like I have a say in the matter."

"Don't pretend I'm making you do anything against your will. You're the one driving."

"I just don't see why we had to go to a studio so far out of the way," she said.

"Well, Merrill insisted. Didn't you, Merrill?"

"I just didn't want to go to that studio beneath the bridge. We're not The Three Billy Goats Gruff." Merrill gave each cheek another slap. "What are we going to play, anyway?"

"Old songs. Songs we used to play with Pop," Buddy said.

"Haven't those already been recorded hundreds of times over?" Merrill asked.

"Not by us," Buddy said.

"Whatever you want, Bud," Merrill said. "I am ready to go 100 percent."

"That'd good," Olivia said, gliding the car into a spot on the lakeside. "Cause we're here."

As soon as they walked through the doors of Phillips Sound and Motion, Merrill rushed to the bathroom. Buddy couldn't remember seeing him run like that in years. He started to follow him, but Olivia grabbed Buddy by the arm.

"You'll embarrass him," she whispered.

"What big brothers do," Buddy said, shaking free of her grip and walking down the hall, slowly though. He didn't want anyone to think his middle-aged brother needed his help -- that Merrill might not have forgiven.

* * *

Like nearly every manmade structure in McGill's Landing, the studio was located near a lake. Of the three that dotted the center of town, Phillips Lake was the largest. The studio's parking lot backed right up to the water and there were a couple of young guys fishing off the back of a pickup. A hint of rot hung strong enough in the air to make Ray hope they'd throw back anything they caught.

The cinderblock building painted a fading red, looked to be a place where dreams flickered briefly before sinking into the dirty water. It was the type of place that catered to amateurs; the kind of place Ray knew well. In need of the bathroom after one too many cups of coffee, Ray was directed to the end of the hall after checking in.

"Is someone in there?" Ray asked, finding Buddy outside the bathroom.

"Yeah, my brother. He might be awhile too," Buddy said. "We're going to record and he gets, you know, nervous."

Retching erupted from behind the door. It was so loud and painful that the splashing that followed sounded like relief. Buddy cringed through a smile, trying not to look embarrassed for his brother. He shrugged and nodded at Ray, who couldn't hide the uncomfortable look on his face. Buddy took it as a rictus of disgust not realizing that Ray was squirming with commiseration.

"Kind of a ritual for some musicians, from what I've heard," Ray said.

"Tell me about it," Buddy said then stepped closer to the door as it seemed Merrill was done. No sooner had he put his hand on the door to open it and take a look than the terrible sounds started up again.

"Listen," Ray said. "I have a meeting I need to freshen up for. I'm just going to slip into the ladies' room. As long as you're standing there..."

"I'll make sure no one bursts in on you while you're in the girls' room," Buddy said.

Ray nodded in thanks and stepped inside. The sounds of Merrill getting sick were even louder in the ladies' room. Ray tried to be quick, feeling embarrassed for this stranger in a way he seldom was at his own behavior in similar situations. Not that he threw up in places where he did business. Ray'd always been successful in keeping that sort of humiliation behind the doors of bars and taverns -- places he rarely frequented after.

"Is your brother going to be alright in there?" Ray asked Buddy as he returned to the studio lobby.

"I hope so."

"Thanks for making sure nobody got an unpleasant surprise." Ray offered his hand. "My name's Ray, Ray Davis."

"Buddy Cyzek," Buddy said, offering his hand limply.

"The Polka King?"

"That's me, alright. But I don't wear a crown or nothing."

"Say, Buddy Cyzek. You're famous around these parts," Ray said. "I've seen your records on studio walls from here to Cleveland and Baltimore and beyond. I sell microphones."

"Is that right?"

"We've met once before. At The Shelby Hotel in Pittson. A good while ago."

"No kidding? I just came from there, as a matter of fact."

"So did I," Ray said, swallowing the bitterness of that memory. "Didn't stay long enough for our paths to cross again, I guess."

"You don't say?" Buddy said and listened as the toilet flushed, hoping the worst was over for his brother.

"Do you remember having drinks in your room once? You let me play your accordion."

"That doesn't sound like something I'd do," Buddy said.

"You physically kicked me out when it became obvious I couldn't play."

"That sounds more like me," Buddy said, smiling at Ray and hoping he'd be gone when Merrill reemerged. Buddy was sure he'd hear it from his brother, if he'd dragged him out sick all that way and then was caught reminiscing with a stranger.

"You know what I hate?" Andy's voice crackled to life, hushed and uncertain. "When you've just finished a threesome and your mom and sister go right back to nagging you."

"Your brother's sick. In kind of a funny way, I guess," Mark said, stopping the playback. "But look I'm just the producer. What do you want here, a big laugh, a small laugh? Maybe one that sounds...I don't know...just generally confused and maybe uncomfortable?"

"Let it play," Angus said. "Cue it back up and let it play through."

Mark nodded and pressed the button. Andy's voice repeated itself.

"You know what I hate? When you've just finished a threesome and your mom and sister go right back to nagging you."

"Man, that's sick," Mark said, shaking his head.

"Shh," Angus said. He leaned closer to the board, listening.

Some snickers rose from the crowd. Glasses clinked above the low murmur. The room sounded weary and sad.

"I told you he was a mutter fucker." Angus's angry, whiskey-drenched growl came through the speakers.

"There I am again." Angus melted back into his armchair. "Drunk, but not drunk enough to claim I didn't know what I was saying."

"Why didn't your brother ever come back at you and put you in your place?" Mark asked. "That's what comics do, right?"

"My brother would never pick on a drunk. He didn't even tell me it bothered him until...well...I never found out it until...it was too late."

"You never thought he was bothered by it?"

"Everyone seems stoic to a drunk, Mr. LeSides." Angus shook his head. "Can't you put something over my voice? Cover me up? Erase me?"

"I could just cut it before you come in. I'll have to finesse it thought otherwise it'll sound abrupt."

"Sure, let's do that. Can you also stretch out the laughs to make it sound like the audience really roared?"

"Will make it seem like a real sick crowd."

"Calling it a crowd is generous. Barely ten people were there that night."

"Is that right?" Mark asked. "I can make it sound like a hundred."

"No one would believe Andy ever played in front of that many people. Not with his material. I love my brother and all but, look, he was just starting out."

"How long ago is this from?" Mark asked.

"Like a year or so ago," Angus said. "He was going through a kind of midlife crisis, I guess."

"What's the biggest crowd he ever played in front of?"

"Thirty-eight people saw him at the Winchester Gaming Grounds and Casino."

"Thirty-eight can make a lot of noise," Mark said.

"Not that group of half-soused blackjack losers and slot jockeys," Angus said. "All they did was drink and sigh. A drunken sigh from thirty-eight people all at once just sounds sad."

"I bet."

"Thirty-nine if you count me," Angus said. "I was supposed to be supporting him but really the nicest thing I ever did was just sit there and sigh."

* * *

Marianne stripped Angus's mattress. The warm stench of nicotine hung in the air, overpowering her guest's faint musk. She sprayed enough Lysol to make a kind of crystal mist in the sun-lit room. With an ill-timed breath, she inhaled the cleaning product, causing her to sneeze violently.

She locked the door behind her and began to wheel the cart down the hall. Another thunderous sneeze exploded through her into the emptiness of the hallway. As she stepped into the elevator, her lower back muscles began to spasm, tightening her in a grip of pain. She struggled to get the cart into the elevator. Her back tightened against every inch of movement. Leaving the elevator once it landed in the lobby proved even more difficult. Marianne gritted her teeth and pushed the cart as far as the front desk. Pain convulsed through her back and down her legs as she reached for the bell. She rang it twice, meekly, before finding the strength to come down on it hard. The ding reverberated through the lobby.

"Bruno," she cried when he finally showe in a t-shirt and jeans. "What have I told you about dressing properly when you come to answer the bell?"

"Why're you ringing it?" he asked. "What's wrong?"

"I hurt my back."

Marianne splayed her hands on the desk and forced her body upright. She trembled, eyelids fluttering. Bruno rushed over and took her in his arms.

"How?" he asked.

"Cleaning Mr. Sperint's room," she said, finding just enough mobility to slide along the desk and out of his grasp.

"You want a chair or something?"

"No," she gasped. "Put the cart away. I can't push it any further and please, some aspirin from the closet. It's in the back."

"In the back? Where?" Bruno asked pulling the cart with him into the closet.

"Behind the shower caps and shampoo. They're horse pills...big ones."

Tiny stars of dust flickered beneath the naked bulb dangling in the closet. Bruno rummaged through packages of ant traps and dental floss, knocking several mini-bottles of shampoo off the shelf as well as a couple of doorstops. Finally, in the far back corner, he found a plastic bin filled with small individually wrapped packs of ibuprofen.

"I need some water," she said, then snatched the packet from his hand as soon as he got near enough, tearing it open with her teeth.

Collapsing onto the desk, Marianne hid her head in her arms. Every movement sped pain more acutely down her back. She stifled her tears, choking back a whimper. The pill rolled around her mouth like a lump of chalk. Crying in the lobby in front of an employee wasn't professional. Clawing inside for some sort of reserve, she straightened herself, the pill now clutched between her teeth. She slipped her shoes off and let Bruno take her. Delicately, with a touch of her shoulders, he steered her through the apartment and helped her into bed.

"Water," she said, taking the pill from her mouth.

As she waited for the interminable seconds to pass before he reappeared, she shifted in bed. Each position felt comfortable for only a second before the pain reasserted itself. She scooted to the side of the bed. Opening the drawer of her nightstand, she took out a hot water bottle

Bruno brought her a mug full to almost overflowing. He didn't let go of it until she took it with both hands. Water sloshed out of it onto the front of her top and the sheets. She looked at Bruno as she exhaled a moan from deep in her chest, the effort of that exasperated breath was all she had in the way of a reprimand. After swallowing the pill, she held up the hot water bottle.

"This filled with hot water please," she said.

"Hot water," he said, racing from her room without it.

"Wait, wait," she said, the words snapping at the air but not loudly enough to bring him back.

After a few minutes, he carried in a tray with a silver teapot whose belly was enscribed with the hotel's insignia. A ribbon of steam twisted from its spout. He sat it on the nightstand, his shaking hands rattling the pot as he put it down. She handed him the rubber bladder.

"Why on earth did you bring that thing in here?" she asked, "Where did you even find it?"

"In the kitchen cabinet beneath the junk drawer with the old receipts and stuff," he said. "I thought it'd be easier to pour."

But he managed to make a hash of that as well spilling a stream of boiling water onto the carpet. He had to do a dance to avoid burning his feet. He tried handing the water bottle to her once it was full but it was too hot for him to hold, so he dropped on the bed next to her.

"Sorry, I've never filled one of those before."

"It's fine," she said, filling that descriptor with every ounce of its mild reproach. "Thank you."

"Do you want some tea or something? There's all this extra hot water," he said, picking up the teapot.

"No, but thank you."

"Should I leave it here?" he asked.

"Just go change your clothes. You have to watch the desk for me. I need to lie down."

He nodded and left the room, shutting the door gently. Marianne looked over at the teapot. At one time years before, they used to have a tea in the lobby each afternoon at 4. She'd been much younger than Bruno when she circulated among the guests with that tray. The pot would be on it along with an assortment of tea bags. She was always so worried about burning a guest with the hot water, but of course, she never did.

Then a mild yet persistent wave of pain, like a breeze, pushed aside a curtain and another buried, more indelible moment surfaced. She was a girl in the apartment kitchen, waiting to start the tea party she was supposed to have with Mother and Daddy. It was to begin directly after lunch but her parents were in the midst of another terrible fight. It had begun at the kitchen table and was taken into their bedroom. She no longer remembered the matter which lay at the heart of that particular disagreement, but it no doubt had to do with her father working too much, supposedly caring more about the hotel than his family.

Shattering the fluttering calm that had taken hold since they'd left the kitchen, their bedroom door slammed loudly enough to make Marianne jump in her seat. It took a few moments after that violent sound for the quietude to reassert itself. She got up and opened the kitchen door just enough to see her mother was in the living room, putting on her coat then pulling on her gloves. Marianne wanted to call to her but was afraid. She decided to wait until her mother had left the apartment and was in the lobby. There, at least, she would have to deal with Marianne's questions calmly if not warmly.

"Where are you going?" she asked, her mother moving quickly towards the revolving door.

"Out and down into town," her mother said.

"Where's Daddy?" Marianne asked.

"Something in Room 304 needed his immediate attention. Could not wait, apparently."

"Who'll watch the desk?"

"I cannot be a prisoner to this place any longer," her mother said, coming to her and hugging her and kissing her forehead.

"A prisoner?" Marianne asked as her mother walked back to the door.

She pushed through and was out on the sidewalk before Marianne could remind her about the tea party. It was not unusual for them to fight, but it was for her mother to leave. Standing at the desk, trying to look her professional best, this notion began to bother Marianne more and more. She worried her mother would never come back.

Though it ran contrary to the nature her father had so instilled in her, she left her post and took the elevator up to the third floor to find him. The door to 304 was partially opened. She could hear him muttering to himself -- not that the words were distinct but the sound bore the flavor of his grousing.

"Daddy?" she asked, knocking on the door.

He threw it open, then stood swaying in the doorway as though he might fall over. His shirt collar was undone, his face a molten red. His thumb and forefinger pinched the neck of a tiny bottle.

"What're you doing up here?" he asked.

"Mommy's gone away," she said.

He pursed his lips and nodded as though this was not news. After finishing what was left of the tiny bottle, he put it in the pocket of his blazer. Then, looking behind him at the room, he shut out the light.

"Let's go down," he said.

His steps were crooked going down the hall. He veered from one side to the other -- his lumbering form reckless. Not wanting to get in his way, Marianne stayed several steps behind. At the elevator, he put his arm out to use the wall for support and missed, falling to the ground. The empty bottle plus a couple of other full ones spilled from his pockets. Seeming not to notice them, he got up and opened the gate for the elevator.

"Not so steady on my feet today," he said.

Marianne picked up the bottles and handed them to him. He took them with a sigh of thanks. His breath was hot and sweet.

"We were supposed to have a tea party," she said to him, her voice low.

"We will. We will," he said. "I'll put up the sign and we'll go into the apartment."

On the ground floor, he regained his bearings. He held the gate open for her. There was no swerving or wavering in his steps as he led her into the apartment after putting out the RING BELL sign. Marianne hoped they wouldn't be interrupted.

"The water's gone cold," she said, filling his mug.

"Cold tea's alright with me," he said. "Come sit here."

She sat in his lap, something she'd not done in ages. She felt awkward and heavy atop his thighs. He adjusted her one way then next until he was comfortable.

"Can I tell you something a big girl should know?" he asked. She nodded.

"This hotel, our hotel's my life. Do you understand that?"

"I...I think so," she said, not certain that she did.

"It is my life," he continued, "it represents family and duty and all of the other things I've been telling you are important. And you know what?"

"What Daddy?" she said, anxious for him to get to the point as she'd become uncomfortable wedged between him and the table.

"One day, this hotel, my life, will be yours. Now, isn't that wonderful?" he asked and kissed her gently on the temple.

"Wonderful," she repeated and slid off of his lap. "Daddy?"

"Yes," he said after a slurp of tea.

"Where did Mommy go?"

"She'll be back," he said, then closed his eyes as though he might fall asleep right there at the table.

After sliding off his lap, she filled his cup back up to the brim. This roused him enough to offer her a smile. She sat across from him, sipping her tea, hoping he had no more big girl things to tell her. She only wanted to know when her mother was coming home.

* * *

Mark peeled the label, leaving white streaks of paper on the bottle. He rolled it into a cone and placed it in one of the four grooved slots atop the ashtray. Smoke came thick from his nostrils as he took a long sip.

"Sure I can't get you something more?" he asked Angus.

"No. I'm fine with soda."

Angus lit a cigarette and pulled the ashtray between them. He waved towards the bartender who stood drying a glass. Balding with long sideburns that just failed to meet below his chin, he sneered at them, as though they were only a few fluid ounces away from becoming a hassle. It was almost enough to make Angus want to drink until he got so loaded he threw up all over the bar, just to see how deep that spiteful look could get. Bored bartenders were always his favorite ones to annoy.

"So, you don't drink, huh?" Mark asked.

"Not anymore," Angus said.

"Used to though?"

"Too much, too often," Angus said stirring his soda, rushing a fresh batch of bubbles to the surface.

"Say no more. I've seen a lot of that in my line of work. A lot of talented men and women undone by the juice. You in a program?"

"Of sorts," Angus said, thinking of the amount of explanation needed to make that anything but a lie. "I haven't had a drink since Andy..." He paused to gather himself, his emotions threatening to steer his thoughts away from the lies he'd so come to cherish. "It's been six months. I haven't had a drink since his funeral."

The bartender brought Mark another beer and refilled Angus's soda. Mark again peeled the label from his bottle, rolled it into a slender cone and placed it next to the first one he'd made.

"Keeping track?" Angus asked.

"Sorry?"

"With the labels. You trying to keep count of how many you've had?"

"No. Just a habit, I guess. Don't know where I picked it up."

"I only ask because, when I was first trying to rein in my consumption, I used to keep the caps from the bottles in my pocket to help me keep track."

"Did it work?"

"Not really. Just made my pockets heavy." Angus patted at his pocket, where the caps would've been. "Now I'm drinking too much soda. It bloats me." He considered the tiny bubbles gathering around the straw.

141

"One vice at a time." Mark reached over and gave Angus's shoulder a sympathetic squeeze.

Angus agreed by taking a long draw from his cigarette. He exhaled a double-headed snake of smoke through his nostrils. He wanted to tell Mark about Andy, about what had happened and why he was doing this recording. They'd been working so closely on it that the bubble of professionalism that encased them seemed to get thinner each day, until it felt as though he could trust the truth to pierce it. But he still didn't know the whole truth, at least not well enough to admit it to himself. The words that formed it, the ones he'd have to speak caused enough pain while still locked in his head. He ashed, accidentally knocking one of Mark's label cones into the ashtray.

"Sorry," he said, retrieving it and putting it back in its place.

Buddy looked over his shoulder, across the rows of chairs at the tiny woman seated in the corner of the waiting room. Leaning her dyed blonde head against the wall, she wore glasses so huge they distorted her face. Her smudged mascara had turned her eyelids black and streaked her cheeks. She'd been sitting there since he and Olivia had arrived and still hadn't moved other than to shake and whimper. Buddy envied her. She looked as though she'd already heard her bad news.

He and his sister had met only briefly with a doctor, a white-haired woman with a square jaw that, combined with the severe expression in her eyes, made it appear as though she was always prepared to enter and then swiftly exit a tragedy. She confirmed that Merrill had suffered a stroke and that they were doing all they could to stabilize him. Buddy wasn't sure what that really meant and was relieved that Olivia hadn't asked.

"You must be hungry," he said, just above a whisper as he leaned into her, brushing her shoulder lightly with his. "I'll go get us something to eat."

"I'm not," she said, her voice flat and barely audible.

"We should eat, Liv. We don't know how much longer it's going to be."

"Don't you want to go out and smoke a cigarette?" she asked.

"I thought it might seem selfish, you know, under the circumstances."

"Why would you think that? Go ahead, have one. Just don't have a stroke while you're doing it." She chuckled slightly, almost painfully. "*That* would be selfish."

"You sure?" Buddy opened the front pocket of his overalls, teasing a cigarette out of the pack. "Is there anything you want? Soda or snacks or something?"

"No, I'm okay."

"Nothing from the machine?"

"No. Just go ahead, Bud. There's nothing you can do anyways."

Buddy patted the top of her head before going to the elevator. After Merrill had collapsed in the studio, Buddy wasn't immediately concerned. In fact, his first impulse had been to feel embarrassed for Olivia. Her shrieking had seemed overly dramatic at first. Merrill had simply tripped or so he thought. Only after he saw Merrill's eyes roll back and something like death freeze over his face did he cry for someone to call 911.

Feeling it conspicuous to light up too close to the hospital, he walked a block down the street past a line of cabs. He tried to enjoy the smoke, to not think about what still awaited him but the nicotine failed to calm his nerves. After he finished, he felt no desire to go back inside. He lit another, trying to enjoy every puff. The second one proved as disappointing as the first. Halfway through, he mashed it out under his foot and walked back towards the hospital.

He thought about hailing one of the taxis, heading back to his sister's house, jumping in his wagon and just leaving. Olivia would've been fine without him. She hadn't said a word when he didn't come home for his father's or mother's funeral. She knew he found his place in things difficult when there was nothing he could do. He had little use for sitting around waiting for the inevitable or sharing maudlin memories.

* * *

Bruno didn't care for the proprietary way Rick pulled the kitchen chair out before he sat down, as though it was his appointed seat. He'd only been in the apartment for a few hours. It wasn't as though he'd be cleaning rooms or hauling laundry later. The way Bruno saw it, Rick should've behaved as a guest who'd merely been granted the temporary privilege of entering the apartment.

"So, it's time to start again," Bruno said.

"We only have two hours left. There's a lot we need to cover. Your mother sent me some of your homework from last year."

"She did? Why?"

"I needed to know where to begin. I was impressed, Bruno. It was pretty good, most of it. I read the paper you wrote for the standard exam's English section, the one on the Walt Whitman poem. What did you get on that again? Do you remember? Wasn't it an A-?"

"No," Bruno said with an air of satisfaction. "It was an A. It really wasn't that hard."

"That's what I thought," Rick said. "It didn't seem like you worked on it much."

"What?"

"It didn't seem that hard to write. I think you can do better." He pulled two books from his green knapsack. "I thought we'd try some Whitman to start."

Rick laid a dull grey book down on the table. Bruno dragged his thumb down the side and sliced the book open sluggishly. The brittle pages turned with a crinkling sound.

"What's the matter?" Rick opened his own copy, bending the covers back and cracking the spine. "I thought you were a big Whitman fan. What was that you wrote about seeing the poet's true heart or something?"

"Are you like making fun of me or something?" Bruno asked.

"No. Not exactly but it was just in reading your essay I came to wonder if you've ever even read any Whitman?"

"Hey," Bruno said, allowing his voice to get loud. "an A's an A. You can't go back and change the grade."

"No, but I'm your teacher now," Rick said calmly. "And I want to see what you can do with a gentle shove -- academically speaking."

Bruno slammed the book shut and passed it across the table. After flashing his own copy, Rick flipped his pupil's book open and slid it back. He shook his head as he did so with the air of a man used to controlling a conversation without having to resort to words. Taking it with one hand and pulling it only a fraction towards him, Bruno forced a hard frown he hoped gave the impression that he could become difficult.

"Poetry's not going to help me with anything. Poets don't run hotels," he said.

"It might broaden what you know about yourself," Rick said. "I think that's worth your time, don't you?"

* * *

Buddy's stomach gurgled. He felt dizzy. Olivia remained expressionless, her back locked upright and rigid. It looked as though she was capable of sitting there forever, steady in that position and staring at the double doors marked by the huge red cross. Suddenly, they swung open, the cross splitting in half. A nurse in a pink uniform passed them with a smile on her way to the elevator. Buddy sensed his brother suffering somewhere behind those doors and turned away from them as they closed.

Merrill had always been the health nut of the family: the vegetarian, the vitamin popper. Buddy was the drinker, the smoker, the unhealthy one, always out on the road working. None of this should've been happening to Merrill Cyzek, with his life of moderation, teaching music and directing the marching band at the high school.

"Say something, Liv," Buddy said.

"It's not going to be good news. When they make you wait this long it's because they're trying everything. That means they don't know what to do."

"Let's go somewhere," he said. "The wait's killing me."

"Strange choice of words, Bud."

"It's just...I'm hungry. We got to eat."

"What if the doctor comes?"

"How long do you want to wait for that?" he asked. "We can't do anything here but worry. I'd rather be worried and full, than worried on an empty stomach."

"I don't know." Her lips quivered slightly. Buddy hoped she wouldn't cry. He hadn't the energy to hold her. "I don't think I can eat."

"Never been a problem for me," Buddy said.

Bright lights reflected in blinding white puddles from nearly every surface, giving him a touch of a headache. He felt the cigarette pack through the fabric of his overalls. For the moment, it was enough that the pack and the future chance to excuse himself remained close. Steps approached from behind the swinging doors. Another nurse, this one in a uniform covered with cartoon mice and cats, smiled in a courteous, noncommittal, nurse-like way to those assembled beneath the glow of the waiting room's television.

"Look, Liv." Buddy paused to choose his words with care. "We both know the news might be tough to hear but...let's take a break. Let's go down to the cafeteria, just for a few minutes."

"Let me go tell the nurse we'll be right back," she said.

* * *

"*I am to wait,*" Bruno said in a stilted, bored monotone. "*I do not doubt/I am to meet you again/I am to see that I do not lose you.*"

"Good, Bruno. Better job taking your time. You still sounded robotic, but it was better. Now, what do you think that poem is about?" Rick asked.

"It's a poem to a stranger." Bruno's eyes searched the air above Rick's head.

"It's titled *To a Stranger*. You needn't have read more than the title to have gleaned that much. What do you think he's saying to this stranger? Who is this stranger to him? What is his relation to the speaker?"

"The speaker doesn't seem surprised to see them," Bruno said, his words shaped like a guess.

"He doesn't?" Rick asked.

"No." Bruno glanced back at the poem, disbelieving Rick was taking it so seriously. "It might remind him of someone he knows. It also seems like he's kind of stalking them."

"Really? Stalking them? Why do you think that?"

"It says..." Bruno paused to find the words on the page. "*You don't know how longingly I look upon you.*"

"But is he stalking or simply observing them?" Rick asked. "They're strangers after all. Can you really stalk someone you don't know anything about?"

"But he doesn't think they're strangers. He thinks he knows them. I think that's what this poem's about."

"Okay." Rick nodded. "I guess I can buy that."

"Can we be finished with poetry then? I read that one like three times in a row." Bruno flipped the book closed.

"You've suffered enough." Rick stuffed Whitman back inside his bag and removed a thicker, much less worn book. "Time for the exciting world of algebra."

"I'm pretty good at math."

"I know you are," Rick said. "I have to warn you though, I'm pretty good too."

"You should be," Bruno said. "You're like twenty years older than me."

"Not quite," Rick said, sounding amused. "Anyway, it doesn't matter how much older I am because I've always known the secret to being good in math. You want to know what that is?"

"Showing my work?" Bruno asked.

"Yeah, that helps. But the real secret?" Rick motioned for Bruno to lean closer to him and dropped his voice to a stage whisper. "Anyone who has a teacher's manual can be good at math. All the answers are here. They never change and are completely incontestable. Monkeys can be made to look smart at math with this." He tapped the teacher's copy with his fingers "I should know, I was taught by one."

Bruno laughed, trying to shake off his new tutor's obvious efforts to win him over. The problems proved to be easy. He took his time over them, nonetheless. Even if Rick could produce no evidence he'd earned fraudulent marks on those, he was wary of not appearing to work. As he sat there pretending to think about how to solve for (x), he found himself wondering about the poem and about how Rick had forced his thoughts in a different direction. It wasn't something his mother had ever done. And though he resisted it at first, Bruno felt as though a door in his mind had been cracked open, one he didn't even know had existed. Were there to be more poetry covered, though he'd not act outwardly excited, Bruno was interested to see where the work might take him.

* * *

As Ray watched the turtle crawling across his hood, he thought he was dreaming. Then he noticed the clicking of the turn signal and a hissing sound coming from beneath him and realized he'd driven his car into a ditch. He didn't know how long he'd been there or even where he was. He had no memory of leaving the bar he'd stopped in. It was hard to remember exactly how much he'd drunk there, though he had a dim inkling of a bartender remarking that he seemed to be "in a bit of a state."

The last thing he could clearly recall was the man stumbling out of the bathroom at the studio and collapsing right there in front of him. Something ghastly came over the stranger's face. His eyes had shone white as pearls. That could've been me, Ray had thought himself with the sound of the man vomiting still echoing in his head.

He struggled to unclick his seatbelt. A tree had shattered the passenger seat window and taken off the headrest. That could've been Bruce, he thought.

He killed the engine, listening for sirens. It was now just an accident. He'd lost control of the car. There could be no criminal complaint against him. Opening his door, he stepped out into a muddy creek that ran up to his calves. He helped the turtle off of the hood, then climbed up to the road. There were no skid marks that he could see, only the tracks of where his tires had matted down the tall grass.

Twice, he got sick walking down the road. His head spun. The vision of that stranger kept haunting him. Squatting down, he threw up on the edge of the macadam. It was lucky, he thought, that it'd happened apparently miles from anywhere but now he had to walk to find out how far that was.

Bruno took a moment before dialing -- phone to his ear, line buzzing blankly. His feelings for Rick now were far beyond those he'd felt only a few days ago, when he'd first called. Then, there had still been strong vestiges of his boyhood fantasies, of the first ones he'd experienced back when Rick was still his tutor. Those had been merely about physical encounters, about scenarios Bruno neither could imagine entirely nor resist trying to call forth. Having learned something so intimate about Rick's life, having learned about Tristan made Bruno want to spend more time with him. He now felt he truly had something to learn from his former tutor.

After dialing the phone, Bruno listened impatiently to the purr of its ring, which sounded nothing like the abrupt trill of the antiquated phones used at the Shelby. It would be enough to hear Rick's voice, feel his breath over the line. All the time he spent in confusion and it turned out Bruno just wanted to know someone else was there to hear him, to talk to him, to know him.

"Hello," Rick said.

"Hi...it's Bruno."

"Bruno, it's early."

"I know, I'm sorry...I just...I wanted to" Bruno said, his voice wavering with his nerve. Panicked, he no longer remembered how he wanted this call to go, what he really wanted to ask. He'd found the old book of Whitman poems stashed in a kitchen drawer but couldn't remember what he wanted to tell Rick about it, where and how he thought the conversation might go from there.

"What is it, Bruno?" Rick asked.

"How are you?"

"Tired."

"And how is Tristian?" Bruno asked, fumbling around for the question he'd hoped to raise more elegantly.

The line crackled with impatience. There also came the sound of some shuffling of fabric as though Rick was still in bed and searching for the proper position from which to address the issue. For a moment, Bruno worried he'd gone too far and betrayed Rick by prying into something he wished to keep private.

"He's sick," Rick said finally.

"I know. I know what he…"

"No, no. I mean he's got a bad cold now. He's been getting those a lot lately."

"It's not really right of me to ask, I guess, but I know how serious it is to need someone like that," Bruno said almost to himself as though it were an answer to a quiz he hadn't realized he'd prepared so well for.

"So you know," Rick said, clearing his throat. "I knew you were smart."

"Thanks." Bruno had wanted to tell Rick about his mother hurting, about her needing him but felt she should have no place between them any longer.

"It's nice of you to call."

"*Journey to the Center of the Earth* is playing with James Mason and Pat Boone," Bruno said, suddenly remembering the one thing he would not allow himself to forget. "I was going to try and see it, if you think you might like to come up and go too."

"I haven't seen that one in years. But I don't think I'll be going anywhere for a while. I have to try and help nurse him through this."

"Yeah," Bruno said then took a deep breath in place of asking Rick more about Tristian.

"But you should go. Tell me what you think."

"Okay."

"I mean it. Go see it and call me," Rick said over some coughing happening near him. "Your assignment is to give me a full and well thought out review. Nothing sloppy. Tell me what the movie meant, what it was trying to say."

"To me?" Bruno asked. "What it meant to me, you mean?"

"I'd love to know."

He put up the sign and went to check on his mother, bringing her some coffee and toast. The hot water bottle had fallen off the bed and lay half-crumpled next to it, the bottom bulging against the carpet. A pained look gripped her face even with her eyes closed. Bruno put the tray down next to her, hoping to just make enough noise to wake her. She was so often in motion, it felt strange to stand over her while she slept, like he was seeing her as she wasn't meant to be seen.

When her eyes opened, he jumped back and made as though to pick up the water bottle. In that instant, she looked so confused, so old -- lost in her own room. He wanted to tell her it was okay but just looked away. When she got her bearings, she pushed herself upright, grimacing with pain.

"You need to empty it before you can put more in," she said, using her fists to again readjust her position. "And it needn't be boiling hot. Regular hot tap water will do. I nearly burned myself with it yesterday."

"I brought you some breakfast," he said, gesturing to the tray on her nightstand.

Once more she put her closed fists down on the mattress, this time moving closer to the nightstand. Taking the mug with both hands, she blew into it and took a sip. Every movement she made took such effort. He wanted to help her but found himself watching instead.

"What're you going to do about your back?"

"I'm going to lie here until it feels better. The water bottle will help."

Taking his cue, he took it to the bathroom sink and dumped it. As he waited for the water to get hot, the need to get out of the hotel grew urgent. Even if he wouldn't see Rick, he wanted to go to the Thompson, to sit in the same seats where they'd sat and watch the movie closely. He wanted to make a full report on it, teach his old teacher something he didn't expect to learn. Bruno could no longer think of him in the kitchen, for there lingered the memories of his boyhood desires. Things were different now, the outside world felt theirs in a way the kitchen never could.

Rather than just give her the water bottle, he slid it under her back. He helped her with her pillow too and asked if she needed more coffee. He wanted to make sure she was as comfortable.

"Can I go for a run or maybe to the movies later, if you're feeling better?"

"Who would watch the desk? I need you at your spot. We have a guest, Bruno," she said, cringing as she raised her voice.

"I know. I know. I just need to get out. I need some fresh air."

"Fresh air? In that old firetrap of a movie house?"

"I want to see *Journey to the Center of the Earth*."

"Your job's here," she said. "I may need you to make up Mr. Sperint's room. You know I would like to be able to trust you, to give you more freedom, but you have to earn that. I can't have you gallivanting all over town when we have a guest, especially when I'm not at my best."

"I know where my job is Mom," he said. "I just want to see a movie. It's right across the street. I won't be gallivanting anywhere."

"I tell you what, go clean Mr. Sperint's room," she said, "then we'll talk about an afternoon furlough."

* * *

Angus hung the DO NOT DISTURB sign on his door. He couldn't sleep and didn't plan on leaving the room until his appointment at the studio. He put on the television, lay back on his bed with the pillows propping him up and tried to find something to watch. He flipped through the channels, but the news didn't hold his interest, neither did any of the movies or talk shows. A children's television show caught his attention for a while, mainly because he couldn't figure out what the two clay animals it featured were supposed to be.

One more session with Mark would do it, surely no more than two. Then he'd know if he'd redeemed himself enough, at least to sleep. *Do not blame yourself,* Andy's note had read. Angus had stopped reading it right there, then crumpled it up, threw it over his shoulder and walked out of the hotel where they'd been staying.

As the television's blue glow flickered over his eyes, he was reminded of being backstage at a little club outside of Buffalo -- an early date on Andy's "tour." A radiator's water pipe ran up the corner of the wall. It was hot, the air smelled of mold. Paint peeled from the ceiling. A muted TV glowed from one of the other corners.

Angus stretched out on a loveseat, a drink in his hand. They were both hopeful then, excited about what they were doing. Andy paced the room trying to get ready.

"Relax, Andrew," Angus said, "have a drink."

"Haven't you already used up all of my coupons?"

"Our coupons, Andrew. Our coupons. We're a team remember. Talent," Angus said, raising his class to his brother, "and management," then, taking a sip.

"We should act like a team, then," Andy said.

"What do you mean?"

"Just don't drink so much, okay."

"Hey, Andrew, brother, I got it under control," Angus said, raising a hand-held tape recorder, "Look, my latest idea to help you improve your act. I'm going to make a recording of it for you to listen to later. The type of thing only a great manager would come up with."

"Just try to manage not to get falling down drunk and keep your ideas to yourself while I'm on stage."

"You need to relax."

"Just leave me alone when I'm on stage," Andy said, his voice rising and shaking. "Keep it to yourself."

"This," Angus said, holding up the recorder again, "is something you will thank me for."

He'd failed to record that set because he forgot to bring any blank tapes. He asked around in the audience for some and even pestered the bartender. They'd all looked at him like he was crazy or maybe just really drunk. Angus shook off the memory by switching off the television and then shut his eyes, hoping to fall asleep.

* * *

Bruno had never sped the cart as quickly from the elevator then down the hall as he did on that day. Not once, but twice, he had to stop to retrieve a can of Pledge that fell off. When he arrived at Mr. Sperint's room to find the DO NOT DISTURB sign, it seemed so miraculous, he squatted down to look more closely at the card to make sure it was true.

No sooner did he get the cart back downstairs and into the closet than he was rushing across the street, still in his uniform, to the theater. He didn't want to miss a minute of the movie. He wanted to watch it closely enough to talk to Rick about every single scene. So focused was he on rehearsing this future phone call with Rick, he almost rushed right by him on his way into the theater.

"You're in a hurry," Rick said.

"What are you doing here? Is Tristian..."

"He overheard our call and didn't want me to miss the movie. He hates the way I fuss over him. Said he needed a break, so here I am. I was just going to see if you were at the hotel."

"Why didn't you call? If I knew you were coming I would've..."

"Changed clothes?" Rick asked. "I can't believe she let you out of there in your uniform."

"I didn't want to miss the matinee," Bruno said.

"Shall we?" Rick asked and they made their way to the ticket booth.

Inside the theater, they were alone. There was still time to talk before the movie started and yet Bruno found himself unable to do more than look over and smile. His former tutor didn't notice, lost, it seemed, in concerns Bruno was trying so hard to imagine the precise source of. All of the questions he wanted to ask Rick, all of the thoughts he wanted to share, all of the words that kept Bruno's mind whirling since their last visit now seemed beyond his ability to express them.

When the movie started, Bruno found it hard to concentrate. Rick's presence was distracting, even as it felt remote and distant. On the screen, Pat Boone rode a wave of salt through a winding tunnel, brightening the whole theater with a white glow that lit the tears streaming down Rick's face. Bruno rubbed Rick's arm. At this, Rick got up from his seat.

"Where are you going?" Bruno whispered as he got up to follow.

"I've got to get back, Bruno," Rick said, choking down a tremble, once they were out on the street. "I'm sorry I didn't mean to ruin it for you."

"It's okay. The special effects were kind of cheesy anyway."

"They were," Rick said with a laugh like relief. "It doesn't really hold up."

"I have so many things I want to talk to you about," Bruno said. "I don't even know which thing to start with. Can we go somewhere and talk, just for a little while? We'd have some privacy in the lobby, I think. I found that old book of poems by Walt Whitman."

"Did you?"

"I thought we could talk some more about them."

"I'm sorry but like I said I have to go back to him. I shouldn't have left but he's so bossy."

"Will you come up again, maybe when he feels better?" Bruno asked. "Or can I call? Like I said, there are so many things I don't know about."

"There's only one thing you need to know and it's to get out of this town. Go someplace, any place. See more of the country, of the world. Just don't stay here. You'll never belong here no matter how long you live."

"I want to but..." Bruno said, bruised a bit at the severity of Rick's tone as though he'd made a grave mistake just by being born there.

"I know," Rick said, offering his hand.

Bruno took it. They stood on the sidewalk holding hands, the shake always about to happen and ruin the moment. Then Rick let go and, in his release, Bruno thought he detected a farewell.

"Will you come up again, sometime?" he asked.

"I'll try," Rick said.

Bruno walked with him to his car. Rick was crying again. As he opened the door, Bruno grabbed his arm and, half pulling him back, held him. It seemed to Bruno a great deal of time passed before Rick relented and wrapped his arms around him. After Rick pushed away and got in his car, he blew Bruno a kiss. Not knowing how to respond, Bruno smiled, then watched Rick disappear around the bend on the road down into town. Wiping away tears, he felt full of life, full of his tutor's words, even if they asked the impossible. Slowly, he crossed the street and went back inside The Shelby.

16

The whole way down the dimly lit stairwell to the basement of St. Justin's, Ray kept promising himself it would all be over soon enough. Pungent with ammonia, the air stung his eyes. When he found the room where the meeting was to be held, he wasn't sure he could go through with it, still convinced he wasn't one of those guys. He willed himself inside and circled around the ring of empty chairs a few times before sitting down. He turned his head to find a large portrait of Jesus behind him. It was painted in such a way that the eyes seemed to follow him as he moved his head one way, then the other.

He wasn't sure he belonged here, though clearly, he'd crossed a line. The tow truck driver, Bo, had turned out to be something of an evangelical for the sober life. He wasn't a talkative guy, at first. They spent most of the ride from the service station to the crash site listening to some Christian channel -- preachers and organ music followed by news from a biblical perspective.

"You didn't do that by yourself," Bo said when they came upon Ray's car.

"I don't know how I did it," Ray said, his head still pounding.

"You had some help, alright. You drank your way in there. And now Jesus is working through me to get you out."

Ray didn't really want to hear any of it, but he listened. When they got back to Bo's garage he made a deal with Ray, the tow would be free and he'd even set Ray up with a cheap, reliable rental car if he promised to go to a meeting.

"What about my car?" Ray asked.

"Let us pray," Bo said, bowing his head and bringing his hands together.

* * *

Buddy stomped on the reel of tape and rammed his shoulder into the fridge, rocking it against the wall. Its door sprang open. He slammed it shut. When he heard Olivia's heavy feet coming down the stairs, he bent down to gather the broken reel, picking at the shards of plastic and unwinding the mangled tape. Pulling back his forearm to rip more tape from the spool, he accidentally struck her across the nose. She grunted and screeched, slapping at the air where his arm had been. He barely noticed, concentrating instead on placing what remained of the plastic reel beneath his boot. He stomped on it, sending plastic fragments scuttling across the floor.

"Buddy!" Olivia clawed at his shoulder as he stomped away. "Buddy, what are you doing?"

Plastic crunched under his feet as he stumbled around. Kicking at some of the pieces, he shook her off. Buddy grabbed a bottle from the kitchen table and took a heavy gulp of beer. It dribbled on to his chin and down the front of his shirt.

"I'm getting rid of these," he said, wiping his mouth on his shirt sleeve.

"God, Buddy!" Olivia felt along her nose where she'd been struck. "Why are you doing that?"

"Do you have to ask?" Buddy unspooled the tape from another reel and wrapped it around his forearm.

"He's not even on them," Olivia said.

Buddy stood a reel on its side and then rolled it across the floor. The music he'd spent so long laboring over trailed behind it -- a shiny brown tail. He tore at the tape that remained wrapped around his forearm.

"What does that matter?" He finished his beer and belched.

"You've worked so hard." Olivia buried her face into her cupped hands and began to cry. "He wouldn't want you to ruin them. He'd want to hear it."

"No, he wouldn't. He never really liked my music or any of our family's music."

160

Olivia grabbed him by the shoulders and pulled her brother close, taking him in her arms. His head instinctively found that crook between her shoulder and neck, the one he'd learned about before he knew anything else. She rubbed the back of his head. Olivia, the big sister, had always been the most reliable source of comfort, the only one he'd ever really come to count on. Buddy's tears began to darken the white collar of her pink nightgown.

* * *

Marianne brushed her hair from over her ear before touching it to the kitchen door. She wasn't spying, she told herself, simply making sure they were getting their money's worth. After years of doing the tutoring, she knew how difficult Bruno could be, especially when engaged in a lesson that failed to hold his attention. His voice came through in the bored monoton that had lately become his new default setting. Unable to tell what he was reading, she tried to listen closer.

"Better." Rick's voice was so loud and sure by comparison. "Now comes the hard part. What do you think the poem's about?"

"About?" Bruno mumbled with petulant frustration.

"What was it about, in your view? What do you think the meaning of the poem was?"

She should've moved on and allowed them to continue the lesson unobserved. But she wanted to hear her son's answer. Marianne was troubled by the idea that she didn't know her son as well as she wished. They never bonded over matters concerning the hotel the way she and her father had. What bothered her more was that she didn't even know what to ask him, what answers she needed, what about him was knowable and what he would always need to keep to himself.

"Start with the title," Rick said, his voice clear and confident.

"*Are You the New Person Drawn to Me,*" Bruno said, softly but clearly.

"Why do you think it asks that question?"

"I don't know," Bruno mumbled, his voice now trailing off into boredom.

"What's the poem doing?"

"Not rhyming?" he huffed.

Marianne found his performance uninspiring so far. She'd hoped that a young man like Rick would energize her son. She'd agreed to allow artsier subjects like poetry into the curriculum because he'd been so passionate about the need for it, especially for a boy Bruno's age. Really, she would've been more comfortable with Rick teaching the most basic things mandated by the state. From what she was hearing, poetry seemed to be something of a waste of time. She stepped away from the door to leave them to their lesson, unsure of what, if any, value it held for her son's future.

* * *

"Is this where the meeting's being held?" Andy's tiny eyes darted about the room, as though he was unsure whether to focus on Jesus or Ray or the empty chairs. Ray thought he looked too bright, his complexion too healthy to be an alcoholic.

"Yep," Ray said. "That's what I'm here waiting for."

"Where's everyone else?"

"We could be it."

"Just us? Hopefully, at least one more person's coming." He took a seat across the circle from Ray. "I'm Andy."

Among the folding chairs and cold carafes of coffee, Ray expected everyone he met at AA to seem like a stranger. He didn't give Andy his name, just a quick smile. Another alcoholic shuffled in; he offered no other sign of his presence beyond the dragging of his feet. A woman with bags of drooping pink flesh below her eyes, made even more apparent by her heavy makeup, nodded to everyone around the circle like she was greeting old acquaintances. Her smile, both friendly and fearful, came as though from a distance then slowly melted to nothing. Then, an elderly man with dull eyes and shaking hands stooped into his seat without looking at anyone except for Jesus, whom he greeted by making the sign of the cross.

Ray looked them over, trying to measure them, trying to tell if they wore their problems on the outside. It wasn't hard to find them worse off, more beaten looking. They looked to Ray emphatically alcoholic somehow, hard-bitten by the disease. A man with thighs so flabby the seams of his brown slacks almost cried out waddled to the center of the circle of chairs. The glow from his eyes was partially washed away, as though he was looking from behind frosted glass.

"Hi everyone. I'm Gene. I'm an alcoholic," he said, hitching up his pants over his hump of a belly only to have them droop back down.

"Hi, Gene." Everyone except for Ray and Andy responded with only mildly strained enthusiasm.

"It's great to see everyone back here," Gene said. "We have a couple new, ah, faces, a couple of, ah, new friends joining us. They don't have to say anything for now if they don't want, but we appreciate them coming and appreciate their, ah, support. Since everyone is here for everyone else, let's, ah, welcome them."

The group mumbled a greeting, more a general exhalation of empty syllables than words.

"Let's open up the floor now." Gene took the empty seat next to the woman. "Who'd, ah, like to start?"

Andy raised his hand, waving it back and forth listlessly like a pupil trying to confess to something his teacher already knew him to be guilty of.

"Go ahead, new friend," Gene said.

"Thank you." Andy stood up and coughed into his hand.

"Can we know your name?" Gene asked. "Just your first name. We're all friends here, so we try to keep, ah, introductions somewhat informal."

"Andy. My name is Andy."

"Hi Andy," everyone said.

Ray immediately detected something phony in the looks of sympathy the circle offered. To him, their disguises of soulful compassion really spoke of glee; glee at being a little less alone in the thing for which they felt the most shame. Standing in silence, Andy looked to the door, then around the circle, then back at the door again.

"I'm not sure I should even be doing this. You see, my brother told me to meet him here and if he didn't show..." Andy paused, his chest heaving as though he'd run out of air. "I could tell you all that he has developed a serious drinking problem. His name is Angus and he's...I'm sorry, I shouldn't be here..."

Ray had no one to meet him anywhere. He had no siblings and had been estranged from his parents for so long he couldn't even be sure that they were both still living. Of all the people he did know, Ray had broken too many promises to make even the smallest request of them. Alone in a room full of drunks, Ray thought only of leaving, but couldn't find the strength to rise from his chair.

"It's okay, Andy," Gene said. "Everyone here has a member of their family who's, ah, an alcoholic, even if it's just themselves." He paused, smiling over a brief twitter of laughter. "It was good of you to agree to, ah, come for your brother. This can be hard, a very hard thing for someone to do for the first time. Stay with your brother, Andy. He'll, ah, need all of your support."

Ray turned away, despising the smile smeared across Gene's face. He looked at the door then back to the ground, determined not to speak, not to be drawn in by the looks of encouragement around him. He was there but the notion that he hadn't made good on his promise to Bo nagged at him. Taking a deep breath, Ray trained his attention on the next speaker and wondered if maybe they'd all once felt as out of place as he did.

* * *

Bruno stared at the numbers and letters describing the word problem. As Rick read it aloud, he watched his lips form the words, making little more sense to him than they did on the page. All Bruno could think about was the poem, about all of the questions he had about it. He wasn't sure how to voice the feelings and thoughts it'd inspired.

"Was it really about him being, you know, gay? Like preferring men and it was the secret of his life?" Bruno asked, almost in a whisper. His mouth formed the last word deliberately, as if uncertain of producing it.

"This?" Rick playfully gestured at the math book in front of him. "I don't think so. I think it's about carrier pigeons, distance, and wind speed. Haven't you been paying attention?"

"No, I mean the poem we just read," Bruno said.

"That's a very mature question, Bruno." As he spoke into the teacher's copy before him, Rick's voice became quieter, more serious. "Shall we look at it again?"

"Can't you just tell me?"

"Sure. I can tell you my opinion, but it's important to keep in mind that we're talking about poetry. It's not like math. There's no right or wrong answer, no teacher's manual...just opinions, those well-considered, unfounded and every iteration in between." Rick set the math book to the side. "I would say that the poem, in my semi-considered opinion, is about finding that no matter how much we might feel for someone, how strongly we might be attracted to them, there's so much going on under the surface that it's almost impossible to know them well enough to validate the strength of those feelings."

Bruno's head swam in a sudden current of emotions. He searched for some safety in the book before him, his eyes tracing the page. The word problem still remained unintelligible. All he could get hold of was the sense that something he'd always wanted to know was slowly being revealed.

"Do you agree? What do you think, Bruno?"

"I don't know," he said. "I'll have to think about it."

"That's great," Rick said.

"What?"

"You do have to think about it. Poetry takes time and contemplation to understand. In an afternoon, you've learned how to study poetry as well as people who've studied it for years."

"Really?"

"I should know. It took me years," Rick said.

When Rick smiled after saying that, Bruno felt a charge go through him. The edges of a barely remembered dream flashed through his mind. In it, his tutor lay beneath the blankets of a bed in one of the rooms. He beckoned Bruno to join him, pulling back the sheets to reveal the full length of his sculpted, alabaster body. Just as Bruno felt he was about to be carried away by the remembered force of the dream, by the erection snuggling up against the zipper of his pants, he dove back into the math problem. It took a moment before his mind would let go of the image. Then mercifully, the equation came back into focus; the pigeons, wind speed, and distance described by the words and accompanying diagram were all so wonderfully safe. He began scratching away at the half-used pad of hotel stationary.

"This one's a bit more straightforward, isn't it?" Rick asked. "The math problem."

"Yes...straightforward," Bruno said.

Rick took his copy of Whitman from his bag. He placed it off to the side. Bruno glanced at it for only a second more than he could bear. He wished Rick would've just left it in his satchel.

"We can go back to it, if you want. The pigeons will wait." Rick reached for Whitman.

"We should move on to the math."

"As you wish," Rick said. "Is everything okay?"

"Yes. Fine," Bruno said, without looking up from the problem.

With greater speed than usual, Bruno figured that of the three carrier pigeons, 'Bird A' would make it to its destination first. He showed Rick his work, watching as it was checked. His tutor's red pen hovered but never dove to mark the page.

For a time, Buddy stayed on the road, polishing what remained of the tapes he'd salvaged but lacked the same zeal he had when starting out. Sometimes he had to pull over because he suddenly found himself crying so much, he couldn't see the road. Other times, he'd glance up in the rearview miror and see Merrill sitting there, ready to play just as he had been on that terrible day.

The wake had been packed with former students of Merrill. It'd moved Buddy to see them all come and pay their respects to his brother, their former teacher. Later, in talking to them, he understood the impact Merrill had made on so many lives and how many of them he'd helped turn into lifelong music fans. It was, Buddy had to admit, the secret ambition of every musician to touch so many lives in just that way. It revealed to him what his polka almanac really was, a vanity project that he and a few others would enjoy but would really do nothing for the music.

He remembered too the way the bright sun reflected off the windows of the cars that packed the funeral home's parking lot. Lowering himself onto the back bumper of his station wagon, he smoked half a cigarette before the thought of Olivia's frown invaded his psyche. He opened the trunk, removed his accordion and silently tapped out a mournful song but stopped short of making it sing.

Back inside, he ducked to get away from his sister's glare. Olivia's expression of distaste was so severe she looked like she was about to consume her own lips. Buddy accepted a couple of condolence nods as he retook his spot next to her.

"Are you going to play?" She gestured at the accordion.

"Not sure." He loosened the strap so that it dipped down to hide his potbelly. "Do you think I should?"

"Why did you bring that in here?" she asked, her voice climbing above a whisper for the first time that day.

"I thought I'd give it to Merrill."

"You're going to put *your* accordion in the coffin?"

"I've got others in Erin's garage."

"She hasn't gotten rid of them?"

"I hope not. It hasn't been that long."

"Well, take it off for now. Everyone'll think you're going to play something," she said.

"Do you really think our friends would think it odd to play something for him, right now?" he asked.

Buddy bent down with a grunt and took up the accordion. Too choked up to sing, his fingers picked out an old, half-forgotten melody that summoned a vision of his brother as child watching him play. Buddy had given Merrill his first lessons on the instrument.   The room turned to him, silence prevailed as they all listened. Buddy couldn't remember the last time he'd played for a crowd that size. They clapped gently when he finished. Then, he took a look around the room before laying his instrument on his brother's chest.

"I'm giving you this because you were always a better player than me. Even if you never wanted to be, you know it and I know it," he said. "Pop always said so. Since I never got you to play it again, I'm giving you this in case you get the urge, and they don't have polka in the next world."

* * *

Determined to keep going to the meetings, though he still wasn't sure he needed to, Ray had no problems finding them in the small towns he traveled through. They were usually at schools or churches, tucked away in basements where the musty air made him feel like a prisoner newly in his cell. He'd always been good with strangers when he drank but now found himself subdued, worried his fellow drunks could already tell what his secrets were.

A lump of a man with sore looking eyelids glanced at Ray before returning to the paper folded over his thigh. Across the circle from him was a redhead who, while not exactly young looking, had a freshness to her, a brightness to her face that made Ray's heart race hard enough to remind him that life had things to offer beyond his problems. The woman's skin showed no signs of the patchy dryness he'd come to recognize in the faces of other drinkers. He moved the chair next to her, its skittering sounded abrupt in the quiet room. Allowing himself one more glance, he sat down.

A younger man with headband encircling a head of unkempt, curly hair sat down across from them. He glanced nervously at everyone but said nothing. A short, thick man in a rumpled grey blazer and a pair of blue trousers squatted into his seat carefully, as though his hips were a crane setting down a load. A large man in overalls drinking a Diet Coke arrived next. He looked over the room, appearing confounded. He circled the chairs once before sitting next to the guy in the jogging suit.

"Do we look unsavory?" the woman asked Ray.

"What?" he whispered.

"No one wants to sit next to us. Thank God you sat next to me. These meetings can give a girl a complex," she said, cocking her head towards Ray and offering her hand. "Haven't seen you here before. I'm Veronica."

"Ray." He gave her hand a squeeze. "This is my first time at this meeting. Trying to get in the habit, but it's hard. I travel."

"Really? You like the bad coffee that much?" she asked.

"Not many places left where you can get free cookies and lukewarm coffee simply by self-identifying oneself as a victim of the dreaded demon alcohol."

Smiling, she took his eyes with her as she turned away, getting her phone from her bag. She swiped at the screen, at whatever was more interesting than Ray. He focused on a square pool of light shining on the linoleum between his feet. If she'd laughed or even let him look at her for just a flicker longer, he might never have gotten up to speak.

When he did, he was surprised how much came out. With that whole room looking at him, he felt compelled to give some accounting of himself. He talked not just about his car ending up in a ditch, for if that were truly his lowest point he would have been the luckiest there, but about the whole blur of his life -- all that he'd lost.

"So, I'm going to do the work to rebuild some trust and hope to see my son more often," he said as he began to sit back down, shaken by the torrential confession that he'd let flow. "Maybe even take a trip with him, just the two of us."

After the meeting, he ran into Victoria again at Mung's Diner, which was across the street. She invited him to sit down, putting her phone back in her purse for the first time, it seemed to Ray, since she'd picked it up. He was still shaken a bit by what he'd done, proud and ashamed and bewildered and unburdened all at once. He thought about reassuring her that his shaking was due to nerves, he wasn't suffering from delirium tremens but decided they had both heard enough talk about the dire effects of alcohol at the meeting.

In his best impersonation of someone completely at ease, Ray stretched out his arms across the back of the booth. He fought the compulsion to ball up his hands and instead forced them to lay flat. The light in Veronica's hazel eyes looked to be one of bemusement, her smile just slight enough to almost appear mocking.

"The coffee in this place is awful," she said, after a scowl inducing sip. "I can barely stand it."

"Better than the stuff at the meeting." Ray took a sip, holding the cup with both hands and trying to keep it steady. He put his mug down and pushed it away.

"Bad habit. I need the caffeine," Veronica said.

"I know what you mean. I always end up getting hotel coffee when I'm on the road. It's awful, but I keep getting it anyway," Ray said, taking his mug again.

"It's surprising," she said in between another sip and scowl. "The things we do out of habit, out of a lack of creativity. Because we don't know or want to think of how to be any other way."

"A lack of creativity." Ray nodded, fingering his mug and pushing it away.

"My son's like that." Veronica paused and looked up at Ray as though to gauge his reaction. "He's got this plastic duck on wheels with a string that he pulls all over the place. Sometimes, he'll put its beak into his mouth like he wants to eat it. The second he can taste it, he gets a terrible look on his face and starts bawling. But it's like he only does it when he's bored."

"How old is your son?"

"He'll be three soon."

"Mine's fourteen," Ray said.

"You don't look old enough to have a teenager."

"His name's Bruce," Ray said. "I don't get to see him much because of my work."

"I'm sorry," Veronica said. "I'd hate being away from my treasure."

"I wish I led a stable kind of life. I'm out on the road so much."

"Are you and Bruce's mother...? Forget it. I shouldn't be asking."

"No. It's okay." Ray tried a laugh, but it came out hollow. "We never even got married. We talked about it, but no I'm unattached. How about you?"

"Same," she said. "Better unattached than detached, I guess."

Ray laughed, though he didn't know what she meant. He took another sip of coffee and scowled. She did the same. Like at the meetings, the coffee at the diner seemed to be just drinkable enough that one could almost hide behind it.

* * *

Buddy tossed the empty bottle at the plastic reel floating away from him. When it made contact, a soft splash sent ripples across the water, shimmering in a sliver of moonlight. Submerged briefly, the shell bobbed back up and floated next to the bottle. Since Olivia hadn't allowed him to destroy his tapes in peace the last time he was at her house, he was now determined to drown them in her lake.

He coughed with his whole body until his ribs ached. He flung another reel into the water. Part kite, part discus, it landed with a polite splash. Pulling on the tape, he created a tiny whirlpool atop the dark meniscus.

Steps crunched on the gravel behind him. He didn't have to turn around to see who it was. Buddy chugged down the rest of his beer and opened another.

"Drink, Liv?" he asked without turning around.

"What are you doing back here?" she asked.

"I was too drunk to think of anything better to do with them." Buddy took a loud sip from his bottle. "Still am. Care to join me?"

"Who'd help us get up the hill and back to the house if I got drunk too?" she asked. "I do hope you're planning on staying at my place. You're not driving anywhere."

"It's just the two of us out here. The last of the Cyzek Family Band. What'll we do, Liv? What do we play now?" Buddy belched with enough gusto to rock him back on his heels.

"You are going to pick up all these bottle caps, right?" Olivia asked, kicking at some caps that had become embedded in the dirt.

As clouds devoured the moon, brother and sister stepped closer so they could see each other's face. Olivia hugged her arms to her chest. Buddy took off his jacket and dangled it in front of her.

"Here, take this."

"I'll be okay," she said, taking it anyway.

Buddy wrapped it around her, pulling her towards him. She tried to smile, but her face was too creased and puffy. Merrill's death had aged her.

"It's just the two of us." Buddy staggered away from her after another sip. "He loved this place. He loved your house, loved the water down here."

"He did." Olivia pulled his jacket around her, turning to watch the moving clouds as they released the moon. "Are you throwing all of those tapes in?"

"In tribute to him!" Buddy raised his bottle into the air. "Merrill always thought music sounded better played nearer to nature. It's one of his theories that I'll always carry with me."

All at once, Buddy felt exhaustion seep into his blood, into his bones. He collapsed, his legs sprawling out before him so that he resembled a toddler who'd failed at walking. Sitting his bottle to the side, he looked up at his sister; the reemerging moon glowed on the tear running silver down her cheek.

* * *

Ray turned on all the lights in the hotel room, then one by one, turned them off again. He closed the bathroom door, then opened it and turned the bathroom light off and on -- the same with the fan. He hadn't expected to be this jumpy. Since parting with Veronica at the diner, seeing her again was all he could think about. Now that he'd waited so long to call, he was as nervous as a high-schooler asking his crush to the prom. He sat on the bed and looked at his phone for a while, wishing it could make the call. Then, he flipped it open and dialed before what was left of his nerve left him.

"Hello," Veronica said, after only a ring and half.

"Hi, this is Ray...Raymond," he said, feeling his pulse race.

"Ray Raymond." She giggled. "How are you?"

"Nervous," he sputtered, trying to generate some saliva between his parched cheeks. "I haven't done anything like this in a long time."

"That's okay. It's been a while for me too." She giggled again. "I'm glad you called. I wanted to ask you out to dinner."

"You wanted to...me...dinner..."

"I'm surprised I'm not hearing a 'yes' in there, Ray. I took you for a sure thing."

"Yes," he said. "Yes, let's have dinner. Let's do that."

"Weren't expecting, that were you?" she asked.

"No," he said. "You can't imagine how hard I had to think about a way to do this, how to ask. I made it harder than it needed to be, I guess."

"I know what you mean. It all feels strange. But that's fitting, given that we'll have to act like kids all over again. No cocktails, skip the house wine. I haven't done that since I was in high school."

"Me neither," he said.

"We'll have to treat ourselves, split an apple cobbler for dessert or something...something datey."

"I can't remember the last time I had dessert," he said.

"This's what they mean by starting over."

* * *

When over halfway into Bruno's school year with Rick, Marianne had still not heard back from Pittson's historic preservation office about setting a date for their visit, she had to take a hard look at the numbers. Business had not been good since Buddy had checked out. In fact, it had been non-existent. The money her father had left her was dwindling even faster. She called the office handling her application again and again but never heard back. She did consider that they might've been busy, though it seemed hardly credible. For even if every crumbling down factory and boarded-up bowling alley in town applied for historic status, it surely shouldn't take that many months to get back to her about a date on which to meet. As they said, one could not fight city hall, especially in Pittson where, since that building had burned down three years before, it'd become a moving target.

The meager fee she was paying Rick was no longer affordable. Thankfully, she'd looked into the state tutoring requirements and found a loophole that would at least allow Bruno's education at home to continue. She only needed to get Rick to agree. She asked him to come in early one day. They met in the kitchen. She gave strict instructions to Bruno not to leave the desk.

"You probably are expecting some bad news," she said to Rick once they were seated at the kitchen table.

"I hope it's not something I've done," he said.

"No. But...well, we have to tighten our belts around here and I can't keep paying you," she said. "I don't know what I'll do."

"You're letting me go?" he asked.

"I'm sorry Rick, but I don't know what else to do."

"You'll have to send him to the school down in the valley, I guess."

"No. I couldn't do that. Not with the school year more than half over. Besides, I need him here with me in the hotel. It's to be part of his education."

"Right," Rick said, "but I don't see what else you can do. I mean, I like Bruno and you and coming here to your wonderful home, but I need to be compensated for my time."

"I understand," she said, removing the form she'd stashed in her pocket, "I just need you to do something for me. I found this." She spread it out on the table before him. "It states that you will be unable to finish the school year and name me as a qualified replacement."

"But you're not certified, are you?"

"Don't need to be, if you'll just vouch for me on this form," she said, her hand shaking as she passed him a pen. "Please. You can see he's a smart boy. I must've been doing something right, even if the state doesn't regard me as qualified. Please, just sign."

Rick took the form but not the pen. She didn't want to beg him but felt desperation rushing out of her with every breath. It was bad enough when the state had taken control of Bruno's schooling from her. Now she'd handed it to this young man, no more than a few years older than her son, whose lessons had seemed to her to be less than entirely pragmatic. She'd overlooked the poetry even though she hadn't approved. And now she found herself begging this aesthete with her eyes to give her back oversight of her own son's education.

"It says here if he fails the end of year exam, I could lose my certification," Rick said.

"He won't. I promise you, he won't," she said.

"I know he won't," Rick said, scraping the pen across the table towards himself. "Does he know about this?"

"I was hoping you'd tell him that we had a disagreement about your methods and decided to part company. I don't want him to worry about this sort of thing."

"Business stuff, you mean," Rick said, signing the form. "I'll tell him it nobody's fault. We just agreed to disagree."

17

"Fucking sit down! Fucking get off the stage! Sit motherfucking down!" Angus' voice, full of anger and drink, sounded like a mouthful of barbed wire.

"I can try to dull that down," Mark said, sliding a lever on the mixing console. "But it'd be easier to just cut it out altogether."

"How's it going to sound?" Angus asked. "Will it be terribly abrupt?"

"It comes right after the joke. I can finesse, but it'll be hard to make it sound completely natural. It sounds like you're on stage with him."

"The tape recorder was right next to me."

"That would explain it." Mark reset the levels. Green and red lights took turns flashing on the board. "You've been difficult to erase."

The urge to find a proper place to start a bender, to down drink after drink until it felt too good to stop, now lingered large in Angus's thoughts. In the back of his throat grew an itch like a whiskey burn. Nothing else was going to make it go away.

"You want to hear this again? Or do you want to take a break?" Mark asked, hunched over the board, his finger hovering above the PLAY button.

"Let's hear it."

"I'm going to make you as soft as possible." Mark adjusted the levels with a light touch.

"I was thinking about getting a dog." Andy began. He paused to clear his voice.

"Sit down." Angus could still be heard in the background, no louder than ice tinkling.

"Then again," his brother continued, "I don't want to have to feed it or walk it or clean up after it. That's just not me."

"Sit down." With a soft touch on two of the blinking sliders, Mark faded Angus further into less distinct ambient noise.

"I mean, I want a dog to love me for me. Is that so wrong?" Andy asked.

"Fucking sit down...fucking get off the stage..."

Angus scratched at his throat, thinking he could almost feel the scars inside from all that drinking and yelling. To heal was an on-going process, the therapists at the clinic were always saying. Things suppressed resurfaced. Old wounds reopened. He had begun to trust all of this advice, because he could see getting sober really had been the easy part. They'd been right about that.

* * *

The pain ebbed and flowed, returning with enough strength to make Marianne cry out. Her agony felt beyond the power of her meditations. Though she could easily identify the place of the discomfort and isolate it, she could not pierce it, could not break it into smaller pieces no matter how tightly she squinted her eyes and tried to focus on it.

With a shaking hand, she picked up the phone and held it against her chest. Fighting the urge to call her son, she dropped it back down onto the receiver. She wanted to trust that he was at his post, that he was making the hotel his only priority until she got better. The night before, when she had explained to Bruno that there would be no jogging or movies for a while, he'd responded cheerfully like a prisoner who already knew his escape plan.

Struggling to move, she thudded the headboard against the wall as she reached to pry the phone from its cradle. Pinning the receiver to her chest, she laid her finger on the 8, but didn't press. She breathed through the pain. Though it didn't exactly pass, the agony waned to mere discomfort. She put the receiver back down.

No sooner had it come to rest in its cradle than it rang. A trilling, invasive sound that found her pain and shouted inside of it. She picked it up and paused to drink in the gentle relief she found by stopping the noise.

"What is it Bruno?" she asked, guessing incorrectly.

"Is this Marianne Shelby of The Shelby Hotel?" a voice which was not Bruno's asked.

"Yes. It is. I am. How can I help you?"

"Good afternoon, Ms. Shelby my name is Ron Schnell with the city's office of historic preservation, how are you today?"

"I'm well, sir. And how are you?"

"Listen, I know you've called the office once or twice to check up on your application and I wanted to tell you, we finally found the time for that meeting we've been meaning to take with you."

"It's been almost two years."

"I know and apologize for the delay. State funding is often an issue. Are you still interested?"

"We are. We definitely are," she said, able now to ignore the pain and push herself into a more upright position. "I'd love to do it as soon as someone from your office can come up here."

"It'll be me doing it. I am the office, you see," he said. "That's another reason why it's taken so long, sorry to say. Pittson's a town full of old buildings with stories the owners think need to be preserved and well, I can only do this part-time."

"I completely understand," she said, thinking that like him, she was her hotel.

"Would tomorrow at 2 suit you?"

"Yes, yes it would," Marianne said, her mind too buzzed from sudden adrenaline to say anything else.

Only after she hung up, did she realize what she'd committed her aching back to. This task was far too important to entrust fully to Bruno. Mustering strength, she lifted herself out of bed and gently crashed against the dresser. She gripped its edge and dragged her body toward the door. With a firm grip on the doorknob, she rested, thankful to have made it that far. All she had to do was make it across the hall to the bathroom. There she would find the horse pills that would reduce the spiking sensation along her spine.

Before she could advance any further, another jolt in her back struck her. She fell against the door, opening it for a brief second before slamming it shut. The tightness felt like a nest of angry wasps stinging her lower lumbar muscles. She rested her head against the door and forced herself upright. The bathroom, no more than a few steps away, no longer seemed possible. Once the pain subsided enough for her to move, she dove back into bed.

Marianne struggled to reach out and dial the phone, her back muscles threatening to tighten with every inch she stretched. She settled back into position, suffering in the very same spot where her father had died. She thought of his last days, hoping the memory of being with him before his passing might soothe her own pain. Where the nightstand now sat, there had been a chair from which Marianne had watched him slip away.

He'd never missed a day of work until he got sick. Marianne had just turned 24 -- more than old enough to take care of things. Still, she had found it a struggle to work at the pace he had set in handling all the day to day tasks without assistance.

His health deteriorated rapidly. Still, he refused to go to the hospital. As late as the night before his final day of life, he promised to be back on his feet, telling Marianne not to worry about taking out the trash. That next morning, she went to sit with him just as she did before the beginning of each of her shifts during that dark time. His face was yellow and bloated, his eyelids a bright, painful pink. She thought it good that he was at least sleeping rather than coughing. She watched his chest rise and fall, fearing he'd stop breathing if she looked away. One of the chair legs on which she sat was slightly shorter than the others, so she had to concentrate on being extra still.

She stayed and listened as long as she could, but the sense of duty her father had impressed upon her was keen. That day, she performed her tasks with a sense of purpose that would've made him proud. She managed not worry about him too much, not realizing she'd already seen him alive for the last time.

The spasm finally retreated long enough for her to pick up the phone. She dialed 8. Bruno didn't answer until the middle of the third ring.

"How can I help you?" he asked.

"What took you so long to pick up?"

"Hey, mom. Feeling better?"

"No." She grunted. "I need another pill for my back. Someone is coming tomorrow and I have to be upright to see them."

"So, I've got to keep on manning the desk by myself for the rest of the day?"

"Listen, Bruno." She was in too much discomfort to be properly aggravated. "You'll be in a better position to bargain about your schedule if I'm not in pain. Now please, bring me one of those big, fat pills."

"Should I put the bell and sign up?" he asked.

"Just bring me the pill please, Bruno. I can't move. Do you understand? I'm in pain."

"Okay, okay, I'll get it..."

"Paralyzing pain."

"I said okay."

She'd never told Bruno about the proposed visit or even the application. She'd meant to but then as the days and weeks and months went by without a response, it became one more thing that would've made difficult her job of getting him to take pride in his work. Now maybe he would see, would understand not just the need to take pride but the joy it could offer. People cared about The Shelby. Someone had taken notice.

When he came to her door, she responded to his knock impatiently. There was no time to spare. He handed her the pill and a glass of lukewarm water. The look on his face was as tender as she'd ever seen.

"Slow out there?" she asked after washing down the pill.

"No slower than usual," he said.

"Bruno." She laughed. "You are developing the sense of humor necessary for the uneven life of the hotelier."

"So, do you think I can go see a movie tomorrow?" he asked.

"*Journey to the Center of the Earth* still playing?"

"*The Third Man.*" Bruno sat on the edge of the bed and took the glass from her.

"Another classic," she sighed. "I guess if we can manage to get me out to the desk tomorrow."

"Really?" He rose from the bed quickly, as if sitting any longer might draw her into a debate.

"Just go finish your shift tonight. And make sure to put the bell on loud so that we hear it in the apartment in the off chance we get a late-night visitor."

"Okay," he said. "Need anything else before I go?"

"I want to tell you about some changes that might be happening here soon. There's someone coming to see me tomorrow and tour the hotel."

"Tour the hotel? Who?"

"Someone from the city. They are interested in possibly making our little establishment a historic landmark."

"Really?" he said, sounding more impressed than she could've hoped. "Historic? Will we still live here?"

"Yes and operate the hotel but the designation should help boost the business, which as I'm sure you've noticed has declined a bit recently."

"So, what, they're just going to like put a plaque or something outside the building?"

"And we'll be on the register of historic places and we'll get a stipend from the state and local governments to help cover the expenses of running a landmark."

"But we'll still be just a hotel?"

"Yes, but a historic one."

"Am I going to get a bigger room?"

"No. Nothing will change except for our status. We'll be a spot of interest, Bruno. Enthusiasts from all over will want to come and stay here."

"You mean there are people who want to stay in old hotels?"

"Of course."

"Why?"

"To be surrounded by the history, I suppose. I've been telling you that this is something special, this place makes our lives special."

"What time does this guy come tomorrow?"

"Two o'clock, so we need me to be better by then. Otherwise, you'll have to show him the place and try to fake being proud of it."

"You can take one of those every four hours," Bruno said. "And I won't have to fake it. I just don't like standing out in the lobby for hours every day."

"I know but we must be at our posts, here. It must always look busy, especially when it isn't," she said.

* * *

The sun drowned beneath a sky of velvet pink. Torn into edges by the purple beginnings of night, clouds shimmered with all the sulfurous colors of the day's combustion. The wind drove through them, tearing the formations apart with a breath of cold.

Angus turned up the collar of his suit coat after taking the cigarette Mark offered, then leaned in to take some of his flame. He thought of how little of Andy there was left to hear. Soon, he'd learn if his plan was a success, if the worst of his heckling had been drowned out by a sea of laughter. Someday in the far future, he might not even remember that he had been recorded at the show - - there might only be Andy.

"There's no other way to take what I'm about to say, other than to know I say it to everyone I work with." Mark spoke from one corner of his mouth, the other pinched around a cigarette. "In a couple of days we'll be done, and I'm going to hand you the finished product. We'll go over it, make sure it's good, it's what you want, but before you walk out of here with it, you'll need to hand me that last check."

"I understand. I will," Angus said. "Of course, I will."

"I figured, but it's still something I have to say," Mark said. "I got stacks and stacks of reels in my office of people's work who didn't or couldn't pay me. Got a whole shelf of this one band, Grand Plasma. They recorded for weeks and weeks and couldn't make that last payment. All that work now just sitting there collecting dust."

"What will happen to the tape if they never pay?"

"Technically, it's my property so I can do what I want with it. I could rename the band Lesides and release it if I really wanted to, but it'll just sit there."

"If they never pay will you just throw it away someday?"

"Can't do that," Mark said, shaking his head. "Musicians were bestowed God's greatest gift. They bring harmony to the universe, all of them, from polka to hip hop. I'd never get rid of music just because God made the mistake of giving humans that gift."

"What if I didn't pay? Would you throw Andy away?"

"Well, I'm fairly certain you'll pay."

"But if I didn't, if something happened," Angus said, unable as ever lately to shake the notion that some unplanned catastrophe awaited him.

"No, I couldn't throw it out because I know it means something to you, just like the music means something to the musicians, even if they let other things get in the way." Mark dropped his cigarette to the ground and mashed it out. "Commercials, promos, stuff like that I'd toss but that kind of stuff always gets paid for, because its sole purpose is to make money for someone."

"Don't musicians do things for money?" Angus asked, finishing his in the same manner.

"They think they do sometimes, but it's because they don't respect the extent of their gift. One of the kids from Grand Plasma was going around a couple of years ago, trying to shake down studios for money, saying they owed him. When that skinny punk showed up here, I threatened to kick his ass."

"Because he didn't respect his gift," Angus said.

Mark nodded and held open the door.

* * *

The next morning, Marianne managed to get out of bed. Most of the sharpness of the pain had gone away and been replaced by more of a dull ache. She felt stiff and tired. It took several cups of coffee to get her going. Bruno was already at the desk, unable to hide the look of near excitement on his face. She stood next to him and they both watched the door. Not in years had they stood there side by side with so little friction frying the air between them. Each was silent, afraid to speak as though they could ruin the moment by giving voice to their anticipation.

Promptly at 2, the doors swung open. Ron Schnell strode in, unbuttoning his tweed jacket; a clipboard in one hand and a briefcase in the other. He made notes as he inspected the lobby. Smiling, he swooped by the desk to look over the elevator, whistling to himself as he did so.

"Ms. Shelby," he said finally slinging his briefcase atop the front desk. "I'm Ron Schnell."

"Yes," she said, taking his hand. "And this is my son Bruno."

"A family business. We do like that. And the elevator over there, is it inspected regularly?"

"I keep everything up to code," she said. "There's no cutting corners here."

"Excellent, excellent," Ron said. "I wonder, young man, if I might entrust you with my briefcase. From my day job, I'm afraid. Insurance. Very tedious. Nothing but actuarial tables and policy brochures in there but I'd like it if you kept an eye on it while your mother shows me around."

"What would you like to see first?" Marianne asked.

"The room you're proudest of as long as it's part of the original construction."

"412, it is," she said and led him to the elevator.

He seemed giddy at the prospect of riding in it. Inside, he inspected the button panel carefully. He touched the gate after she closed it. All the while, he made notes on his clipboard. Marianne was anxious for a glance at it but restrained herself.

"This sure is a beautiful building, you should be quite proud," he said.

"We are," she said, battling a pinch of pain that spiked when the elevator came to a rest.

"I must say this is a rather nice place to visit compared to most of the locations in town that put in an application."

"We're glad you're finding it enjoyable."

"Most places want historic status on the strength of being a site of one kind of anti-union violence or another," he said, following her down the hall. "Why, just yesterday I was on the premises of a former cracker factory where Pinkertons had killed 14 men around the turn of the 20th century."

"I had no idea those sorts of things had happened here."

"History loves a martyr, Ms. Shelby," he said as she opened the door to 412.

On that visit, 412 was agreeably free of Ray's ghost. Marianne was too consumed by Ron Schnell's inspection. He took in the view, rubbed the carpet, ran the sink, even flushed the toilet. She wanted to ask what he was looking for but also wasn't sure she wanted to know the answer. It was better to let him do his work and stand idly by as though he was a guest trying unusually hard to decide if the room was suitable.

He had her show him a room on every floor. She kept to the rooms which had no or a few minor alterations over the years. He took his time at each stop, making notes and asking the odd question about lamps or faucet fixtures. It wasn't until they had visited the last room that her pain came back. Marianne just hoped she could hold on until he left, thinking any lack of poise on her part would have a negative effect on their application.

"I don't much go for suspense in this job," he said once they were back in the lobby, "so I will say I think this will make a fine addition to register the historic places of Pittson."

"Really?" she asked, her voice high and joyful. "That's wonderful news. Did you hear that Bruno?"

"Great mom," he said with a voice that betrayed some actual enthusiasm.

"I'm going to give you these tax forms to fill out and a brief questionnaire purely to include in a brochure about the area's historic places," Schnell said, removing some pages from the back of his clipboard. "Make sure to get these in by the due date. The state doesn't mind our office taking its time, as you may have noticed, but requires punctuality on your part."

"We won't," Marianne said and bit down hard against the knot in her back reasserting itself, though it seemed to matter little now if she came undone.

Back in her bedroom, she held the forms to her chest as she collapsed onto the bed. What had seemed like giving up on the hotel two years ago now looked more like its salvation. She knew there would be much work to do to make sure the place always looked it best but felt safe to rest.

18

As Veronica stirred, Ray removed his hand from her back. Smiling at her through the darkness, he couldn't remember the last time he'd been with a woman. For the first time since trying to get sober, he didn't mind being awake so early in the morning. He got out of bed quietly, hoping not to disturb her.

He closed the bathroom door softly behind him. The light on the back of his charging phone lit the white walls and porcelain tub a subterranean green. When they'd got back to the room, he'd called the hotel and chatted with Bruno. Even as he was doing it, he was conscious that the character he was trying to portray, the committed father, was not going over. It'd been weeks since he and Bruno had spoken and they didn't have much to say to each other. Ray's promise to see him soon must've sounded as hollow as every other thing he'd said. He'd just felt that he needed to do something to make sure Veronica stayed. He couldn't believe she'd even agreed to go out again let alone come back to his place for a cup of bad coffee.

Their last date had been a disaster. At first, they'd found that outside of drinking and parenthood, they had very little to talk about. Sober, Ray realized his stories from the road were tedious and that few people cared about what he sold. He'd even spilled water on himself, not once but twice. It had been so bad that as he drove back to the motel where he was staying and found himself at a stoplight between two bars, he decided it was time to knock the rust off. Sober Ray wasn't someone anyone wanted to be around.

He pulled into the parking lot behind a place called Hilltop, though there wasn't a hill in sight, not even a mild gradient. Inside it was dark, the air smudged by the neon signs hanging on every available piece of wall. Ray felt calm for the first time that night, maybe for the first time since he'd run his car into that ditch and made a real effort to quit drinking. The stool, a bucket seat, was comfortable enough that he could see himself drinking until close. He was just about to order when Veronica walked in. She shook her head when she saw him. Ray couldn't tell if her smile was admonishing or guilty.

"Did you follow me here?" he asked.

"Looks like we had the same bad idea," she said, "or maybe you followed me here."

"Yeah, bad ideas," he said, still unsure if he should order or not.

"So, I guess it went as bad for you as I thought it did," she said.

"I'm sorry, God, I can't stop apologizing lately. I guess it didn't go too well for you either."

"It's funny because I had a fine time," Veronica said, "but then I got in my car and started driving and thinking that maybe you didn't have such a good time. You were so nervous. You didn't even try to kiss me."

"I guess I just don't know how to do anything anymore. Thought maybe a drink would help."

"Funny thing about being sober," she said, placing her hands on the back of his stool and her chin on his shoulder, "you think it'll make life simpler but it turns out drinking just helped you complicate things in a different way. Life's still here waiting for you to make a mistake."

"So, I'd guess you'd say drinking right now would not be a great idea."

"I thought it was what I needed walking in here, but seeing you...yeah, let's go," she said, picking up her chin and turning his stool so that it faced away from the bar.

In the parking lot, he walked her to her car. She surprised him by holding his arm. Then again by reading his intentions and unlocking the door of her car so he could open it for her. Once she was inside, he leaned over and they kissed. They made plans to meet again the next time Ray was in town.

She appeared to have fallen back to sleep when he returned to bed. Ray wanted to take her in his arms, to feel her body pressed against his. He tensed as the urge to reach out for her grew stronger. He wondered if he could've felt that way for anyone when he was drunk. Curling himself back into a ball, he turned away from her, careful not to take more than his share of the sheets.

Bedsheet allocation had been a source of contention from the very beginning with Marianne. In the early days of their romance, when petty annoyances were taken as blessings, the arguments were playful, a mere lark played by two lovers still dazed by the novelty of sharing such an intimate space. With time, her complaints took on a nastier edge, as though Ray was using those sheets to cover more serious faults.

"You move around so much while you're in bed, I swear you must be exhausted when you get up in the morning," Veronica said, her voice muffled partially by her pillow.

"Sorry." Ray rolled back towards her.

His eyes rode the line of her body as it curved beneath the sheet. Reaching across, he lightly drew a piece of hair from her cheek.

"It's been such a long time," he whispered, grateful that she was tired enough not to ask him to finish the thought.

* * *

Awakened by his own snoring, Buddy sat up, letting the cool night air wash over him as he tried to remember where he was. His groggy confusion lasted until he realized he was on Olivia's back porch. He'd fallen asleep on the lumpy couch whose vinyl cushions now clung to his bare arms.

He groped his way through the dark to the kitchen, banging into the table. An empty bottle fell to the floor and clattered across the linoleum. He hoped it hadn't awoken Olivia. At the bottom of the stairs, he took a moment to steady himself by gripping the banister. His bulk produced whining protests from every step. The knee he'd slammed into the table also let its displeasure be known with a wince-inducing ache.

Olivia's immaculate, tiled bathroom glowed silver in the full moon shining through the window. In the medicine cabinet behind the bathroom mirror, Buddy found a bottle of aspirin. After swallowing a handful, he put his face beneath the tap and slurped. His knee throbbed. He'd go back to Erin and see his kids, he silently promised his reflection in the mirror, as soon as Olivia seemed herself again.

He'd been making that same promise to himself for a few weeks now. She'd retreated and been made small by Merrill's death. He didn't know enough about what she was like when she grieved to understand if it was serious or not, but it worried him. Plus, it was easier to fool himself into thinking his stay there was for her, than face his own fears about trying to find a way back into his own life. He sat down on the toilet, pressing his feet down on the tiles. The chilling sensation on his soles made him feel better.

* * *

Each toss answered a turn, a flip of the pillow. Each movement, each new form carved out atop the mattress by her body brought sleep no closer. The space between Marianne and the possibility of rest widened with each intrusive thought.

The hotel alone had always been enough to keep her up, even when business was up but now that they were really struggling, the possibility of sleep had become ridiculous. She'd called the office of historic preservation again, just to see if there had been some problem with the forms and when they would like their tour of The Shelby. Once again, she'd gotten a machine telling her the hours and asking her to leave a message. She'd left one already, earlier in the week, so she hung up.

Marianne had looked at the numbers and extrapolated out into the future and it wasn't bright. Even with Rick French gone and Julia off the payroll, they'd be lucky to last another couple of years. There simply wasn't anything left that she could truly cut back on. Hiring Julia had been a mistake, but she'd felt nearly burnt out by the start of the past summer and Bruno wasn't willing or ready to take on much more work.

Her father always spoke of the future of the hotel with such confidence even when business was down, but she didn't think he rested any easier. Mother never seemed too anxious to help in that regard either. She was never satisfied. When the place was full there was too much work, when they had open rooms there wasn't enough money coming in. There must've been a time when she'd been more optimistic about the hotel's future, but Marianne couldn't remember it.

Flattening her pillow, she thought of what it was like after her father had passed, when her mother came back. They held each other in the lobby, each weeping on the other's shoulder. Then, her mother steered her to the couch in the lobby. She sat and had Marainne lay her head in her lap. She stroked her daughter's hair and whispered comfort. It had been many years since Marianne felt like such a child, so vulnerable, so cared for.

The next day, her mother had a property accessor visit. When she found how little she could get for the place, her mood changed. They couldn't afford to keep it going, she lamented, pounding her fists upon the desk, and they couldn't get a good price for it either. Marianne watched from the couch, wanting to lay back down under the protection of the mother she'd forgotten she so needed.

She didn't know how much longer she could keep the truth from her son. It wasn't yet the time, she felt, to worry Bruno unduly. He already knew that business

was bad. There was still some money for now, there was still some time.

She buried her face in her pillow one last time. Sleep was not coming. She felt her way through the darkened apartment, out into the lobby and down the stairs into the basement. In a cobwebbed corner on the opposite wall from the washer and dryer, rolls of weather stripping lay atop one another on a stack of window screens. Two seasons' worth of dust had turned the stripping a mottled grey. She tucked a few screens under her arm and wore a roll of tape around her wrist. She'd fix up the windows on the top floors in case they had a sudden surge in occupancy and make them ready for summer with new screens. Preparing for the future was the only way she knew of ensuring it would still be there.

* * *

As she slept, Olivia looked at peace for the first time in weeks. Buddy wondered if she was dreaming of their brother. He wasn't about to wake her. Still feeling groggy, a warm tickle started in his ear. He yawned it away.

Dawn began to drip a golden light through the window. The sun's rays crept over the sheets and danced on his sister's face. Creases around her mouth and on her cheeks emerged with that first light. Her eyelids fluttered open.

"It's just me, Liv," Buddy said.

"I see that," she said, pulling the covers up to her chin. "What are you doing in my room, Bud? Yours is down the hall."

"Waiting for you to wake up."

"Why?"

"I think I know what to do. For Merrill, I mean. Something that will really mean something to him. I've spent the morning thinking very sober thoughts about our little brother," he said, his voice loud and tender, like a love song in a crowded dance hall.

"Sober thoughts?" She sat up in bed and tucked her wiry white hair into the collar of her nightgown.

"Sober thoughts, about Merrill and my future, all of that." Buddy leaned over the bed.

Olivia yawned with her whole body. She stretched her arms over her head, her back cracking as it arched. Reaching out, across the bed, she put her hand on his.

"Your future? You mean you're finally going to leave my house?"

"I'm going to become a teacher like Merrill."

"Are you?" she asked, mockery resting across her brow, eyes twinkling. "A teacher? Is that what you want to be when you finally grow up?"

"Did you see all those kids at his wake? Well, I say kids but some of them were Erin's age." Buddy slipped his hand out from under hers. "They all loved music. It's a real loss to this community not just us."

"Bud, they aren't just going to let you waltz into some high school music room and take the band over. You know that right?"

"Of course, I do. That's not what I'm talking about I'm talking private lessons in my home."

"You're going to be heartbroken when you realize how few people actually want to learn the accordion in a trailer," Olivia said, sitting upright. "No offense, Bud."

"I mean, I'd teach guitar and piano as well then try to steer them more or less in the direction of the accordion."

"More or less, huh?" she asked then coughed out a laugh. "How're you going to get a piano in that trailer of yours?"

"Erin has one at the house."

"She does, doesn't she? Is that still your idea of your home?" Olivia said. "I take it she knows very little, if anything about your plans."

Buddy's chuckle soon turned to a hard cough that made it difficult to catch his breath. Olivia slid over to the edge of the bed and rubbed his back. After the cough died down, she took his hand and held it in both of hers.

"You need to go to her." She squeezed his hand until he looked her in the eyes. "I've loved having you here and I appreciate you being by my side all this time, but now you've got to go and try to make it right with Erin. See your children, Bud. That's what Merrill would want you to do. Appreciate the things he never had."

19

A cool wind bearing the crisp promise of fall accompanied Angus on his final walk down the steel stairs of Mount Kneebow. It would be the first time he visited the studio without sweating until it felt like he was swimming in his clothes. He stopped halfway down to bask in the breeze and prolong his final trip there. Soon, he'd have to face whether or not he'd succeeded, whether or not it would make up for what he felt he'd pushed his brother to do.

Stalled traffic clogged the road at the bottom. Cars surged forward and stopped. Angus waited for the light to change. Like the traffic, the light took its time. Angling his slender frame between two motionless vehicles, he kept his head down as though embarrassed for the drivers. Halfway across the bridge, he paused again, watching an empty barge float downstream bound for Castle Island. With a smile, he recalled a scheme of Andy's to stow away aboard a cruise ship and attempt to pass himself off as the onboard entertainment.

"So this is it, my man," Mark said and wrapped Angus's less substantial hand in his own.

"I guess we'll be done today." Angus's smile hid none of his apprehension, twitching and faltering before melting back into the beginnings of a frown.

"I think you're going to like it. Your brother sounds like a real crowd pleaser."

"I can't wait."

Mark led him to the white room in the back of the studio. The fluorescent light humming overhead was all that could be heard. Mark slid a piece of paper across the table.

"When we're done, you'll sign this," Mark said. "It just says you've heard the finished product and found it acceptable. Then, like I said, you just need to cut me a check. Sound okay?"

"Sure."

"Now we're going to go through this track by track. If there's anything you don't like, let me know. We've still got a chance to get it right."

"What if we can't?" Angus asked.

"I've done right by you so far, haven't I?"

"You have."

"I'll go load it up and we'll get started. Relax, you're going to be happy with it, I guarantee."

Angus nodded. Back in the clinic a fellow patient, whose name he could now no longer remember, had warned Angus the project could kill him. Angus had found all of the rehabbers and recoverees to be dramatic in that way, especially those who'd been through the program once already. For them, every choice was a matter of life or death. He used to be able to laugh at the amount of fatalism they were able to inject into every moment of their lives but now saw wisdom in their caution. If he heard the tape and felt that he had failed his brother in death as much as he had in life, he'd never be able to face it.

* * *

Dressing for work pleased Marianne more than she'd expected it would. She knew they needed to be granted landmark status for the money, but now that she was on the doorstep of achieving it, found herself feeling proud of it in a way she hadn't imagined she would.

Ready to take on the burden of the hotel all on her own again, she ignored the returning pain as she brushed her hair and pulled it into a bun. She knew that if her father could've sensed what she was feeling, his heart would have swelled. The hotel hadn't been given up but changed into something more. Only the ringing house phone could break her from her reverie. She yelled for Bruno to answer it.

* * *

Bruno stood at the desk, baring his mother's voice for as long as he could. She'd been unbearable the last couple of days, treating him like an underperforming employee. New tasks were heaped upon him daily and if he wasn't being bored to death standing there at the desk, he was cleaning rooms or being sent to the basement to dig up relics of the hotel's past. He could've let the line ring dead but then he'd never hear the end of it, and all he wanted in that moment was to come to the end of whatever mania had taken hold of her.

"The Hotel Shelby, how may I assist you this morning?"

"Ah, Bruno, is it? I'm Ronald Schell, I visited your hotel a few days ago. How is everything up there?"

"Fine, sir. Getting more historic by the hour," Bruno said, thinking of his recent trip to the basement in search of ancient alarm clocks.

"That's...good to hear. Getting ready for the change, I take it. I know your mother had lots of ideas about how she wanted to present the Shelby on its dedication day. I should mention that that'll still be several months away."

"She certainly has ideas, yes sir."

"Good, good. Anything to put the public in better touch with the area's history will do," Schnell said. "I wanted to call and just remind her that the deadline for submitting those forms is a receipt date. Yes. Not a postmark date. And please tell her that the state is absolutely firm on that deadline. They'll take any excuse not to fund this program, I'm afraid. So if she hasn't yet, tell her be sure to send those forms off today."

* * *

Wheeling the cart from the closet, Marianne ignored fresh twinges of pain riding the length of her spine. Bruno went to say something to her but she waved him off as soon as he opened his mouth. She was in no mood to hear his whining about needing a break to go running or see a movie. There was much to do, the least he could offer was to stand behind the front desk as agreeably as he could manage. She pulled back the elevator's gate. Her attempt to stand straight sent more telling spasms on the ride up. Ignoring these warnings, she wheeled the cart down the hall to Mr. Sperint's room. And though her steps were off balance, she kept a crooked line.

Stripping Angus's bed released a combination of body odor and nicotine. Marianne was struck again by how masculine the willowy little man smelled. She took in his scent, again, allowing herself to almost get lost in it. Ray's ghost no longer lingered so presently in the air, not even enough for her to have to push it away. 412 was hers completely again.

* * *

While the disc played, Angus could feel the tension leaving his body. He even smiled and nodded, catching his producer's eye. No longer was there even a trace of his cruelty. Angus allowed his bony frame to find its sink points in the chair, a posture of relaxation rather than defeat.

"Everything good so far?" Mark asked.

"I think so," Angus said. "Could you turn it up a little?"

"This one'll go at the beginning on the final copy," Mark said and twisted the volume knob. "Once you're okay with the quality, I'll sequence it, if that's alright with you. Then you cut me a check and it's yours."

"Sounds great," Angus said.

"If I seem a little nervous, it's because I just escaped from a cult," Andy said, accompanied now by a couple mild guffaws that grew louder as Mark turned up the volume.

"It was kinda tough on me. Kirk, the Neogod, saved everyone by having sex with their wives, daughters, and girlfriends. He took one look at my Shawna and said we were good. He didn't need to save us." Mark filled what had been an awkward pause in the act with some heavier laughs. "He said I'd be saving a lotta men by keeping her all to myself, until the end of time." An even heavier burst of laughter followed. Angus chuckled to himself. Again, there was no trace of him. He couldn't even recall the taunt he'd uttered.

"It sounds utterly natural. Incredible work," he said. "How'd you pull this off?"

"The thing was to isolate your brother's voice. You wanted to pay tribute, so I focused it all on your brother."

Mark took the cigarette from his ear and motioned for Angus to follow him. Angus pulled his own pack from his trouser pocket. He planned to leave Mark the rest, banishing another vice from his life in the process.

* * *

The morning sun had a drowsy effect on Bruno as he jogged across the forsaken ball field. It was as though autumn had risen that morning all at once, and summer had retreated far into the distance. His legs felt tight and heavy. It'd been a few days since he'd gone for a run.

Soon, he and his mother would be spending hours every morning sitting across from one another at the kitchen table, going over accounting, math, and whatever else she deemed necessary for the future she'd been cornering him into his whole life. Each lesson, each example used, practically every utterance she spoke lately made it apparent how much more tightly their lives revolved around the hotel. Now that they were historic, there would likely be a whole new field of otherwise useless facts for him to memorize.

As he made his way up the dirt path that led to the top of the hill, he checked to make sure the book of Whitman's poems he had tucked into the back of his waistband was secure. When he'd found it in the kitchen drawer a few days before, he hadn't known what it was at first. Some papers had been piled on top of it, as though his mother had wanted to hide it from him. Cracking it open, it was more the sound than the sight of it that transported him back to the brief school year when Rick had been his teacher.

Since their last attempt to see a movie together, he hadn't seen or heard from him. The book of poetry was all he had to hold on to of their time together. He could look at the book and think just of Rick the teacher, not the man whose lover was dying. It was the way he wanted to remember Rick now -- selfishly as though Rick might still be his.

At the top of the hill, he paused to rest in his customary spot at the base of the transmission tower. He removed the book, flipping it open to a dog-eared page. After sitting down, he read aloud: *"Among the men and women the multitude,/ I perceive one picking me out by secret and divine signs,/Acknowledging none else, not parent, wife, husband, brother, child any nearer than I am,/Some are baffled but that one is not—that one knows me."*

∗ ∗ ∗

Angus did not stop off, instead getting back to the hotel as quickly as he could. The clanging echo of the metal stairs grew louder, the higher he climbed. He'd never noticed that sound before, had never taken those steps with such speed. He was out of breath by the time he reached the top. His head throbbed. As he passed Marianne at the desk, he kept his head down, returning her greeting with barely a mumble.

Back in his room, he experienced a moment of sheer panic during the interval of silence between the time in which it took his computer to read the disc and begin playing it. He worried that there had been some mix up, and the disc he'd spent so many sleepless nights agonizing over was blank, while the finished one was lost somewhere in Mark's studio. Then came the voice of some anonymous nightclub MC whose name he didn't remember: "Now, let's welcome to the stage, Andy Sperint."

Sitting on the bed, head bowed listening, Angus became truly aware, maybe for the first time, that his brother was somewhere else -- somewhere Angus could not go. He laughed and cried as he listened to the disc again and, in this way, began to measure the distance between him and his brother. The recording felt less like a tribute and more like a map that reminded him of where he was and how the rest of the territory, known as the past, fit together. No longer was it so important that Angus had been scrubbed from the recordings, but that Andy was there, sounding confident and thanks to Mark, properly appreciated. When it was over, he wiped the tears from his eyes and face, then played it again.

* * *

"Where have you been?" Marianne asked after waiting for Bruno to get close enough to the desk so that she didn't have to yell, even if that was the volume at which she felt like speaking. "Out running, I take it."

"I needed to get out okay?" he said. "I figured you were busy, so I didn't want to bother you."

"I was Bruno. I was bothered," she said. "I came back from cleaning Mr. Sperint's room only to find the desk empty. It bothers me that you just don't..."

"That I don't what?" He turned with his well-practiced wounded look.

"You didn't even leave a note. I know you really couldn't care less, but I am trying to turn this place into something. Now get a quick shower and put on your uniform, so I can do the laundry. We'll have to get to your lessons later."

He'd planned on telling her about the call from Schnell when he'd gotten back from his run, but her order to take a shower made him think again. He resented that demand more than any of the others she'd made in the last couple of days. He was sick of being treated like a child.

Bruno hadn't even seen the forms since she'd taken them from Schnell. If she wanted to make it all her problem, he had no trouble ignoring it. He smiled to himself at the idea of her scurrying around in a panic, should it turn out that she'd made a mistake.

* * *

The hotel room felt safe to Angus. He could no longer be so sure about the world outside of it. He played the disc over and over again, searching for some resolution or sign that the past had been altered. He expected something inside of him to change, that the burden of his brother's death might be lifted through this project. The more he heard Andy, though, the more wrong he felt he'd been. That tickle in his throat, the one that wanted to be burnt with whiskey nagged at him. He turned down the thermostat, once he began to sweat. Something inside now wanted to be set loose.

As he listened to his brother joke once again about embarking on a bit of sexual espionage involving their parents, he thought of how Andy loved trying out inappropriate material. Back when they were altar boys, Andy would take the time they spent preparing in the vestibule to make the most blasphemous remarks. On one unusually hot Sunday morning, they were waiting for Father McNally and sweating through their vestments, when Andy gave him a disgusted look.

"Gross," he said, "look at how much you're sweating."

"So are you," Angus replied, giving his armpits a sniff.

"I got some meat on my bones. You're too skinny to sweat. Skinny guys aren't supposed to sweat like that."

"What?" Angus asked, testy from the heat. "You don't know what you're talking about."

"Really?" Andy asked then swung his arm to point at the painting of the crucified Jesus that dominated the back wall. "Look at our Savior dying on the cross without so much as a bead of sweat. Wasn't he under some enormous pressure? Don't you know how hot it gets over there in the Holy Land? Hotter than here, that's for sure."

They laughed, not caring if the parishioners sweating it out in the pews heard them. When Father McNally finally arrived, they found their altar boy faces. Though it was hard not to snicker looking at the priest with his white hair soaked with sweat, his ruddy complexion blood pink. As soon as Mass ended, McNally left hurriedly, neglecting the one duty he enjoyed the most: finishing what was left of the sacramental wine.

Before his brother could see him do it, Angus had finished the wine left in the chalice and filled it back up from the jug. Andy giggled nervously as he watched him take another sip. Angus finished half of it, staining the sleeve of his robe crimson as he wiped it across his mouth. He forced the goblet into his brother's hand.

"We'll get caught," Andy said, holding it away from his body as though the wine was threatening to jump into his mouth of its own accord.

"Come on, have one for your sweat-free Savior," Angus said.

They laughed again before Andy drank. He finished what was left, coughing after it was gone. It was the first time either of them got drunk. They enjoyed the feeling of elation accompanying them on their walk back to their dorm through the heat of an early summer. They covered for each other a little later when they each had to puke. Angus laughed through the whole thing, but Andy had not found it as funny. He worried the house master would discover them at any minute.

After listening some more, Angus gave up and stopped the playback. Lifting an empty glass, he imagined it full of whiskey, then downed it. He rolled off the bed and headed for the bathroom. The tap ran so cold, its offering so drinkable. He wanted to regard it as a sign from his lost brother. Ever since the experience with the warm wine that afternoon so long ago, Andy steadfastly refused to drink anything that hadn't been properly chilled.

Squatting at the intersection of two streets, the pawnshop looked sad as a beggar. The air inside smelled of rust and yellowing paper. A display case featuring chainsaws, weed whackers, and every other manner of outdoor tool was protected by a heavy padlock. The one behind that was wrapped by four heavy chains to protect the cache of guns and jewelry, displayed with no more fanfare than the gardening tools.

Standing behind a cash register at the back, a kid inspected the split ends of his long hair. It made his eyes cross. He didn't notice Buddy at first.

"You open?" Buddy tottered towards him. The kid never lifted his eyes. "Are you..." Buddy stopped a few feet from the kid.

"Usually the door being ajar is a clue," the kid said, keeping his eyes on his hair. "Buying or selling?"

"Looking to buy."

"Looking to buy what, exactly?"

Buddy studied the instruments hanging on the wall behind the register, taking in the trumpets, saxophones, violins, and guitars. None would do for what he had in mind. Near the top, the blue plastic of a kid-sized accordion tried to shimmer from beneath a layer of dust.

"How much for that?" He pointed.

The clerk tucked a clutch of his hair behind his ear and turned around. His jeans drooped off his skinny hips, offering an unnecessary view of his red and black checkered undershorts. He was all bones and hair and a stretch of skin. Buddy wanted to buy him a sandwich.

"Which one you want?" the kid asked, searching the wall as he hitched up his sagging jeans.

"The little squeeze box up there," Buddy said, nodding his head to encourage the kid to look higher.

"That thing?" The clerk pulled a ladder down to the end of the row. He grunted as though each step took considerable effort. "15," he said reading the tag.

"15 bucks? That seems steep. It looks cheap from down here."

"What do you want to give me for it?" the kid asked.

"10 seems fair to me what do you say?"

"It's an accordion right?"

"A cheap-looking one," Buddy said. "But that's alright. It's for kids. More like a toy."

"I sure don't know no kids who want to play accordion. Ten'll do," the kid said.

"I think you'd be surprised," said Buddy as he looked the instrument over.

He could only get the straps of the child's accordion under his knuckles, which made it hard to play, as did the breath-mint-sized keys. Still the more the clerk cracked his knuckles as he pulled a bored face, the louder Buddy played. He wanted to prove something to the kid about music but would settle for just annoying him. Once Buddy had finished, the kid shrugged and went back to the register, counting the money in it like it was real work. Buddy put the instrument down on the counter.

"See. This thing can play rock and roll. I can make it do whatever I want."

"I'm not sure I'd exactly call that rock-n-roll," the kid said. "Don't know what I'd call it, man."

After handing over the money, Buddy tucked the instrument under his arm. He moved away from the counter, holding the kid in a deep glare. He felt he only had to break wind hard enough to knock him down.

Placing the accordion in the passenger seat of the station wagon, he secured it with the seatbelt. He then shut the door with care, as though for a sleeping child. He knew which of his children would take to it and the thought of the look on her face had him finally, actually racing to what had once been his home.

* * *

Fiddling with the radio, Ray tried to read Veronica's face as he passed each station. Her smile was a riddle that offered no clues. After settling on a morning news program, he relaxed back in his seat, enjoying the novelty of being a passenger. The ride to his hotel parking lot was too brief.

The sun broke low over a line of hills, the sky a dazzling orange. The motel looked dingy and pale in the early light. Ray pulled down his visor. There were only two cars in the parking lot. One was a spotless white BMW pulled perfectly between two spaces, the other Ray's dusty rental, a Ford Taurus, sitting crookedly in its spot.

"There I am." Ray nodded in the Ford's direction. "I've been renting it long enough it's practically mine."

She pulled in beside the Taurus and turned off the radio. Ray grew short of breath. When he looked over at Veronica, she looked away.

"So, I'll be back around here in a week or so," he said, cracking the door, his words competing with the car's beeping alert.

"I'll have to think about it," she said, not even glancing at him. "This has been fun, but I need to be sure where it's headed."

"I know you need to...I have a son too. I...," Ray said, one foot out of the car. "Maybe I can visit you again sometime? See your place in bright daylight?"

"Listen, the last couple of weeks have been fun, but I don't think it's a good idea for us to keep seeing one another."

"You don't?" Ray asked, getting back in the car.

"I'm at a place in my life where I need more than a fling and...," she said, breaking off then turning to him. "I don't think this's headed where I want it to go."

Ray nodded. He flung the door open again and climbed out.

"Sorry," she said. "There isn't anything else to say. We'd just be bad for each other. I need to be in a program and away from men for a while. Don't take it.... it's not you, it's...look, don't take this the wrong way, but I don't need another drunk in my life. I'm more than I can handle most days."

"I guess you're right."

"It really has been great, Ray but you're a salesman. You're on the road. I understand that kind of life but I need someone grounded. I need someone..."

"I get it. I get it," he said. "I can't pretend to be that reliable right now."

"Unreliable Men Anonymous is the group I really need," she said.

Unsure if he should take that as the insult he felt it to be, Ray stepped away from the car slowly. He wanted to offer her the chance to take it back, to take everything back. Turning the radio on, she waved to him but didn't say a word. As he placed the key in his door, he heard Veronica pull away, as though she had been nothing more than a considerate taxi driver, waiting to make sure her customer got safely inside.

Halfway through the revolving door of The Shelby, Ray paused and backed out. The surge of purpose and energy that had been propelling him over the last few days and weeks -- maybe even months if he looked closely enough at the immediate past -- no longer felt so near at hand. He'd not visited his son in two years and choked by sudden guilt, tried to do a quick accounting of the interval. There had been a period of drinking and trying not to drink with some successful sales trips thrown in. Then, he'd met Veronica and failed to get the relationship as far down the road as he'd thought it could go.

A lot of the time since then had been dedicated to grounding himself. He'd gotten a two-bedroom apartment in Wheelington, so that Bruce would have a place to call his own when he visited. At least a couple of months had been spent setting that up.

Mostly, he'd been working on himself, making his life smaller to accommodate the rather big piece that staying sober now represented. He'd found a regular meeting and when he traveled showed up at the same ones often enough to be a semi-regular. He even asked Bo, his old tow truck driver to be his sponsor, who'd agreed with predictable enthusiasm.

Ray knew he hadn't called his son often enough. The infrequent ones they did have were short. He was more of a face to face guy and consoled himself with the thought that his son was the same. He put his hand up to the glass of the door and peeked inside. The young man behind the desk no longer looked quite so awkward, quite so much like a boy. His shoulders and chest were filled out with muscle; his once oversized facial features now perfectly in proportion. These changes hadn't been apparent during those calls; his son had always still seemed a boy. Visiting Marianne and Bruce, who'd been wounded the most by his drunken cowardice, was the last and most important step in his recovery. Once it was done, he could finally say he was starting over.

Towards the end of his relationship with Marianne, when his drinking was at its worst, he would try his best to act sober in front of her. He practiced walking and talking before confronting her, always finding the act more convincing than she did. Now, he realized that actually dealing with her while sober was going to be even more difficult than acting like he was. All of the work he'd done on himself, all of that self-examination, all of the hours spent in meetings, would amount to nothing, if he was anything short of convincing.

He thought of their last conversation, about her ultimatum that he be sober for two years. Whether or not she'd really meant it, he'd been holding onto it all that time. Sometimes, it represented the hope he needed to keep going; other times the resentment he needed to plan his return. Whatever it was to him in that moment, it proved enough to get him to push all the way through the doors.

The lobby still smelled the same as he remembered; open, expectant and bored like a dog yawing. He tried not to wince as he drew closer to the desk, spotting his own teenage affliction spilling across his son's cheek. The two years he'd been holding onto now tucked firmly by his side. "You're either ready or you're not," Bo had told him, "thing is, there's only one way to find out."

"Dad?" Bruno asked, sounding uncertain.

"Are you still going by Bruno?" Ray shook off his stupor and strode confidently towards the desk.

"Yes dad," Bruno said. "No one calls me Brucey. I tell you that every time we talk."

"It's been a while," Ray said.

"I never expected you to actually come back here," Bruno said, a tone more challenging than hurt.

"I've been saying sorry all my life to you so let's hope this is the last time. I'm sorry I haven't been around or called as much, but I've been working on myself, trying to get better." Ray pulled his suitcase from the floor and slung it atop the desk, beating his fingers on the worn leather.

"Yeah, you've told me," Bruno said in a tone that lacked any hint of conviction. "Thanks."

"You don't have to thank me. I'm not doing it to be thanked. I just want to create the space for me to say from the depths of my soul, that I'm sorry, truly."

"Okay, dad."

"In person."

"Okay. Whatever you say."

"To you and your mother."

* * *

Angus grew thirstier with each successive playing of the disc. "Celebrate," a voice in his head whispered. The more he listened to his brother, the more real and insistent that voice became. It would be just one last time, one final, reasonable celebration. Surely, Angus hadn't ruined himself enough that he couldn't enjoy something as momentous as his brother's first comedy album. Anything short of a few drinks would not curb his cravings or appease the ghost in his head. If he was going to do it, he'd act as though he was under Andy's watchful eye. Andy always stopped when his toes went numb. He said that was how to tell when you'd had enough.

* * *

Bruno stared at his father's nose, cracked with capillaries and swelled at the tip. It was a face he hardly remembered. His voice was different in person -- quieter, more breathy and less sure of itself. The closer the old man got, the more he spoke, the less Bruno recognized him. He'd grown used to seeing his father in distant memories, fleeting glimpses that faded out before he could make sense of them. On the phone, it was always easy enough to make up some excuse to get away. Relief sounded with the whine and clank of the settling elevator.

"Mom." Bruno moved out from behind the desk to block the cart's path back to the hidden closet. "Look who's here."

Ray watched with a frown as Bruno rushed to hug his mother, too lost in his own confusion to notice how awkwardly she received her son's affection. She seemed even more surprised when he took the cart from her and guided it into its spot in the closet behind the desk. Then, he disappeared behind the door of the apartment. As Marianne switched places with their son, Ray shrank away from the desk like a destitute lodger who'd come to settle an account in serious arrears.

"Ray," she said, hard and heavy like a curse.

"Marianne." Ray cleared his throat. "You look good. How's business?"

"Fine."

"It's good to see you. Good to see you...see you both again." Ray halted, gulping audibly. "I'm sorry, I've been away so long. You've been getting my checks?"

"I've been cashing them, haven't I? Is that what you came to ask?"

"No." Ray's eyes darted away. "No, it's not. I came to apologize too, for the way I used to be."

"Used to be?" she asked.

"Yes. I want to apologize for the person I was."

"Cause you're different now, yet again?"

"I believe so, yes," Ray said. "I've made some big changes to my life and am ready to be more involved in Bruce's, sorry, Bruno's life."

"He's told me about some of the things you claim you've done to get a better grip on adulthood."

"You make it sound like..." Ray laughed nervously, a quick chattering sound that lacked joy.

"Like it's not that easy." Marianne slid the register in his direction. "You're only here as a guest until further notice."

"It isn't easy," Ray said and took the book, signing it in a hard scrawl.

"Very well. Mr. Davis, is it?" Marianne made a play of reading the register as though to learn his name. "I have some work to do. If you need anything, don't hesitate to ask my son, who will be back and manning the desk in my stead."

* * *

Angus had listened to the disc so many times that it began to feel like it was playing in his head. Andy's voice lurked just behind his thoughts. He considered it might've been what he'd really been searching for all along -- not just to immortalize his brother but to become one with him.

He finished another tumbler of water but like all those he'd drank before that, it only made his thirst worse. The glass had become so smudged by his touch that it appeared frosted. After rinsing it out, he filled it yet again and thought of that gold communion chalice and how cold it'd felt against his lips and how warm the wine had gone down all those years ago.

It wasn't the first secret they'd kept together, but the first time Angus had been aware that the two of them keeping secrets was like being one person. He drank the latest glass of water quickly in a single swallow. Bloat formed as a bubble he could feel inside of his stomach. Pressing play again, he lay back on the bed, hoping his brother's voice might send him off to sleep.

* * *

Ray retreated to his room on the second floor and reassessed the situation. The key was to make his pitch about Bruce, Bruno, whatever he wanted to be called. He would appeal to the idea that the boy would benefit from his influence -- that he could not only be an example of how a man could change his ways, but also offer Bruce the opportunity to show the kind of grace and humility that came with forgiveness. True, he'd also be giving Marianne the same chance to show those qualities, but Ray knew that sort of thing would only carry weight if she were to discover it herself.

When he got off the elevator and found only his son in the lobby, he relished the pride he felt. His heart leaped in his chest at the man his boy was fast becoming. To him, that feeling was the surest sign yet that he was a real father and ready to show it.

"Bruno," he said. His son stood straight. "Can we speak in private?"

"What for?" Bruno asked, turning away from his father and pretending to sort things in the closet behind the desk.

"Look, you're my son. And I think I owe it to you to try and establish, reestablish, some kind of bond. I'd like us to know one another. Why don't we..." Ray gestured to the couch. "Have a chat. Face to face, man to man." He sat down, patting the empty cushion next to him.

Ray waited as Bruno lingered in the closet, doing whatever meaningless mundane chore his mother, no doubt, had deemed crucial. It seemed impossible that the boy didn't feel trapped there. Still, Ray knew he had to be cautious, there was no telling how contagious Marianne's pride was. Bruce had never seemed that enthusiastic about the hotel over the phone, but then he never seemed enthusiastic about anything, least of all talking to his own father.

Finally, Bruno came over to him. His posture as always too straight. He sat down as far from his father as he could get, wedging his substantial frame against the opposite arm of the couch. Ray could only think of how much easier he thought this all would be; his mere physical presence, sober and committed did far more work in his imagination than it was capable of in reality.

"What's new?" Ray asked.

"The hotel's been granted special status. We're going to be a historic landmark. Did I tell you that?"

"Right, you did. Been in the works for a while, I take it?" Ray asked, patting the cushion between them. "Remind me what that means. Will it still be a hotel or just like, a what, a tourist destination?"

"No, we'll still be a full-service hotel just one with special landmark status."

"Great. That's great," Ray said, taking his son's hand and shaking it. "Congratulations again to you both. She was always so proud of keeping things the way her father had them, I'm surprised she agreed to such a thing."

"She's really excited about it."

"She should be. She should be. And you?"

Bruno ran his hand against the grain of the couch arm, turning it darker, and shrugged, then ran his hand back over it. The upholstery returned to the original shade of blue. Heaviness nestled on the free cushion between them, born of the silence of two relative strangers, each struggling to remember who the other really was.

"So, listen I don't want to make this all about me," Ray said, "but I have some things to tell you that I need you to try and understand. Like I've been saying, I was sick and I'm getting better. I know that I haven't been who I should be as your father."

Ray chopped at the air with the double blade of his joined hands. They trembled slightly as he drew them apart. He ran them through his hair, then put them over his face.

"I understand." Bruno nodded.

"You do?"

"You think you're better. I get it," Bruno said, hoping to sound like he really knew what that meant. "You told me before on the phone."

"I did talk about some of this on the phone, didn't I?" Ray asked, tilting his head back as though a better way of putting things would ride the air down to him. "I don't just think it, I am, son. I want more than for you to just forgive me. I want you to know about life. My life, I mean."

"Oh...kay." Bruno said.

"And I want to know about you, about your life. More than just what we talk about on the phone. I'm not much of a phone guy."

"What about it?" Bruno asked. "What about my life?"

"I don't know," Ray sighed. "God, I guess I should've written things down." He reached for his pockets as though stage notes might be hidden inside. "Tell me about your schooling."

"Well, you know mom's been tutoring me."

"That's good," Ray bobbed his head. "She knows what to teach you?"

"I guess the state provides some guidelines. But she mixes in some bookkeeping and other hotel stuff. You know, for when I take over."

"The business, of course. What subject's your favorite? You still good at math?"

"It's not that difficult. I wish she was teaching me something else."

"Like what?"

"I don't know, like poetry," Bruno said, only just then having realized how true this was.

"Poetry," Ray whispered as though uncertain of the meaning of the word.

* * *

Angus drew his last clean suit off its hanger, slowly and deliberately, so as to enjoy the moment. With excitement and fear coursing through his system in equal measure, he found the buttons of his white dress shirt difficult to fasten. Once he'd slid the trousers up his skinny legs, he took his shoes into the bathroom and sat on the toilet.

Gathering a healthy gob of saliva against his lips, he spat on the toe of the right shoe. As he rubbed it with a washcloth, Angus promised himself that he'd keep it under control tonight. He was only drinking one last time to celebrate his brother's life. Tonight, all that he did would be done in Andy's honor.

As he did the same to the left shoe, he thought of how, back in the heaviest of his drinking days, so many celebrations ended in sorrow. The same thing had happened every time; the same person got hurt and accepted his apologies. Now, he planned to adhere to the kind of rules his brother had always suggested. He was ready to listen to more than just his brother's jokes. Now, he was finally ready to hear more than just Andy the comedian.

Without lathering, he shaved his slender face, noticing how gaunt and pale he'd become since he'd gotten sober. Angus needed to bring the red back to his nose, the pink to his cheeks. He put on his shoes and wiggled his toes to make sure he could feel them against the hard leather -- to make sure he could feel his toes for when they went numb.

* * *

A moment passed before Marianne realized she was watching them from just inside the apartment door. With Bruno at one end of the couch and Ray at the other, they seemed almost like strangers simply passing time, waiting to go to their rooms. Ray worked his hands through the air and spoke without taking his eyes off the ceiling, as though sculpting the truth from his own hot air. The fact that they were father and son, forever bonded by blood, settled and thickened inside of her. She felt a small twinge of bittersweet joy when Bruno seemed to flinch from Ray's attempt to lay a hand on his shoulder.

Marianne knew well that lying touch of his, she'd been fooled by it many times. She shut the door behind her and took up her post at the front desk. Bruno stood up and approached her quickly. Their embrace was more comfortable than the one he'd smothered her with earlier that morning. Marianne silently gave a quick thanks to Ray for giving her Brucey back, suddenly so affectionate and dutiful.

"I've got to finish those accounting problems," Bruno announced on his way back inside the apartment.

"Marianne." Ray repositioned himself on the couch. He curled forward rigidly, his elbows resting on his knees, holding tight to his salesman's courage and concentrating on maintaining the confidence in his voice. "Good to see you again. We have a lot to discuss. I understand congratulations are in order for The Shelby achieving landmark status. I would think that will amount to some good advertising."

"Reintroducing yourself to your son?" she asked.

"Yes. You could say that," he said, trying not to sound hurt. "I've been trying to make my amends. We have spoken over the phone. I do call, you know."

"You're really on a mission this time, aren't you Ray?"

"I am. I guess. I'm here to make my amends with the both of you."

"Like a holy crusade," she said, her eyes growing wide. "Looking to forgive yourself in a day for years of neglect."

"What do you want from me?" Ray asked. "I've stayed clean practically a whole 24 months just like you demanded the last time I was here. I'm a different man now. And I'm here to prove it."

"Then I guess congratulations are in order for you as well."

"Don't you think Bruce...Bruno deserves to see that and understand that people can change?" he asked.

"More than you deserve to believe it's true, that's for sure."

"It was the deal we made," he said, his voice rising. "Remember? Two years sober. I've done it."

"It wasn't a deal, Ray," she said. "It was something I said to get rid of you. Something I never thought you could do. Something I still don't believe to be possible."

The elevator came to rest in the lobby with its usual shutter, giving Marianne a chance to break from the conversation. She walked back towards the desk, breathing deep calming breaths. The last time she'd argued with him in the lobby; she'd promised herself to never again allow him to rattle her to the point that she lost hold of herself.

"How are we today, Mr. Sperint?" she asked as he emerged from the elevator.

"I'll be out for a while, I guess," he said. "I won't need dinner tonight."

"That's fine, Mr. Sperint," Marianne said. "Have a nice afternoon."

Even after he'd managed to maneuver through the revolving door and out into the street, Marianne managed to suppress the urge to take on Ray at an angrier, wholly unprofessional volume. Wearing discomfort in the wrinkles of his brow, he wiped the back of his hand over his perspiring forehead. At least, she'd made him sweat.

"So, you do have an actual guest," he said.

"We do and as you can imagine there're other important changes happening too, so I need Bruno here," she said, throwing her head back. "There are so many reasons I won't let him go away with you that I don't have time to list them. I hope you can understand, at least, the idea that there's a lot of work here to be done."

"I just want to spend some time with him," Ray said. "And maybe not now but at some point, I'd like him to come..."

"You're free to see him here," Marianne said. "But you are not taking Bruno out on the road with you. Not now, not ever."

"But..." Ray cleared his voice and leaned forward. "Marianne, can I..."

"I'll even give you a discount on the room -- our new friends and family rate."

"Perfect," he said, leaping to his feet. "You're holding my son for ransom from me."

"I need to keep an eye on you," she said. "Is the money an issue? Won't you just write it off anyway like a bar tab?"

"I'm not here for business," Ray said over his shoulder, just before going through the revolving door.

Out on the street, he gave it an extra spin, nearly falling over with the effort. He started down the road that led to the stairs descending Mount Kneebow. For the first time in months, his resolve to stay sober threatened to desert him. He hoped to find someone to vent to at the Northpark Lounge. He just wanted to talk and drink until he could no longer remember how he'd hoped this day would go.

* * *

The dark amber liquid sat just beyond Angus' reach. He leaned forward, resting his elbows on the cushioned upholstery of the bar's edge. Every time he reached for it, the strength needed to lift the glass seemed to leave him.

"You gonna drink it or just admire it, hun?" Lois asked as she wiped down the empty bar on either side of him. "If you're waitin' til five, you've got about a half an hour."

"I'm waiting to hear from someone." Angus kept forcing his mind to throw up images of Andy, listening for his ghost. He wanted to do this together. He wanted to find Andy or at least his voice still humming somewhere in the background of his thoughts.

"It's just a meeting, just one meeting," Andy had said, handing Angus a glass of water. "I mean look at you. You're a mess."

Angus sat up and took the water. The sheets cold and damp against his skin. He'd hoped his brother hadn't noticed he'd wet the bed, but now that he was coming at him again with the AA stuff that hardly seemed to matter. His teeth felt mossy, evidence he'd gotten sick the night before. Across the nightstand, a swath of more concrete evidence of that fact was drying. He could be sure Andy had noticed that.

Angus felt trapped. Andy took a seat at the desk across the room, prepared to wait, it seemed, until Angus agreed to go to one of these meetings.

"I had a rough night. I'm sorry," he said. "Things got away from me."

"Things have been getting away from you lately like you're Godzilla," Andy said. "I'll go with you to the meeting, if you promise to go. You don't have to do it alone."

"I don't think I have a problem," Angus said and started suddenly to cry. He hadn't felt it coming on. It just rose within him as he began to speak. "I just don't know what's wrong with me."

Andy came to the bed and took crying Angus in his arms. He rocked him without trying to stop his brother's blubbering. He just let him weep until it was done.

"Please promise me you'll go," Andy said once it'd calmed down. "You can't go on like this. We can't go on like this."

"Okay, I'll go. I'll go," Angus said. "Just to hear what they have to say."

"You mean it?" Andy asked.

"If I don't you can tell whoever's there that I have a problem," Angus told him through his sobbing. "Blab it all out to a bunch of complete strangers."

"You haven't been in for a while," Lois said, flipping a coaster in his direction.

"I've been up at the hotel," Angus said, glad to be freed from a memory that he certainly hadn't been searching for.

"The Shelby huh? I've lived here all my life and never been inside. Hear it's nice, though," she said. "You want a pack of smokes or somethin' while you think it over?"

"I think I quit for now."

"Smoke 'em while you can, hun. Rumor has it the city's going to do away with our exemption," Lois said as she slipped through the swinging door behind the bar, her white head disappearing like a cloud back into the kitchen. "Holler back if you need me. I'll just be sorting some spoons."

Angus was never comfortable drinking alone. He wished someone else, anyone else would come through the door. He wanted someone to brag to, someone he could tell about his brother and the comedy album they'd made together, drowning himself in the fantasy of Andy's fame with a complete stranger.

When Ray arrived a few minutes later, he was sweaty and out of breath from the walk. He sat several stools away from Andy. Looking down the bar, he smiled firmly and nodded his head.

"Lois on today? Anyone on today?" he asked.

"She's in back," Angus said. "She said to yell if she was needed."

Taking a clutch of napkins, Ray wiped his brow. Once he was done, he picked at the paper shards that stuck to his nose and his chin. Angus took up his glass and swirled it around, giving it a sniff before putting it back down.

"If you just give a yell, I'm sure she'll come eventually," he said.

"I can wait," Ray said. "I'm not sure I want a drink. I'm not even sure I should be here."

"Neither am I." Angus lifted up his glass. "I haven't so much as touched this. Ordered it like I really wanted it and now…I don't know."

Ray half-rose from his stool and threw the napkin in the trash behind the bar. He drummed his fingers on cushioned bar rail. Leaning over a bit, he tried to peek into the kitchen.

"Thought I had this all figured out," he said. "Nothing went the way I thought it would today, so I figured I'd come in here and gather my thoughts. What's she doing back there?"

"I think she said she had silverware to sort," Angus said, pushing the glass away from him. "Didn't I see you in the hotel, talking with Ms. Shelby?"

"Oh yeah, you were the guy in the elevator."

"That's right," Angus said. "Walk down here, did you?"

"Stormed's the word I would use," Ray said

"I've been asking myself why I came here, maybe I'll ask you."

"Why did I come down here or why did you come down here?" Ray asked. "For a drink, I'd guess."

"If you're like me, you're looking for some excuse to start letting go of that rope a little bit."

"Is that what I'm looking for?" Ray asked, putting his phone on the bar and spinning it. "A rope loosening excuse?"

"Yeah, I'd say so."

"And what makes you so wise to the ways of the world, guy?"

"I'm not," Angus said after a half a laugh. "It just seems to me we're a couple of fellows with some doubts as to what we thought could be accomplished here, and maybe we need to listen to those doubts."

"Maybe," Ray said and ordered a Coke when Lois came back.

* * *

When Bruno heard the elevator land a couple of afternoons later, he wished he had a room to clean or some other thing to do. His father had been pestering him nonstop since Mr. Sperint had left. He wanted to talk to Bruno about life, about decisions, about his future. Every afternoon, they'd sit on the couch and struggle through the latest topic. Bruno felt cheated in having Rick replaced by his suddenly overeager father. His dad smiled as he approached the desk, Bruno already knew what he wanted.

"How are we today, Mr. Davis?"

"Don't," his father said, "don't do that to me. I've told you, I am here, before you at the front desk as your dad, today and every day. Okay?'

"It's just...I'm supposed to be working."

"I know. I know your mother thinks this is what you need, but I want to offer you a chance to see something more. Don't you ever want to get out of here?"

"I do. I go..."

"I'm not talking about going across the street or running around the top of this slag heap," his father said, sounding pained. "I want you to see some of the world with me, just for the afternoon."

"I don't know," Bruno said, feeling much the same childish gravity the hotel had exercised on him two years before.

"Let's just see if your mother thinks you're mature enough to make this decision."

"What do you mean?" Bruno asked.

"Why don't you go ask her if you can? See what she thinks of you. Aren't you curious?"

"About?"

"She lets you man the desk, thinks you're old enough for this apprenticeship. Let's see if she understands that you are old enough to get in the car with your father for a couple of hours this afternoon."

"You want me to ask for time away?" Bruno asked and hearing the question phrased in such a way did indeed make him curious.

"I've already asked. She told me 'no' but that's because it was my idea. What if it were yours?"

Not certain he wanted to go, Bruno turned to the door for the apartment and let himself in. He closed it firmly but gently behind him in case his father tried to listen for how he asked. Bruno was sure he wouldn't be as assertive as his father would've wanted.

His mother was in the kitchen crying, an envelope sitting on the table had half-spilled its contents. He'd never seen her like that. Her eyes welling with desperation, her breathing so shaky, it disintegrated here and again into blubbering sobs. With a trembling hand, she gathered the forms up and put them in the envelope as she turned away from him.

"These forms for the landmark status," she said, choking back a whimper, "needed to be in today. I can't find anyone to take them."

"Dad has a car, maybe…"

"No. Not him."

Bruno put a hand on her shoulder and slipped the envelope out of her grip.

"What are you doing?" she asked, her eyes red and full.

"They have to be in," Bruno said.

"But do you even know where that address is?" she asked.

"You had me memorizing the streets and drawing maps of Pittson for guests since I was old enough to hold a pencil," he said over his shoulder as he went through the door. "I'll find it."

He passed by his father sitting on the lobby couch. Bruno said nothing to him as he picked up speed through the revolving door. Out on the street, he broke into a sprint. Down the metal stairs, he went without hesitating. They clanged and swayed with each of his steps, but he pushed away the fear that sound used to conjure and kept going. At the bottom, he crossed the street picking up speed on the bridge. Past the Northpark Lounge he went, then the recording studio, then the crumbling remains of The Fireman's Arcade and one empty parking lot after another. The rusted smokestacks of dormant factories towered over him like the battlements of defeated kingdoms. He knew he'd find the right office and once he did, he might just keep running until he'd gone too far to ever turn back, until he found Rick and showed him he'd figured out how to escape.

22

A pine shrub reached out a limp tendril. Buddy snatched it between his fingers and broke it off. He remembered planting the bush shortly after he'd bought the house. Adjusting the straps of his overalls, trying to make it so the big front pocket hid his belly, he rang the doorbell, leaning into it with the whole top half of his body.

He looked around as he listened to the chime. Erin's battered blue hatchback sat rusting in the driveway in the same spot she always parked it. The lawnmower had been left under the weeping willow in the yard just as it had been when he'd last visited. Lost in his admiration of the things that hadn't changed, Buddy didn't notice the door opening.

"Has the road finally lead you to us?" Erin asked.

Her blonde hair, lightened by age at her temples and streaked with grey at the crown of her head, was plaited in two ridiculous pigtails. The drooping skin of her neck and the heavy laugh lines around her mouth spoiled the youth to which she clung.

"I should've called." Buddy tossed the pine stem. "What you been up to?"

"In the basement doing laundry. You must have something you'd like to add to my load."

"You'd do my laundry for me?" he asked.

"Sure, why not?" Erin held the door open for him. "You're bringing in your suitcase, anyway."

"Hard to say no to that." Buddy lifted his suitcase with a heave and squeezed past her into the house.

After being on the road for so long, sleeping in hotels that all smelled of the same artificial cleanliness, he welcomed the smell of burnt toast and baby wipes. When he heard the scream of his son from down the hall, sounding so close to becoming words, Buddy knew some things had changed. Some things were constantly changing.

* * *

Ray rested his hand on the car door handle. Maybe Veronica would appear and see him first. Then he'd know what to do. A light turned a window orange at the far end of her house, which seemed strange in the middle of the day. Sunlight glared down and made everything look as though it was ready to be seen. The chirping of birds sounded lonely on the deserted street. Ray felt that he was the only person on earth. He took out his phone to call her or even just send a text, then thought about what she'd last said to him.

He imagined seeing her at the door, her red hair loosened and falling around her shoulders. She'd open it with that curious smile of hers that never offered purchase for a foothold on her thoughts. Ray pictured her son by her side, a small narrow head, hair red like his mother's but curly. She'd greet Ray in a tone as inscrutable as her smile. He'd do the same, wearing a look that tried to hide his expectations.

Then what? He had no idea how to talk to a kid. He'd never really learned.

Since he'd quit drinking, his thinking had become sharper. There weren't many dull edges to hide behind. He'd inflated his experience as a dad to impress Veronica. Now, they were past pretending.

Starting the car up, Ray let the motor run. He began counting and watching her front door. If she didn't appear by the time he counted to thirty, he'd leave. When that failed, he slowly let the car roll from its spot. Coasting to the stop sign at the end of the street, he kept one eye on the house in the rearview mirror. She never appeared. He turned back towards the highway, trying to think of where he could hawk his wares next.

* * *

Both Buddy's son and daughter had their mother's dishwater blonde hair, blue eyes, and freckles. Both were chubby around the midsection like him. Only Esmeralda had the full lips that was characteristic of all Cyzeks. Hornblower's lips, they were called. As they raced around his legs, Buddy did his best not to stomp them on his way to the couch.

"Daddy?" Esmeralda tugged at his pants.

"What is it, princess?" Buddy scooped her up off the ground and held her high in the air.

"Did you get me anything?" she asked.

"Did you see it in my front seat?"

"No. What is it?"

"You'll just have to wait and see," he said, putting her back down. "It's kind of for both of you."

"You mean we have to share?"

"And I have to teach you how to use it."

"Glenn can't use it," she said. "He's a little too little."

"How do you know that? You haven't seen it."

"He's a little too little for just about everything."

"How bout you, Glenn? You want to see it?"

He scooped his son up for the same treatment. Glenn shook his head, then stuck his thumb in his mouth. He sucked it with enough force to make him drool. Buddy put the boy back down.

"Freeze right where you are. I'll be back."

Buddy tried to get up from the couch but his back, stiff from the road, pulled him back down. The pictures on the walls hadn't changed. There was still lots of him around. Erin would've told herself she'd left them up for the kids, but Buddy knew her well enough to feel safe in thinking that wasn't the whole truth.

"Daddy, I want to go with you," Esmeralda said. "You've been gone a long time."

"I know," Buddy said.

He picked Esmeralda up and held her high over his head. She giggled. Glenn took the opportunity to climb into his lap. Buddy put Esmeralda on the arm of the couch and picked Glenn up. The boy was much heavier. Once he put Glenn down, Esmeralda leaped back into his lap and spread her arms over her head signaling she was ready for another ride. Weary from the exertions of fatherhood already, Buddy didn't know how much longer he could keep it up.

* * *

Bruno finished filling in the boxes with the numbers for a theoretical month of business at the hotel. He wondered if his mother could remember the last time they hosted as many guests as in the problem she'd designed. Even with the inflated figures, the hotel made very little money. He placed his pencil in the ledger book's spine and turned it towards her.

"Done?" she asked.

"I think so."

"You think so?" She pulled the book towards her and began checking his work. "Let's see."

"Would I be learning this in a regular school?"

"You're learning a trade. It's all a part of who you'll become," she said.

"Mr. French said I was doing pretty good with it."

"Did he?"

"He said it was important."

"I hope so. I instructed him to add it to your other studies."

Bruno folded his arms over his chest. Tipping his chair a bit off the ground, he leaned away from the table. He watched his mother flick her pen over the page. As he expected, she did not mark it. He hoped that somehow he'd proven her wrong and she'd allow Rick to come back.

"You did this one right." She pushed the book off to the side. "Let's move on to math."

"What page?"

"I suppose you've mastered this, too?" she asked.

"I'm still good at math."

"Let's see." She moved his math book further beneath him with a nudge of her pen.

"Can we do something else first?" Bruno asked and reached for the copy of Whitman's poems on which he'd been sitting.

* * *

"Where you going?" Erin asked.

Buddy paused, the screen door half open. Esmeralda watched from the couch, smiling with eyes of worry.

"Out to the car. I've got something for them."

"Are you leaving?"

"Where would I go? You have my underwear." He let the screen door fall shut and turned to face her.

"Thirty minutes is usually your threshold." Erin crossed her arms.

"I know but things change. People change. Don't you think?" he asked.

"No. Because what I say is true!" Erin's voice filled with shaking anguish, as though she were about to cry. "You come here to make yourself feel at home, until you remember you don't really like being home, so you leave. Sometimes you say goodbye, sometimes there's a note."

"Erin..."

"It's okay, Buddy. It's okay. I've figured it out now. You don't mean to hurt anyone. It's just the way you are. One day the kids will figure it out, too."

"I want to be a good father, a better father. I've just had to be on the road."

"That's not what I'm talking about."

"Can I just get them their gift? She's been asking for it."

"Is that really what you're doing?" Erin asked, her voice starting to crack.

"Yes." He stepped back inside and took her in his arms. She grasped at the sleeves of his shirt, clutching them in her fists. When he tried to pull away, she deepened her grip. "My brother died," he said.

"God, Buddy. Why didn't you say anything?"

"I don't know. You only met him once."

"Still. Why won't you let us be there for you?" she asked.

Buddy eased himself from her grasp, slipped out the door and made his way out to the station wagon. He took out the mini-accordion and played a few notes. Erin laughed, her eyes shining through the tears.

"It ain't really new," Buddy said as he lumbered back to the door. "I got it at a pawnshop on my way here."

"Are you going to teach her how to play it?" Erin asked.

"I'm going to teach them both," he said. "I plan to teach a lot of kids, accordion, guitar, piano. I've decided to settle down and make a new kind of life for myself."

"Where?" she asked.

He smiled and looked over her shoulder at the upright piano in the next room. She held the door open for him.

"We'll have to talk about this more, Bud," she said as he came inside.

*   *   *

Bruno finished reading the poem without any attempt to hide the smile on his face. He'd filled Whitman's "Beat! Drums! Beat!" with the emotion Rick had always wanted of him. Despite his efforts, the slight frown his mother had worn since agreeing to let him read the poem hadn't left her face.

"Do you know what it means?" Bruno asked.

"No. Do you?" she asked, flipping through her teacher's copy of the math book.

"Mr. French and I would talk about the meanings after I read the poems aloud."

"I know. You told me that before you began reading," she said.

"It was stimulating," Bruno said.

"Stimulating?" his mother repeated, her eyebrows raised. "I'm sure."

"So, do you have some thoughts on this, mom? On the poem?"

"Poetry's just a diversion Bruno. It's not going to be useful to you in your future. How will it help you in running the hotel?"

"I just thought it might broaden my knowledge about myself. That's worth knowing," Bruno said.

"I said I thought it was nice. It's a nice part of life. But you need to learn how to run the hotel because that's who you will be. There are many more important things." She reached across the table and snatched the copy of Whitman away, putting it off to the side. "And I should know. For now, let's keep to the subjects that will help you the most."

After the lesson, Bruno went for a run. He didn't ask, just changed his clothes and ran out of the lobby, ignoring the questions she shouted at him as he went. A gust of wind pushed him down the street. Before he knew it, he'd run to the metal stairway that led down into town. With the rush of disobeying his mother propelling him, he started down.

He didn't make it far. The stairs creaked and swayed under his weight just enough to make him stop. Clutching the handrail, he carefully went back up, worried the whole structure could give way at any moment. Once back at the top, he looked down, wondering if the rest of the world would ever seem real or if it would always be so far away.

About the Author

Jason Graff is the author of numerous stories, a novella, *In the Service of the Boyar* (Strange Fictions Press, 2016) and a novel *Stray Our Pieces* (Waldorf Publishing, 2019). He loves both reading and producing writing that has a strong, clear voice and conveys a deep connection to the characters. In high school, his passion for the written word was ignited when he took a sucker punch for writing his crush a poem. He earned his bachelor's degree at Bowling Green State University and later, his MFA in Creative Writing at Goddard College. The intense nature of that program allowed him to be mentored by a diverse group of talented writers which included: Sarah Schulman, Richard Panek, Darcey Steinke, and Rachel Pollack.

Jason currently lives in Richardson, Texas with his wife, son, and cat. He is currently working on a science fiction novel about the beginning of the end of the universe and another about a romancing con-man. You can follow him on Twitter at @JasonGraffl, on Facebook at Author Jason Graff and/or visit his website: www.jasongraff.wordpress.com.

JASON GRAFF

About the Press

Unsolicited Press is a small press in Portland, Oregon. The small press is fueled by voracious editors, all of whom are volunteers. The press began in 2012 and continues to produce stellar poetry, fiction, and creative nonfiction.

Learn more at www.unsolicitedpress.com.

CPSIA information can be obtained
at www.ICGtesting.com
Printed in the USA
LVHW042038100120
643318LV00003B/568/P